ABOUT THIS BOOK

Is it better to keep quiet or to tell? Is it better to keep your cards to your chest or open up?

Keeping a secret can destroy a marriage. Revealing a secret can destroy a country.

When it comes down to it, though, secrets forever alter the people involved.

Writer and editor Dayle A. Dermatis assembles a compelling mix of stories that run the gamut from crime to fantasy to romance, from happy to sad to thrilling.

They all share one thing: the incredible voices of some of today's top fiction writers.

Secrets Keep Themselves
edited by Dayle A. Dermatis

Electronic edition published 2023 by Soul's Road Press

ISBN: 978-1-946462-24-4

This is a work of fiction. Names, characters, places, and events are either the product of the author's imagination or are used fictitiously, and any resemblance to actual persons, living or dead, business establishments, events, or locales is entirely coincidental.

Inquiries should be addressed to

Soul's Road Press
info@soulsroadpress.com
http://www.soulsroadpress.com

Cover image © anskuw | Depositphotos.com
Soul's Road Press logo: Designs by Trapdoor

SECRETS KEEP THEMSELVES

AN ANTHOLOGY OF PRIVATE WHISPERS

EDITED BY

DAYLE A. DERMATIS

SOUL'S ROAD PRESS

CONTENTS

INTRODUCTION
DO YOU WANT TO HEAR A SECRET?

It's hard to write fiction without the story including some kind of secret. If everything were obvious, would the story even be interesting? In a romance, the hero or the heroine or both might be hiding their attraction to the other. We learn about new worlds and new ways to keep secrets in science fiction and fantasy. And, of course, in mystery and crime, secrets are rife.

Is it better to keep quiet or to tell? Is it better to keep your cards to your chest or open up?

Keeping a secret can destroy a marriage. Revealing a secret can destroy a country.

When it comes down to it, though, secrets forever alter the people involved.

In these pages, Annie Reed delivers another one of her layered crime stories that leaves more victims than expected. Dean Wesley Smith will make you laugh with the antics of his popular character Poker Boy. Rob Vagle and Robert Jeschonek again wrote wonderful stories that defy labeling.

C.H. Hung gave me a moving fantasy story in an

amazing world I hope she writes more stories about, and Stephannie Tallent did exactly that, writing a sequel to a fantasy story of hers that I loved.

You'll read two very different but no less tense historical stories from Dory Crowe and Michèle Laframboise, and a gut-wrenching story from Lisa Silverthorne (I specifically asked her for this one).

Juliet Nordeen provided another nail-biter of a crime story, while C.J. Mattison and Leah R. Cutter gave me very different stories that are both, in the end, heartwarming.

Secrets pervade our lives, even when we try to avoid them, despite Sophocles's wise words, "Do nothing secretly; for Time sees and hears all things, and discloses all."

But never mind that. This isn't a secret at all: you're in for a great read.

—Dayle A. Dermatis
August 2022
West Linn, Oregon

THE FLORENTINE EXCHANGE
DAYLE A. DERMATIS

Libby normally didn't mind the narrow, five-story staircase that spiraled up to their apartment at the top of the 15th-century former monastery, because the lack of elevator was a small price to pay for living in Florence, Italy—and living her dream job in covert operations.

She minded the lack of air conditioning, however, especially on days like this: hot, stuffy, breezeless, with only a few high clouds that did nothing to break the sun's spell. The wooden stair treads dipped and angled, worn by centuries of footfalls; if she didn't step carefully, she'd trip. The only minor plus was that the building smelled of tomato sauce and oregano and onions—a vast improvement from the odor of exhaust trapped in the narrow streets outside.

By the time she'd lugged the heavy bag of clean laundry up the stairs, she was sticky with humidity and ready to peel off her damp clothes and throw them right into the bag. The problem with going to a launderette was you couldn't be naked while you washed your clothes.

She unlocked the door and shoved it with her shoulder —the wood always swelled and the upper right corner stuck—and stumbled inside.

The studio apartment was long and narrow, with unadorned white walls, tall enough that there was room for a loft at one end. You could stand beneath the loft, but only sit upright, not stand, when you were up there. The loft had the only window, so they'd dragged the mattresses up there to sleep, grateful for the cooler night air.

She assumed Antonia had already left for her assignment, but then she heard the toilet flush. The bathroom had been added at a later time, a boxy corner room with a ceiling as high as the loft floor, creating a flat surface above, where they'd shoved suitcases and other things they didn't use regularly. From the loft, you had a view of the dust in the corners.

When Antonia emerged, Libby took in the details in one glance, just as she'd been trained: The fact that Antonia was wearing cut-off grey sweatpants and a red tank top when she should have been dressed for the cocktail reception at which she was assigned to do a data exchange. The fact that Antonia was barefoot, hopping on her right foot. The fact that an Ace bandage figure-eighted around her left ankle and foot.

Antonia—tiny, ashy-blond, and surprisingly unassuming when she was bare-faced and uncoiffed— grimaced. She hopped the few feet to the broken-springed loveseat and collapsed into it sideways, propping her leg up on the far arm.

"What happened?" Libby asked, dropping the laundry on the wooden straight chair that served as a dining chair, desk chair, and the only other seating in the apartment.

"My own stupidity," Antonia said. "You'll have to go to

the embassy event instead. It's a simple exchange. You're ready for it." She glanced at her watch. "How soon can you leave?"

Soon enough, because that was the job. Libby had learned how to shower, dress, do makeup and hair in record time. She didn't wash her hair, just rinsed the sweat off her body under the shower nozzle that stuck out of the bathroom wall, no curtain or surround, one of those weird Italian things she'd grown used to, along with no washcloths and the disturbingly frequent public toilets without seats.

She was here largely as backup for Antonia, a more seasoned agent, and to learn from her. This would be her first solo assignment.

The flurry in her stomach wasn't nerves. Like Antonia had said, it was a simple exchange. She already knew who her contact was; Antonia had gone over that with her as a training exercise. She was finally getting to *do* something that was real, not a test, not a simulation.

She twisted her hair up into an artfully messy knot, the dampness making it easier to style, actually. Long and dyed dark brown, so she didn't stand out. Italian men noticed blonds, fawned over redheads. They commented on her height, five-foot-ten in bare feet (and nobody went barefoot in Italy), but there was little she could do about that except not wear the sky-high heels so fashionable nowadays. Easier to run, maneuver, fight if it came to that, in lower heels anyway.

Before Antonia zipped her into her cocktail dress, a sleek dark red number with a plunging neckline, Libby knelt in the bathroom, pulled out the plastic tub of cleaning supplies under the sink, pried up the false bottom in the cabinet, and opened the small, flat safe beneath.

She grabbed the ID she'd need—the one naming her as the daughter of a diplomat, just the type of person who'd be attending one of these parties—and the tiny thumb drive she'd be passing on to her contact. The drive was smaller than her thumbnail, no more than the part that inserted into a computer and the cover to protect it.

A quick glance in the mirror. Hair good, makeup good. A sedate strand of pearls around her neck, with complementary pearl-and-gold earrings and pin.

Then it was quickly back down the wooden spiral staircase, all five stories, the click of her heels echoing.

Late afternoon sun slanted down the narrow street, turning the sandstone walls to gold and the terracotta roofs to burnished flame. As the blissfully air conditioned taxi pulled into a wider street, she could see the sky cast in shades of butter and salmon, a sight that thrilled her every evening.

She settled back against the seat and opened her purse. It had room for a slim wallet and her passport, lipstick and powder and emergency tampon, and her phone...as well as a secret compartment for her gun. She dipped into the main section to grab the thumb drive, intending to transfer it to the private compartment, but came up with a few coins and *two* thumb drives.

Two identical thumb drives.

She'd washed a few of Antonia's clothes at the launderette along with her own, and when she'd checked the pockets of one pair of slacks, she'd dumped the loose change into her purse. Apparently there had been a tiny thumb drive as well, jumbled with the coins.

She examined both drives. Same brand, size; both black. No way to tell them apart unless she looked at the contents of each.

And that wasn't something she could do in the cab.

———

Antonia waited a full five minutes after Libby's departure, patiently counting the seconds and minutes, just to make sure Libby didn't run back because she'd forgotten something. Antonia didn't expect that. Libby was at the very least conscientious, and at most borderline obsessive; she rarely forgot anything.

She was just young, naïve, and easily manipulated.

Antonia lounged on the sagging loveseat, still and sure, and when the five minutes were up, she sat up and stripped the Ace bandage from her perfectly fine ankle.

Libby would exchange the fake thumb drive with her contact, and Antonia would pass on the real one to someone who was willing to pay a hell of a lot more money than Antonia's meager salary.

She hadn't been expecting glitz and glamor, sure, but she also hadn't expected to be dumped in a shitty box of an apartment that felt like a sauna or to be expected to act as an errand girl.

She was done. Beyond done.

She headed to the bathroom, stripping out of her shorts and tank top on the way, leaving them where they fell, and dug down to the safe beneath the sink. She grabbed her various passports—she'd dispose of the government-issued ones later, keep only the one she'd had made—and the stacks of cash from all over the world, more than enough to get her out of the country.

A few steps across the room and she was at her wardrobe, a prefab, rickety thing tucked under the loft. She'd cultivated a habit of being messy, of scattering things around, to keep Libby from noticing things out of place. Habits were deadly in this business. So instead of putting the clothes she planned to wear somewhere obvious, such as laid out or hung at the front of the wardrobe, she'd tossed them in the bottom of the wardrobe with a few other random items, an ever-changing mishmash.

But the pale pink, three-quarter-sleeve shirt and the oatmeal-colored wide-legged linen pants were gone. The bras, the scarf, the jumble of shoes was still there, but no outfit.

Antonia stared, stunned, for a moment before whirling to scan the rest of the room. When her gaze hit the mesh laundry bag Libby had dropped on the chair by the door, she muttered a few choice curse words under her breath.

When Libby had said she was going to do laundry and did Antonia want her to throw any of her things in, Antonia had called out from the bathroom, where she'd been showering, to grab whatever was lying around—figuring Libby would pick up the items on the bed, draped over the chair, kicked in the corner. She'd never thought Libby would look in the wardrobe for dirty laundry.

But Libby was precise, thorough.

Antonia had underestimated Libby, and that was her own damn fault.

She upended the laundry bag onto Libby's bed, dumping the carefully folded clothes into a jumbled heap, and pawed through. Found her slacks.

The pockets were empty.

Antonia threw the slacks across the room.

Then she stood stock still, took in a low, slow, deep breath, and composed herself.

She had to think, make a plan. Stay focused.

Libby had both drives. The question was, did she realize

it? Probably. Did she know what was on each drive? She wouldn't know which one to exchange otherwise.

Libby followed rules. Her job was to deliver the correct drive. She'd do everything possible to complete that job.

So, Antonia had to get to Libby before Libby exchanged the drive Antonia needed.

Antonia went back to the wardrobe and yanked out a new outfit.

In Italian, Libby asked the driver for a new destination: the Santa Maria Novella station, Florence's train hub. She paid him in cash, with a nice but unmemorable tip, and went inside.

The last of the sunlight streamed through the panes of glass that made up the roof and a sloping wall that reached the top of the ticket counters, dappling the heads of the travelers. A busy time of day, which was good— everyone was focused on their destination, on catching their train or getting outside to continue on their way, and not focused on each other. Beneath the hum of conversation, Libby's heels clicked on the floor of long stripes of veined marble, alternating off-white and dusty rose.

Past the people smelling of perfume and aftershave and body odor, past the ticket booths and machines, past the shops selling sandwiches and coffee and last-minute travel wares and gifts, to the storage room with its walls of lockers, a place for day tourists to store their travel gear.

From one of the lockers, Libby pulled a shopping bag, red with an understated gold logo, from a high-end, expensive boutique. The kind that ladies of leisure all over the city carried on a day of browsing; the kind nobody would look twice at. Her emergency stash.

She locked the locker, pocketed the key. She'd toss it somewhere after she wiped it down, just to be safe.

Back outside, where the sun hovered on the horizon, casting long shadows, she hailed another blessedly air-conditioned taxi to take her to the cocktail party.

She sat in the back behind the passenger seat; the driver would have to turn his head to see her, not just glance in his mirror. Holding her items below his sightline, she pulled a small device, which looked like an external phone battery, from the shopping bag and inserted one end into her phone. In the other, she slipped one of the thumb drives.

Although her phone didn't have all the functionality of a computer, it did have some extra capabilities—thanks to her employer—that would allow her to get a general sense of what was on the two drives.

It was easy to tell the difference, at least. The false drive initially looked as though it contained the correct information, but the files were too small.

Then again, the operative slated to receive the drive wouldn't have the chance to look at it until well after the exchange had been made, and by then it would have been too late.

Libby touched her teeth to her lower lip; not actively chewing on it, though, which would have marred her lipstick.

Did Antonia have a separate job, one she hadn't been allowed to tell Libby about? It was possible, but unlikely. Libby had been sent here to shadow Antonia, to learn from her. As far as she'd been led to believe, they had the same clearance. There was no reason for Libby not to know Antonia's schedule.

Libby shook her head, and put each drive in a separate place in her purse, making sure she knew which one was which. She tucked the device reader back into the shopping bag, beneath the folds of tissue paper that covered some new items from the high-end store, just as the taxi pulled up at her destination.

Whatever weirdness was going on with Antonia, the bottom line was that Libby had a job to do.

She'd worry about the rest of it later.

Antonia slipped into the black skirt that skimmed just below her knees and the plain white button-down shirt, pairing the outfit with low-heeled black pumps. Added a wig: a short black bob. About as unassuming an outfit she could put together, rendering herself as invisible as she could manage.

She was sweating. Moving too quickly in this stifling, monk's cell excuse for an apartment. Speed was of the essence, but not so much that she'd make a mistake. She took another long, slow breath in, out, calming herself.

She considered calling their boss, claiming Libby had gone rogue or some other excuse that would get Libby's fake passport blocked so she couldn't enter the party. But there was no telling how long that would take, and it would put the spotlight on Antonia, too.

She couldn't risk that.

She had to do this herself.

She grabbed one of her few extravagances: a breathtakingly expensive tote bag, buttery-soft black Italian leather with gold buckles. She stashed in it the passports and money, and a few other essentials she'd need over the next few days.

She'd planned to just leave, but now she had to get the thumb drive back first.

When the apartment door stuck, she didn't bother to yank it all the way shut, much less lock it, before she headed down the worn wooden staircase. Let someone steal everything. It wasn't her problem anymore. She wouldn't be coming back.

And depending on how things went down, Libby might not, either.

The cocktail party was being held at Casa Martelli, a fifteenth-century house that had been turned into a museum, still preserved in its original state to show how a wealthy Medici-era family would have lived. Libby had been on the guided tour already; she'd taken advantage of being stationed in Florence by hitting all the sites.

She handed her ID to the black-suited security guard at the door. He scanned it, glanced at the information that came up on his tablet.

"Welcome, Signora Parker," he said in accented English as he handed her passport back.

"Grazie," she responded. "Is there a place I can safely put this?" She held up the shopping bag.

He directed her to a small room set up as a coat check, where a bored attendant—nobody had coats to check on this still-warm evening—took her bag, gave her a numbered ticket, and set the bag next to a short line of leather briefcases, no doubt from diplomats stopping at the party on their way home from work.

She glanced at the slim gold watch on her wrist. She was actually a few minutes early. She had time to order a glass of Pellegrino fizzy water from the bar and fill a tiny plate with a few delicacies: prosciutto-wrapped melon; carefully stacked slices of red tomatoes, fresh white mozzarella and green basil leaves; glistening black caviar on toast points topped with a tiny dollop of cream.

One of the rules was, eat when you can safely do so. You never know where your next meal will be coming from, or what it might contain.

Libby made her way through the room of gold wallpaper, the blue-painted room covered in paintings and a very prominent crucifix, and finally to the one of the rooms with its walls covered with frescoes.

The Winter Garden Room had supposedly been painted to make up for the fact that the house had no outdoor garden space. It was breathtaking. Vines trailed up columns and across the vaulted ceiling. Vine-covered arches opened onto scenes of the city, or of fountains with the setting sun glowing in the distance.

Libby eased her way between partygoers to reach a wall near one corner. Between two painted, vine-spiraled columns and beneath an actual real window, two painted cats played at the edge of a fountain.

She finished her hors d'oeuvres, passed the plate to a red-vested waiter, and sipped her Pellegrino.

A moment later, a man stepped up next to her.

As expected, he wore a pink pocket square with slate-grey dots in his grey suit jacket.

She made a miniscule gesture with her glass. "I believe cats to be spirits come to earth."

"A cat, I am sure, could walk on a cloud without coming

through," he said, finishing the Jules Verne quote and thus confirming himself as her contact.

He was a tall black man, handsome despite the acne scars pitting his cheeks. Or perhaps because of; they gave his face character.

They both spoke Italian, but his had the slightest of French accents beneath.

"You're not who I expected," he said. His expression didn't change, but she heard the thread of suspicion in his voice.

Shit. Antonia should have let her handler know Libby would be making the exchange, allowing the information to pass through the appropriate channels.

Maybe there hadn't been time.

Then again, the second flash drive put Antonia under suspicion in a major way.

Libby had to decide what to do, and fast.

Antonia had the taxi driver drop her off a block and a half away from Casa Martelli. She would have done that in any instance, to disguise her true destination and to give her time to see if she'd been followed. But Casa Martelli was sandwiched in between shops, the entire block of buildings snugging up against each other as if expecting a siege. The only way to the back door was through narrow alleys twisting between those buildings, accessible one street over.

The air cooled a few degrees in the high-walled alleys where the slanted rays of the sun didn't reach. Pigeons cooed in the recesses in the bricks high above as the street noise faded the deeper she went.

Antonia knocked at the back door of Casa Martelli. She had to wait several minutes before someone answered, a harried-looking man who opened the door with an exasperated "What?" in Italian.

Well, dammit. She'd gotten the white button-down and black skirt right, but the waitstaff uniforms for this function apparently also included red vests.

If you were dressed similarly enough, were pretty (or handsome) without being overly so, and had a tray of drinks or delectable-looking morsels, nobody noticed you weren't in the exact uniform of the rest of the waitstaff.

Now, she could either stay with her initial plan of sweet-talking her way in, claiming to be a member of the staff who had gotten lost (and forgotten her vest), or she could go with Plan B.

She'd stick out like a sore thumb without the vest. Plan B it was.

She spoke softly, indicating her throat as if to imply she had laryngitis, and used a mix of broken Italian and English.

The waiter leaned close to hear her.

She jammed the syringe into his neck.

His eyes widened and he gave a short bark of surprise, but thankfully nobody heard. The drug didn't knock him out immediately, but made him both woozy and pliable as it entered his bloodstream. Antonia was able to support him, stumbling, around the corner of the alley, where he finally collapsed. Good. Another member of the waitstaff stepping outside for a cigarette wouldn't see him.

He wouldn't come to until she was well gone, and he'd have a spot of amnesia covering a few hours before his attack.

It took a few moments to roll him this way and that so

she could strip the vest off him. It was far too big for her, but she grabbed a few safety pins from her tote and nipped in the seams, which helped.

She pulled a plastic trash bag from her tote and stuffed the tote into it, setting the bag in the small pile of trash already by the back door. She'd do what she needed to do and be back before anyone cleared away the garbage.

Then she slipped inside, grabbed a tray of bacon-wrapped figs, and popped one in her mouth. The bacon had been soaked in maple syrup, and the taste was incredible.

Tray in hand, she entered the cocktail party.

Libby tapped the gold-and-pearl pin at her shoulder, activating the sound cancelling that would pick the ambient music—a string quartet in the next room—rather than their conversation.

"I think my partner has been compromised," she said to her contact. "She sent me here in her place. Check the information on the drive carefully. She tried to replace it, but I found what I believe is the original, which I'm giving to you."

"Why don't you give me both?" he asked.

Fair question. "I need proof about what she's done."

He nodded slowly, and reached into his pocket, presumably to retrieve the drive he'd exchange for hers.

She'd turned from the frescoed wall once he'd arrived, keeping a casual eye on the room. She saw Antonia, dressed as waitstaff in an ill-fitting red vest, a black wig not disguise enough. She froze.

"She's here," she murmured. "I have to go. We'll reschedule the drop. I'm sorry."

He was already scanning the crowd, but Libby was gone, ducking left and then right through the partygoers, losing herself in the small crowd. It wasn't easy at her height, but most people had imbibed at least one drink, and she'd learned how to hunch, to make herself less obvious.

Her heart pounded in her throat. Antonia must have discovered the missing thumb drive faster than Libby had expected.

If Antonia wanted that drive, she'd stop at nothing to get it. Libby was sure of that. Antonia might be a casual slob, might take her duties lightly, but she had an undercurrent of steeliness that she'd tried to hide from Libby.

Unbeknownst to Antonia, she'd failed at that.

Libby threw her ticket at the coat check attendant and forced herself not to grab her own bag, but let the attendant hand it to her. She had to not be too obvious, too memorable. That meant people would pay attention. Remember her.

She ducked into the ladies room, locked the door, and yanked things out of her shopping bag.

A few moments later, she exited the back door—the waitstaff were too busy to notice her, even as unassuming as she was.

Her shapeless black dress was padded so she looked heavier, and she hunched her shoulders. She'd changed her shoes to black, soft-soled laceups, one of which had a pebble in it to throw her gait off, make her limp slightly. Half of her hair was shoved under a big straw hat that obscured her face; the other half straggled down, giving the impression that her hair was thinner than it was.

The rest of her belongings, including the high-end shopping bag, were stuff in a generic woven-string market bag.

All of it told the casual eye: I'm old. I'm nobody. I'm an average, unassuming Italian matriarch headed home to make dinner.

It was only a ten-minute walk to the Arno River, but she took a good forty minutes, wandering down alleys and side streets, alert to any sign of a tail.

———

Libby was good—Antonia would give her that much. It didn't surprise Antonia; Libby surely would have taken her training seriously, focused on doing everything right.

Unfortunately for Libby, Antonia had put a tracking software on her phone ages ago. If Libby ever found it, Antonia would have said it was a test to see how fast Libby found it. She hadn't thus far.

So as soon as Antonia figured out where Libby was going, she abandoned trying to track her through the streets and doubled back.

She knew how to get there first.

Libby was stepping onto Ponte Vecchio, one of the most famous bridges in the world.

Dating back to the Middle Ages, the stone bridge over the Arno River was lined with shops along each side. Originally butcher shops, they now housed primarily jewelry shops catering to the tourists.

Tourists who were still crowding the bridge on this balmy summer evening, taking advantage of the later shopping hours. Now that the sun had set, the air had cooled, soft on Antonia's face.

Libby would have to fight her way through that throng...but there was another way across the Ponte Vecchio.

In the sixteenth century, Cosimo de Medici had ordered built an enclosed corridor along the top of the shops to ease his passage between his palace and the town hall. About ten years ago, the Vasari Corridor had been opened for public tours. Then, last year, it had been closed again for maintenance.

Antonia knew where the entrance was on this side of the river.

Either Libby intended to lose herself in the crowd—in which case Antonia would be waiting for her on the other side—or Libby knew of another entrance to the corridor—in which case Antonia would meet her inside.

And if Libby doubled back, the tracking software would let Antonia know. She could be at either end before Libby.

Then she could get the damn thumb drive back, hopefully the drive from their contact as well, and be on her way to her money and freedom.

She wasn't going to let by-the-rules Libby ruin everything for her.

Libby cut her way through the crowd, occasionally murmuring, "Scusami. Scusami, grazie." People paid her little mind, barely glanced at her. Her hip hurt, thanks to the pebble that made her limp. She was dearly looking forward to fixing that problem.

It was no doubt the least of her problems.

But she was close to her goal, and she hadn't spotted a tail. She hunched a little shorter, continuing to make her height less conspicuous and give the impression of age. Her soft-soled shoes made no sound on the stone bridge, not that footsteps would be audible above the sounds of chattering tourists.

About a quarter of the way down, she ducked into a shop between the glass cases that bordered the door. She nodded at the shop clerk, and asked, in Italian, for Mondavian gold.

Something that didn't exist.

The man nodded in recognition and drew her to the back of the shop as if to show her what she sought. Once the shop was empty, she slipped through the door into the back storage area.

Then it was a simple matter of sliding a shelving unit sideways, unlocking the door behind it, sliding the shelf back after she'd entered the tiny room, and squeezing into a corner so she could swing the door back shut and lock it again.

She'd paid the shopkeepers handsomely for this, after poring over schematics of the Ponte Vecchio and the Vasari Corridor—private schematics she'd also paid handsomely for the privilege of viewing.

The room she was now in was little more than a wide square chimney with ancient iron hand- and footholds affixed into the stone, leading up. The only light was from a tiny bit that bled around the door from the shop's storage room, but Libby had done this once with a flashlight in her teeth, and didn't need more practice than that.

She climbed the ladder, counting the rungs to know when she'd reached the top. Then, she unlocked the door there and entered a storage closet, and from there stepped into the Vasari Corridor.

The floor was brick-red tiles in a herringbone pattern; the walls were pale cream. No paintings hung on the walls now, as they did when the passageway was open for tours.

The evenly spaced windows high on the outer wall didn't provide light now at night, but a series of pale emergency lights along the wall near the floor, each about a foot long with a molded opaque white cover, gave a little illumination.

Just enough to see the hulking outlines of the scaffolding, the piles of materials, the locked toolboxes.

Antonia had impressed upon her the importance of stashing a go-bag somewhere in the city, in case she had to leave quickly but couldn't get back to the apartment. The train station lockers made sense, because it made it easy to leave by public transportation. Antonia probably had a bag stashed there, too.

Libby seriously doubted Antonia knew she had this one.

She popped open the front casing one of the small modern light fixtures near the floor and used the folds of her skirt to protect her fingers as she removed the hot bulb. Then she carefully unscrewed the fixture, and reached behind to find the small canvas bag she'd left there.

Passport, money, a burner phone. The bare essentials for an escape, in case she was compromised and in danger, and the American Embassy wasn't an option.

She shoved it into her string bag, then removed her shoe and shook out the offending pebble. She didn't bother to replace the light. So what if someone came across it tomorrow? She'd be long gone.

She leaned against the wall. She'd wait a bit, just to make sure no one had followed her onto the Ponte Vecchio below.

Then she heard a noise down the corridor. A metallic hum, as if someone had brushed against scaffolding, then stopped the vibration with their hand on the piping.

Not breathing, Libby slowly, silently reached for her gun, and hid it in the folds of her skirt.

Antonia—or someone—had found her after all.

———

Antonia crept forward, barefoot, her shoes in her tote. The bare, enclosed corridor would amplify footsteps. She'd barely brushed against the scaffolding, and caught it a moment after it hummed, but she still cursed herself, cursed her eyes that hadn't fully adjusted to the dim emergency lights.

Couldn't be helped now.

She was rushing too much. Picking the lock without being seen had taken longer than she'd expected. The noises she'd heard up ahead must be Libby.

She was so over this. Over Florence, over Libby, over the job.

That was no reason to get sloppy, though.

So she changed her tactic and walked up to Libby as if she owned the damn place.

"What are you doing hiding in here, Libby?" she asked. "This isn't part of the drop."

Libby was on her feet, standing next to the net shopping bag she'd been carrying. Her hand was half-hidden in the folds of her skirt. Probably concealing her gun.

She wouldn't shoot unless she had to, though. Libby's training was solid, and she followed rules. Antonia could use that to her advantage, if it came to it.

"I ended up with two thumb drives," Libby said. "That was weird, so I knew something was up. I thought it would be safer to lie low and monitor the situation."

Antonia mentally rolled her eyes. "You panicked. And

your disguise wasn't nearly good enough: I picked you out right away."

"So why'd it take you so long to get to me?" Libby asked.

"*I* was monitoring *you*," Antonia said. "This was a test."

Libby shook her head. "If this was a test, then call HQ and have them confirm it."

Well, it had been worth a try.

"Just give me the thumb drive, Libby."

"I don't have it," Libby said. "I made the exchange."

"Then give me the drive you received."

"I don't have it on me."

"Then take me to it," Antonia said. "Just give me one of the drives—one of the real drives—and I'll be out of your hair."

"You haven't been following me around Florence just to get the drive and let me go," Libby said.

"Okay, then," Antonia said amiably, because she'd long guessed it was going to come to this. "Then I'll shoot you and take the drive."

She saw Libby's hand move in the folds of her skirt.

Two painfully loud reports, almost simultaneous, slammed through the corridor.

Libby's ears rang, aching from the gunshot. But she was alive, somehow. She'd brought her gun out, but Antonia had been faster....

Now, as Antonia spun and crumpled to the ground, crimson blossoming on the front of her white button-down blouse, Libby stared in shock at the tall black man who'd come up behind Antonia. Her contact from the cocktail party.

"How did you...?" She automatically spoke in Italian.

He shrugged as he stepped forward, sliding his gun under his jacket. "When I saw your partner leave after you, I followed her. She didn't expect a tail, so she never noticed. Sloppy."

Libby's cheek stung. She touched it, and in the dim light saw plaster dust and a smear of blood. Antonia's shot had just missed Libby's head, ricocheting off the plaster wall. Some of the plaster must have grazed her.

"But why?" Libby asked the man, her mind spinning through possible scenarios. Her heart was slowing to normal, thanks to her training.

"You said she might be compromised, and I was concerned for your safety. I don't leave fellow agents behind."

Libby knelt beside Antonia's body. Antonia's gun had fallen next to her hand, half under her lifeless form. She leaned closer, peering at her. "That's odd," she said.

"What?" the other agent asked, squatting down on the other side of the body.

Libby shot him in the head with Antonia's gun.

"I'm sorry," she said, only half-meaning it. His damn gallantry had ruined everything. He'd expect her to come with him, sort things out together, be her backup when she gave her report—and she didn't have time for any of that. Her cover was blown here, and he was the only witness. She had to get away before anyone else in the American agency came looking for her or Antonia.

Libby eased the gun, which she'd held in the fabric of her skirt to avoid leaving prints, into Antonia's hand. Let them sort out who'd killed who, the hows and the whys of it.

As for Antonia... Libby sniffed as she checked the

woman's pockets for anything useful—or incriminating. Antonia wasn't much better than a child playing at spycraft. She'd fallen so easily for Libby's ruses: the pretense of following rules, the neatness, the good humor.

Of course, they all had. She'd found it amusing to go through all the training a second time in a new country, passing herself off as an American, never quite doing things perfectly so she didn't stand out, didn't look suspicious. Learning a few secrets along the way.

Her assignment had been to stay deeply imbedded in the American system, but this incident changed things.

It was time to go home.

Elizaveta Papanova was going home, out of the sticky humidity and back to the crisp, chill air of her beloved Russia....

At least until her next assignment.

BRIBING GHOSTS
LEAH R. CUTTER

F u Ran knelt in front of her father's grave. At least
she'd remembered to bring a rough, red-and-black
checked blanket so her jeans wouldn't get too dirty
kneeling on the ground. The August sun beat down on the
back of her head from the clear blue sky, making her wish
she'd wrapped her long black hair up in a bun, getting it off
her shoulders and neck. She wore a short-sleeved white
blouse that her father would have considered scandalous as
it didn't cover her up to her neck, but it was far too warm to
go around completely swaddled.

She also didn't wear any makeup—something else her
father had always associated with the corrupting Western
influence creeping into the mainland.

On the ground in front of Fu Ran sat a paper boat, about
the size of her two hands held together. It had been cleverly
folded out of bright red-and-gold "Hell" money—*joss* paper
to be burned as an offering for the dead. Between the boat
and the unassuming grey tombstone a few feet away, Fu
Ran had stuck nine rows of incense into the ground, three
sticks per row, twenty-seven total: the same as her age,

hopefully a lucky number that day. Sweet smoke curled up from the lit ends, hazing the clear air.

Earlier, that spring, during the *qingming* festival, her entire family had gathered to clean the front area of the grave: her mother, her two older brothers, her grandfather, as well as one of her aunts and three of her cousins. No weeds remained, and the grass in front of the grave marker stayed short.

Now, Fu Ran knelt all alone. No one had dared come with her to visit a graveyard during *gui yue*—Ghost Month.

According to tradition, Judge Yama opened the gates of Hell on the first day of the seventh Lunar month, setting all the wild ghosts free to roam the earth. On the fifteenth of the month, there would be many celebrations and events to feed and entertain the ghosts, who would all (hopefully) leave by the end of the month.

Though Fu Ran's family had made offerings on the first day of Ghost Month to appease any hungry ancestors who came to visit, bad luck had struck them hard. Fu Ran's mother remained in the hospital after the car accident that had claimed the life of Fu Ran's middle brother. Her eldest brother had lost his job. And her youngest aunt had come down with the flu and was still bedridden, the doctors worried and ordering more tests.

Obviously, some angry ghost (or ghosts) was angry with Fu Ran and her family. She'd decided that making an offering in a temple wasn't good enough. The incense and the Hell money she burned there might get lost among all the other offerings and not go directly to her father.

Her family needed an intervention in the spirit world. Who better than her strong, calm, overly principled father? Who'd died only three years before from cancer?

So on the eighth day of Ghost Month, Fu Ran took the

hot, stinky bus all the way to the outskirts of her city, Fuzhou, to visit her father's graveyard. The bus's air conditioning had been overwhelmed by the sheer number of bodies, with mothers and their sisters holding two children each in their laps, sullen teenagers crammed together, even ancient grandmothers stoically standing, their arms wrapped around each other's waist to hold them up.

Though her parents had given her an auspicious name —*Fu Ran* basically translated into English as lucky—Fu Ran considered herself the unluckiest girl in the whole world.

She had excelled during her college exams and had gone on to get an advanced degree in chemistry; however, no job awaited her. With the death of her father, her family had lost their Party connections. No sponsor had come forward to advocate for her.

As a result, she could only get a soul-crushing job in one of the numerous factories that lined the coast, making cheap shoes and clothes to be exported to America, but that wouldn't be putting her education to use. Plus, those jobs didn't pay well at all, and too many factories still had deadly accidents.

She didn't have a boyfriend—not even a secret crush— though her girlfriends teased her she must like *someone*, even if she didn't.

Bills were mounting up. Fu Ran wasn't sure how the family would pay not just for her brother's cremation and burial expenses, but for her mother's hospital stay as well. (It was just too inauspicious to conduct the funeral during Ghost Month, so the ceremony couldn't occur until the following month.)

Fu Ran didn't know if praying to her father would help. She'd found a paper boat because he'd always loved to go fishing on the Min River. He'd told her stories of poling a flat-bottomed boat as a boy, going upriver to where it widened out and a small pool formed where he could almost always find fish.

Fu Ran didn't know what else to do, where else to turn. Her father's old boss, the family's primary Party affiliation, had disappeared out of their lives when her father had died. None of her professors had taken her on as an assistant, despite her high grades. The loss of her brother tore at her chest like an open wound; no amount of fancy surgery could seal the hole.

After she finished her prayers, imploring that not just her father but any and all of her deceased relatives needed to help her family, she set the little boat on fire.

Maybe the boat would delight her father and get him to intervene with the ghosts targeting them.

Or perhaps he'd be dismayed at her whimsy and send more devils to haunt them.

Fu Ran defiantly stood up. The heat of the flames washed across her legs. The scorching sun beat down on her head, making her sway in place. The smell of incense swelled up and made her cough. Dark spots formed in the corners of her eyes.

She blinked.

All but one of the dark spots went away.

She turned to look at the now-moving shape.

It was a man, not a ghost. Definitely not her imagination, either. White shirt, black pants, black hair, dark eyes, tanned skin.

He walked to the tombstone closest to him, then knelt down, looking around.

Then he stood and walked quickly to the next.

Who was he hiding from?

He spotted her standing. He paused and stared hard at her.

Fu Ran resisted the urge to wave at him, just to prove that she wasn't a ghost either.

He shook his head, then changed direction and came directly toward her without pausing again.

His dark eyes drilled into her very soul, holding her captive.

"It isn't safe here," the man said as soon as he drew near. He had a very cultured accent, possibly from Beijing.

He wore his black, glossy hair super short and cute. He had rolled the sleeves of his white shirt up above his elbows, showing off nicely muscled arms. Both his well-made black dress slacks and black leather shoes were scuffed and had streaks of dirt on them.

"Why isn't it safe here?" Fu Ran asked, not wanting to be chased off. This was *her* father's grave, after all. She had every right to be there. "Are you afraid of the ghosts?"

He gave a sharp, barking laugh. "Ghosts?" he asked, looking around. He spied the rows of incense almost burnt to their ends sticking out of the grave. Then he looked at her strangely. "You are a brave woman to make offerings to..." he paused, glancing at the tombstone, "your father, I'm presuming, during the middle of Ghost Month."

"Someone had to," Fu Ran explained. That was all she was planning on saying about the matter. As her aunt always said, wear your broken arm *inside* your sleeve.

The man nodded and bowed his head low to her. "I can only hope that when I have a daughter, she will be as dutiful. But for now, we both need to get out of here."

"Why?" Fu Ran asked, stubbornly crossing her arms when the man reached out to touch her, perhaps hurry her along.

The man glanced over his shoulder. "Spies," he hissed. "Taiwanese spies."

Fu Ran gasped. All her life, the Party had warned about Taiwanese spies. Fuzhou sat directly across the strait from the renegade island. She'd had nightmares as a child about Taiwanese soldiers swarming out of their boats and taking over the city, killing everyone in her family.

She looked past the man, in the direction he'd come from.

She stiffened, shock holding her very still.

Four men stood at the very edge of the cemetery.

"Too late to run," Fu Ran told the man. She reached out and grabbed his sleeve, tugging on it. "Come. Kneel with me. They will believe you are being a dutiful son."

The man glanced over his shoulder, then back at Fu Ran. Relief flowed across his features. The smile he gave her was as dazzling as the sun overhead.

Really, it was just the summer heat that made her knees feel so weak, not his look.

"You're right," he said, gracefully kneeling down on the blanket. "They're just following a man. They don't know me by sight. I'm Zhong Di," he said, putting his hands on the ground and lowering his head.

"Fu Ran," she said as she knelt and did the same.

They each prayed in silence as the last of the smoke from the paper boat rose up into the clear sky.

Just as the men grew closer, Zhong Di reached into the breast pocket of his shirt and took out two more pieces of Hell money. He handed one to her, set his on fire with a lighter and then gestured for her to do the same.

The men abruptly swerved and walked past them.

Fu Ran felt her shoulders drop with relief. Finally, something was going right!

It wasn't until the cemetery was completely empty before Fu Ran spoke. "Why did you have Hell money with you?" she asked.

Zhong Di gave her a carefree grin that made him look even younger and more handsome than he had initially appeared. "It's Ghost Month," he said. "And I've always believed in carrying the appropriate bribes. Who knows when you'll need them the most?"

Fu Ran nodded. A very practical answer. Though the Party decreed that this was the Worker's Paradise and everyone was equal, somehow it generally took bribes to get anything done.

Maybe that was why the Party allowed all the sacrifices during Ghost Month: they saw it as bribes for ghosts.

Both of them rose. The sun was finally hanging lower in the sky, the heat of the afternoon passing. Loud choruses of cicadas sprang up. Zhong Di helped Fu Ran first shake out her blanket, then fold it up.

"Where will you go now?" Fu Ran asked, not willing to let Zhong Di disappear like a ghost.

He sighed. "I could lie and say that I was going back to my apartment, but they might have it staked out by now."

"My middle brother just died. My mother's still in the hospital. My aunt is very sick," Fu Ran said all in a rush. "You could stay in our living room, and sleep on the sofa, but it would still be very unlucky."

She knew that it wasn't proper to invite Zhong Di home. She'd just met him! She didn't know his family or any of his friends.

Plus, he wasn't safe. He was running from Taiwanese spies. Maybe he was a spy himself.

However, she couldn't help herself. There was something about him, maybe how he held himself, or the look of confidence in his eyes, or perhaps even the strong muscles of his arms, that made her throw caution to the wind.

Then again, she'd started the day rashly, making the decision to go to a cemetery during Ghost Month. Might as well continue down that same path.

Zhong Di gave her a smile that matched her reckless feelings. "I accept, but you can't ask too many questions. That wouldn't be safe for you or your family."

Fu Ran considered his statement for a moment. Again, he sounded very practical, an attribute both her mother and her father would approve of. "You will tell me what you can of your troubles?" Fu Ran asked. "Then, tell me the rest later?"

"I promise," Zhong Di said solemnly.

Fu Ran shivered. It sounded like a vow that he'd honor even unto death.

Who was this man? What mysteries filled his life? And how could she bribe him to make sure that he continued to "haunt" her, to stay with her like an old ghost?

The back door to the apartment building where Fu Ran's family lived had graffiti on it already, though it had just been painted an industrial brown not two weeks before. Black and white stickers with strident characters had been slapped on it. Plus some stupid advertisement for an illegal band.

Fu Ran sighed but didn't say anything. She pulled open the door, gesturing for Zhong Di to walk in. He carried the plastic bags containing their dinner. It had been so kind of him to buy enough food, not just for her, but for three additional people as well.

After he stepped into the dimly lit stairwell, she shut the door after him and locked it carefully. The stairway smelled of concrete and bleach. At least it no longer smelled of urine, as it had the previous month when a homeless man had snuck in and spent the night sleeping there.

"Ready for a climb?" Fu Ran asked. While there was an elevator at the front of the building, it was often broken, always dirty, and it made clanging noises that Fu Ran didn't trust.

"After you," Zhong Di said gallantly.

Fu Ran couldn't help but give him a smile before she turned to the prospect of the six flights of stairs that they needed to climb. While she was young and in good enough shape to reach her floor without being too winded, she always felt sorry for the older people in the building. She'd frequently pass them sitting on one of the landings, wheezing and trying to catch their breath.

With Zhong Di following her, Fu Ran couldn't help but show off a little, climbing the bare concrete stairs quickly. She rarely touched the railing. Though it was painted a happy red, it was often sticky or slimy from who knew what.

The sixth floor looked cheery compared to the plain concrete staircase. Lights in red, green, and blue paper lanterns hung from the ceiling down the center of the hall. Fu Ran's family along with the neighbors had painted the walls a bright yellow. Large windows with green glass (reinforced with chicken wire) stood on the right of each door, supposedly to supply the tiny apartments with more light. Ancient red carpet covered the floor, worn bare in many places. The hall smelled of garlic, chicken, and incense—the smells of home—with a faint undertone of more bleach.

No numbers or names marked any of the apartments, of course. It was too easy for evil spirits to follow a person home if they could easily find their address. All the doors had been painted different colors, though, to make it easier for guests to visit.

The old woman at the start of the floor, closest to the stairway, with the strongest Party affiliations, got the lucky red door. Everyone else had to settle for other colors.

Fu Ran happily stopped in front of the dark blue door of her family's apartment. They lived one apartment in from the far end and just across the hallway from the communal showers and toilets for that floor. She hoped that Zhong Di wouldn't think too poorly of them since they didn't have a private bathroom. However, at least they didn't have to go down the street to the public toilets, which were always filthy.

"I don't know who's home," she warned Zhong Di. She didn't know what kind of reception he'd get from either of her aunts, who frequently stayed with them, or her brother.

"Hopefully we have enough food to feed them," he replied with a smile.

"Thank you," she said again as she unlocked the door.

Just inside the tiny alcove, she saw only her eldest brother's shoes waiting there, a pair of worn brown-leather loafers. She hoped he wouldn't be too hard on Zhong Di. Fu Ran slipped off her shoes and put on her house slippers, then handed a pair of guest slippers to Zhong Di.

Thankfully, he wasn't too "cultured" to be ashamed of wearing guest slippers, taking off his shoes and slipping on the guest pair.

The kitchen ran along the outside wall, with a tiny stove that Fu Ran's mother had always worked miracles with, a sink that was barely big enough to hold a dinner bowl, and shelves that rose to top of the eight-foot ceiling, stocked full of instant meals, dried goods, spices, bowls, and chopsticks. It still smelled of rice and pickled fish.

To the left, the apartment opened up into what had originally been one long room. Her family had divided it up to make an extra bedroom for her brothers.

Fu Ran breathed a sigh of relief when she saw the door to her brother's bedroom was closed, with a little placard hanging from the doorknob, showing a red lotus flower.

The sign meant that the person behind the door didn't want to be disturbed. The other side of the sign held a golden laughing Buddha, which, when showing, meant he would welcome company.

Though the concept of spending time alone was frowned on, both of Fu Ran's brothers, and Fu Ran herself, needed it sometimes in order to study.

And now, to grieve.

The living room itself held a low coffee table that the family usually sat around for meals. The white-and-grey top of the table barely had any dents in it despite the numerous children who had banged on it over the years. The legs showed more wear, the gold paint flecking off to reveal the steel underneath. Fu Ran often slid her fingertips along them, as if she could gather strength from their sturdiness.

While the floor itself was concrete, Fu Ran's family had bought several colorful rugs to cover it. Her favorite was made from black, blue, and white cloth all braided together. It sat under the table and provided good insulation from the floor.

They had one black, scratchy couch, pressed up against the wall to her brother's bedroom. Lamps sitting on the wooden end tables at either arm of the couch made the room bright. Folded-up black metal chairs leaned against the kitchen wall, ready for guests.

The wall to Fu Ran's left held a few pictures—school graduations, important ceremonies, her father's death portrait.

Her brother's picture would join there soon enough, something Fu Ran didn't want to think about just yet.

On the right wall were two closed doors: one leading to the bedroom her parents had shared, one going to her own tiny room.

Zhong Di put the bags holding their dinner on the table, then gracefully sank down.

Fu Ran breathed a sigh of relief. At least he didn't seem to mind sitting on the floor.

They eagerly divided up the food, leaving two whole bags for leftovers. Soon, Fu Ran slurped her noodle soup, the broth having cooled to the perfect temperature, with just the right amount of tangy onions in it.

By the time she'd finished that and started in on her rice and stir-fried vegetables, she finally felt human, as well as ready to hear Zhong Di's story.

He'd seemed to come to the same conclusion, and started by saying, "I work as an inventor for...let's just say one of the big shoe manufacturers."

"Really?" Fu Ran asked. "Were you working on different rubber for the soles?"

Zhong Di blinked and nodded slowly. "In a way, I was. Why do you ask?"

Fu Ran didn't like the suspicious look in his eye. "I studied to be a chemist," she told him. "With an advanced degree."

"Oh?" he asked, surprised. "Who do you work for?"

Fu Ran looked back down at her rice. She suddenly was

no longer hungry. "No one," she said. "I had good grades—the best in my class—but no one would hire me."

"I see," Zhong Di said.

Perhaps he did. It wasn't easy for someone as poor as Fu Ran to be hired into a good-paying job. Particularly without Party backing.

"Anyway," he said after a few moments of silence. "I... let's just say I made an interesting breakthrough. When I showed it to my boss, Ya Du, he told me not to continue with that line of reasoning." Zhong Di sighed. He appeared to be choosing his words carefully. "Instead, two men approached me that night."

"Spies?" Fu Ran asked when he didn't speak again right away.

"I believe so," Zhong Di said. "They flattered me. And offered me a lot of money if I would sell them my discovery."

Fu Ran could tell by the way that Zhong Di hung his head that he'd originally been taken in. "What happened?" she asked.

"When it came time to give them the formula, early this morning...I just couldn't do it. I couldn't sell it to them. It was four men. I'd never seen them before. They weren't businessmen. They were goons. I saw them at the end of the street, then just turned and ran. They've been after me ever since." He sighed again.

"Could you sell them a formula that didn't work?" Fu Ran asked. "Alter it slightly?"

"Possibly, but that wouldn't stop them from coming after me," Zhong Di said. "And I can't turn in my boss. He has strong Party connections. It would be his word against mine. Nobody would believe me."

Fu Ran shook her head as a plan came to her.

Why did men always think they needed to do everything on their own? By themselves?

She blamed the West for that corrupting idea.

"I may have a plan," she said slowly after Zhong Di had fallen back to eating. "But it will take some careful timing on both our parts. As well as reaching out to our connections."

"Really?" Zhong Di asked, his eyes gleaming. "I knew that traveling to the cemetery was sure to bring me good luck."

Fu Ran couldn't help but giggle. That was the first time someone had found anything lucky in a graveyard.

Then again, possibly Zhong Di would bring good luck, and not trouble, to her and her family as well.

Fu Ran kept her expression professional, despite how she shook like a little girl inside. She wore a somber, light-grey blouse and a black skirt—her one good interview outfit—with her hair pinned up in a tight bun. Tonight, she'd tinted her lips just slightly pink to make her seem younger, as well as used eyeliner to make her dark eyes look rounder and more innocent.

She didn't squirm in the hard-backed wooden chair that she sat on—that might have overplayed her hand.

Zhong Di's boss, Ya Du, sat and looked sternly at her from across the broad expansive of his oak desk. They were meeting after hours at the shoe factory. He wore the light-grey jacket currently favored by Party officials, though the top button and standing collar dug into his fat neck. His flabby lips and plump face made him look like a toad, while his black eyes were tiny and full of cunning.

The office stank of burnt rubber from the factory despite the cool air that blew constantly from the vents. Bright neon lights buzzed annoyingly above them, highlighting how dingy the place looked. Sad green paint covered the walls, scuffed and peeling. A huge picture of Xi Jinping hung on the wall just behind Ya Du, framed in bright red matting. Various Party awards hung beside it.

No school diploma, however.

"I'm glad that someone had the intelligence to come to me with this," Ya Du said. "And you're sure that Zhong Di has no idea you're here?"

"He does not," Fu Ran said, her voice steady. She suspected Ya Du was trying to figure out just how alone she was and whether or not he could just make her disappear. "Zhong Di said he was going to *hide* his discovery, instead of sharing it with the People."

Fu Ran made sure that she sounded every bit the patriot. She'd considered wearing a jacket with a red star pinned to the lapel, but it had been too warm that evening, plus it felt like overkill.

They needed for Ya Du to make Fu Ran the same deal he'd made Zhong Di.

"So you brought the formula to me," Ya Du said with relish.

Fu Ran wasn't about to tell him that it wasn't the original formula. She and Zhong Di had altered it slightly so it would be sure to fail.

"Of course I would bring it to you! You are his immediate superior," Fu Ran explained. "If he isn't going to take credit for it, you should." She hesitated, and for the first time, added some sadness to her voice. "My family has had so much bad luck this Ghost Month."

"Really?" Ya Du purred.

Fu Ran pushed down on her flush of anger. He sounded like a cat who'd just spotted a wounded bird.

"My brother was killed in a car accident," Fu Ran said softly. The pain constantly tore at her heart, and she no longer had to pretend to be sad. "My mother is still in the hospital because of it." The doctors had finally said that she might be released by the end of the following week, but then she'd have a lot of physical therapy for her broken leg and hip.

And how was her family going to pay for all of that?

"Ah," Ya Du said, sitting back in his chair. He nodded, as if he'd come to a decision. "I have some people who might be interested in such a formula."

Fu Ran frowned at him. She knew she couldn't just jump at the chance he was offering. She had to make him convince her. "I don't understand."

"Sometimes, it's better to help each other along the path, rather than to bask in the sunshine by yourself," Ya Du said, mangling a famous Party slogan.

Fu Ran blinked. "How can we help each other?" she asked slowly, despite her rapidly beating heart.

Good patriot or not, Ya Du would also believe her to be a practical person.

"Instead of selfishly using this formula to better our American masters," Ya Du said, his face scrunching together on the last two words as if they tasted sour, "we should use it to better everyone. In particular, your family."

Fu Ran nodded as if she understood. "And you can help me do that?"

Ya Du smiled broadly at her. "I can! I can introduce you to some people who would pay you very good money for such a formula."

Fu Ran tilted her head to one side, as if considering the

prospect. "Why wouldn't you take it to them yourself?" she asked as innocently as she could.

"I have more than enough!" Ya Du said, his hands spread out as if to indicate the richness of his office. "Besides, I am just a humble servant."

Fu Ran contained her scoffing snort. She'd bet that the Taiwanese agents had paid Ya Du already. And were probably pressuring him to deliver, since Zhong Di had slipped away.

The real reason Ya Du wanted her to approach the agents on her own was so that he could keep his hands clean.

She was about to make sure that Ya Du got his hands dirty, though.

"I couldn't possibly meet with such people on my own," Fu Ran said, shaking her head. "It wouldn't be safe! Or proper," she added, glaring at him.

"You are meeting me here in a factory, after hours," Ya Du pointed out.

"That's different!" Fu Ran said, indignant. "You're a married man, and an upstanding member of the Party."

"True, true," Ya Du said, nodding and preening. "How about this? We'll meet tomorrow night at the Green Tearoom, at eight p.m. I'll make the introductions."

"And this is the best way to help everyone?" Fu Ran asked, as if looking for reassurances. "Including my family?"

"It is," Ya Du assured her.

"Thank you so much," Fu Ran said, rising from her chair, then bowing lowly, as if Ya Du were a great man.

"With pleasure," he said, smacking his fat lips together.

Fu Ran left, her insides shaking but her hands still steady.

Just one more night, and Zhong Di would be free of his foreign ghosts.

Though the Green Tearoom had been built just a few years before, it still felt ancient, with scarred wooden floors, soft amber walls, and discrete lights. The air smelled of refined green tea and lemony cakes. Beautiful pink and white orchids sat on the front reception desk. The young woman behind the dark-oak reception desk wore the replica of an old-fashioned robe and was so covered up, Fu Ran knew her father would have approved.

A large room opened up to the right of the reception desk. Low tables filled the floor, each with comfortable-looking pillows scattered around them. Many men, and a few women, sat at the tables, drinking tea, eating small bites, and toasting one another.

While only the best people with the strongest influence would be allowed in here, it wasn't a place that she ever wanted to return to. She wouldn't be comfortable here.

Perhaps Zhong Di belonged here, but not her. Even though she wore her "interview" outfit again—same black skirt, with a different white shirt, and a discreet black handbag—and maybe she could pretend as though she belonged, she would never actually fit in here. She'd grown up too poor.

The thought made her heart ache.

When the receptionist heard Fu Ran's name, instead of seating her in the public area, the woman led her down a short, closed-in hallway. At the first corridor, the receptionist took a right. Brighter lights shone down here, and soft green carpet muffled their steps. Closed wooden doors lined this corridor.

The receptionist opened the third door on her left, then waited for Fu Ran to enter.

Fu Ran nearly protested. She didn't want to wait by herself in an empty room for spies to come meet her!

Then she swallowed down her fear. She could do this.

She clutched the black handbag she held a little tighter. She wasn't completely unprepared, either.

"Come in! Come in!" she heard Ya Du's cheerful voice.

Fu Ran straightened her shoulders and marched into the room, knowing full well that it could be a trap.

Ya Du sat in the place of honor, at the head of the table. He still wore his jacket that mimicked a Party uniform.

Fu Ran didn't allow herself to sag in relief when she saw that three other places had been set at the table.

The spies would be here.

Before Fu Ran could ask Ya Du about his day, the two spies came in. They looked like the spies who had first visited Zhong Di, as he had described to her, the main characteristic being that they were both so ordinary that it would be easy to forget them. They wore their black hair fairly short. Their eyes were lighter brown, almost hazel color, and their skin looked more tanned. They'd obviously been well fed their entire lives: good fingernails, white teeth, no pockmarks on their faces. One wore a brown Western suit, while the other was in grey, but both were cheaply made.

After the introductions had been made and tea had been served, Mr. Gray (as Fu Ran had tagged the man in the grey suit) asked, "So, I hear that you're a chemist as well."

"I am," Fu Ran said proudly. Then she remembered her

part. "But no one will hire me," she added in a meeker voice.

"We may have need of a good chemist," Mr. Brown said.

"Really?" Fu Ran asked.

She knew she was just playing a part. It wasn't hard for her to sound genuinely excited. She'd looked so long for a real job.

"We would have some tests for you, of course," Mr. Gray said. "But it could be a real opportunity."

"I'd have to think about it," Fu Ran said cautiously, as a good girl would. She didn't add that she would check with her family as well—they didn't need those complications.

Ya Du smiled beneficently at all of them, like a father making a good match for his little girl. "Good! Good! So now that I have made the introductions, I think I should leave."

Fu Ran kept a pleasant smile pasted to her face. He couldn't go. Not yet!

Thankfully, a quiet knock on the door came to her rescue.

"Sir, I—" The receptionist stepped into the room, looking flustered.

Four men stepped in behind her.

Policemen. Wearing olive green uniforms. Not blue.

That meant they were part of the Armed Police Force, who handled security measures, not regular crimes.

"What's the meaning of this?" Ya Du asked, standing and sounding offended.

"We heard there was a meeting here with two Taiwanese spies," the tallest policeman said. He glared at Mr. Gray and Mr. Black.

"These are just two business acquaintances of mine," Ya Du said.

"Right. Business," the policeman continued. "We need to see your papers."

Mr. Gray and Mr. Black reached into their jacket pockets and took out their wallets and their identification papers. Fu Ran meekly handed hers over. Ya Du huffed greatly before he fished out his own.

"What's this?" the policeman asked, waving a five-hundred-yuan note, then pulling out a second and a third.

"Just to show my appreciation for the officers of the law," Ya Du stammered.

Fu Ran couldn't keep a grim smile from her face. It figured that such a good Party member would try bribing everyone he met.

"You're all going to have to come in with us," the policeman said.

"What?" Ya Du asked, puffing up his chest like a stupid peacock. "Do you know who I am? I have important friends, you know."

Another man stepped into the room, pushing past the officers.

Fu Ran blinked, surprised.

It was her father's old boss. Another Party official. Gau Wan.

"I do know who you are," Gau Wan said. He sniffed as if he disapproved of all he saw. "And I have important friends as well."

He looked old, much older than the last time Fu Ran had seen him. Grey hair covered his head, wrinkles marked his face with lines of sorrow, and his skin hung off his cheeks as if he'd lost a great deal of weight. He wore a Western-style black suit, well-tailored, with a white shirt and shiny black shoes.

Fu Ran swallowed down her fear. He wasn't going to turn on her, was he?

As part of the plan, Zhong Di had promised to get a highly regarded Party official to come to the teahouse with the policemen. Hopefully, one who couldn't be bribed by Ya Du.

How did Zhong Di know Gau Wan? Though admittedly, Fuzhou wasn't that big of a city. It wasn't completely unfeasible that the two might know each other. Zhong Di was much richer than Fu Ran, and ran in different circles. The same circles as Gau Wan.

Gau Wan had disappeared after her father's death. Other Party officials had taken note and done likewise, leaving her family adrift. What had happened to him? Some tragedy, she could tell. She suddenly felt guilty for all the angry thoughts she'd had about him over the past few years.

"Let's go down to the police station and get this all straightened out," Gau Wan said. Though he kept an easy smile on his face, his tone brooked no argument.

The two spies looked at each other.

They tensed.

They were going to make a run for it.

Everything seemed to suddenly shift to slow motion.

Mr. Gray started reaching inside his jacket pocket.

Fu Ran just as covertly reached into her purse and wrapped her fingers around the cool glass she found there.

Before Mr. Gray could pull out his weapon, Fu Ran brought out the vial she carried. Neon-green, viscous liquid filled it.

She held it up over the table.

Every eye suddenly turned to her.

"You will go quietly with the police," Fu Ran told Mr.

Gray. "No heroic measures. Or I'll break this over your head and you'll die a long, drawn out, *painful* death."

Mr. Gray visibly gulped and removed his empty hand from his jacket, then raised both hands into the air.

Fu Ran turned her head and glared at Mr. Black. "I have a second one in here for you as well."

Ya Du sneered. "You wouldn't dare."

"What do I have to live for?" Fu Ran said, anger rising in her voice. "I have no father. My mother's sick. My brother is dead. One more tragedy for my family would surprise no one."

She knew even as she said the words that she lied.

She had something to live for. The hope of a relationship with Zhong Di.

However, that hope was ephemeral, as likely to disappear with the bright morning sunlight as mist from the sea.

Ya Du didn't say anything more. Mr. Gray and Mr. Black were frisked (and several more weapons discovered) before they were handcuffed and taken away. Ya Du didn't have to bear the embarrassment of handcuffs, yet he was still going to be seen by some of the more important movers and shakers of Fuzhou in the presence of police as they walked him out of the tearoom.

Finally, only Gau Wan and Fu Ran remained. She took a deep breath and sagged down, resting her elbows on the table and dropping the vial.

"Careful!" Gau Wan said, rushing over.

Fu Ran grinned. "It's just a soporific," she said. "It would have made him feel very sleepy, very quickly. Then like he'd been run over by a bus."

Gau Wan chuckled and shook his head. His smile melted the years away from him. "I need to apologize," he said softly. "For abandoning you and your family. My wife

got sick the week your father died and I lost track of everything else. Zhong Di rousted me, finally reminding me of
my other duties."

"I'm so sorry," Fu Ran said. And she was, though a small
part of her still wanted to yell at him for disappearing years
ago. However, he really did look as though he'd gone
through hell.

"How do you know Zhong Di?" Fu Ran asked as she
stood up. She was still going to have to go to Party Headquarters to tell them about the attempted bribes. As well as
give her statement to the police.

"He's my godson," Gau Wan explained. "I fell out of
contact with him, as I did everyone else."

That explained how they knew each other, and why
Zhong Di had felt he could ask for this kind of favor.

"It was the least I could do, given how I'd abandoned
your family," Gau Wan added, holding open the door for
Fu Ran.

"I see," Fu Ran said.

And she did. She couldn't hope for anything more, like
maybe a job offer or even some money to help cover their
hospital costs. Gau Wan had paid his debt by believing
Zhong Di's story, by not being swayed by another Party
member, and by showing up that night.

"Thank you," she said as he helped her into the back of
a police car.

She didn't expect to see either Gau Wan or Zhong Di
again.

They'd done their part.

Now they'd slink away into the night like the ghosts
they were, and she'd be on her own again.

Fu Ran eagerly strolled through the city park. Water merrily splashed out of the mouths of the stone fish that rose in a tower in the center of the main fountain. The wind carried the smell of the sea. Though no clouds marred the bright blue sky, the breeze cooled everything down.

Just past the fountain, Fu Ran discovered Zhong Di, as the note he'd left her had promised. She told her stupid heart to stop beating so hard. She hadn't seen him for two weeks, not since the night of the police raid on the teahouse.

Ya Du had been publicly shamed and now awaited trial for treason and working with Taiwanese spies. Mr. Gray and Mr. Black had disappeared, and would probably never surface again.

Zhong Di looked so gorgeous resting against the tall edge of the fountain. His black hair shone in the sunlight, his dark eyes sparkled at her. He wore a lime-green short-sleeved shirt that showed even more muscles, grey pants, but only sandals on his handsome feet. Fu Ran couldn't help but feel as though all the air had suddenly thinned, making her lightheaded.

She was glad that she'd worn her prettiest skirt, pale green with the outlines of flowers done in thin black lines. It was short, too—her father had hated that skirt, as it showed off her knees. She'd borrowed white sandals from one of her cousins, along with a peach-colored top.

When Zhong Di pushed himself off the fountain and started towards her, she realized that he had a string wrapped around one hand. A bright red balloon bobbed along in the air behind him.

"Hello," Zhong Di said. He sounded shy.

"Hello," Fu Ran replied. She was happy to be able to get the word out despite her desperately dry throat.

"I wanted to thank you, yet again, for helping me," Zhong Di said.

"It was nothing," Fu Ran said, disappointment stabbing her chest. Of course, that would be the only reason he'd want to see her. He couldn't be interested in her. Not like that.

"So I brought you this," he said, bringing forward the hand with the balloon attached.

"What is this?" Fu Ran asked as she reached for the string and tugged the balloon down. Then she gasped. A Chinese junk was painted on the face of the balloon, floating across a smooth sea.

Zhong Di shrugged, seemingly embarrassed. "An offering."

Fu Ran tilted her head at him, puzzled.

"I know it's tradition to burn Hell money for ghosts," Zhong Di said all in a rush. "I thought...I thought maybe we could start a new tradition." He placed his hand on the balloon string, just above Fu Ran's. "Send our offering up into the sky, straight to heaven."

Fu Ran beamed at him. "I think that's a marvelous idea," she said, letting go of the string.

Zhong Di unwrapped the string from around his palm. He pinched it lightly, then held it out to Fu Ran.

Blushing, she reached out and pinched the string as well.

Zhong Di looked up into the clear sky and said softly, "I want to thank all the ancestors who guided me a cemetery during Ghost Month, so that I might find my luck and my love." He turned to face Fu Ran, his look hopeful.

Nodding, Fu Ran turned her face up as well. "I, too, want to thank all my ancestors for prompting me visit a cemetery, even during Ghost Month, so that I might find my luck and my love."

She looked down at Zhong Di.

The smile he gave her might have been brighter than the sun.

They released the balloon together, and hand-in-hand, watched it sail up, up, up, into the clear blue sky.

THE CUCKOO QUEEN
C.H. HUNG

My husband the king tells me this morning that he has reached a decision regarding my fate. He holds the key to my salvation, but he will not relinquish it without a ransom—one that I cannot pay.

Storm clouds gather outside my bedroom window, framing his slender silhouette in grey. He is handsome in his plumed finery and swan-feather ruff, dressed for our court's greatest celebration tonight. But I much prefer him when he is his magnificent thrush, all brilliant black with a glossy yellow bill, for then I can better see the good in him. Today, his aura pulses with the bold, orange glow of righteousness and determination, as noble as his lineage.

I drop my gaze to the floor before he catches me staring, but I should not have fretted. He pays no attention to me sitting at the edge of my bed, my hands folded in my lap.

Instead, he scans the gloomy skies through the open window, one hand propped on a hip. The sun falls slowly below our clouds. None of the windows in our palace are paned with glass, as covered windows mean imprisonment to so many of us, so the scent of threatening rain fills my bedroom.

"You've tested the roe?" he asks. "The fish will replenish themselves properly?"

"Yes, Your Grace," I murmur. Even though I am his queen, I have not been one in more than name for some time. Not since I birthed our daughter.

"Then after the Fledging," he says, "you will take the long walk down, never to return."

He said "walk" instead of "ride," which means his decision is leniency. But I have little heart to celebrate.

Neither banishment nor death would let me stay with our child. Whatever victory I gained from my husband's small compassion, it pales next to the prospect of never seeing my daughter again.

"Your Grace is merciful," I whisper.

He leaves without acknowledgment, my eyes too dry for tears.

The sky garden lies in the center of the palace, its flora brought from the earth to be transplanted into thick layers of stratus clouds. I know not how the plants have thrived in their foreign environment, only that they have done so. For the first time in the court's living memory, the scent of flowers fills the Aerie from season to season.

I seek the garden's solace now, in the last hours of my time here. Flames crackle from torches posted along the courtyard columns, drenching the garden in deep oranges and yellows. Sweet, delicate jasmine saturates the air, weighing it down as heavily as the white blossoms on their vines.

Ostrich plumes, as delicate and lovely as cirrus clouds, fan into a halo behind my hair, bobbing as I walk and tickling my neck and jaw. My husband hates them, a reminder of the hell that exists for someone who cannot fly, which makes me love their ostentatious allure even more.

In the center of the garden lies a fountain as wide as the wingspan of ten eagles tip to tip, and as deep as I am tall. I sit at its cloud-stone edge and trail my hand through its burbling waters. The evening has not yet fallen deep enough to cool the liquid, and it flows through my fingers as warm as crimson blood.

Beneath the water, silvery scales catch the torchlight, turning golden as they breach the surface. The fish coalesce in schools around me, crowding near, their mouths opening and closing with desperate hunger. They are small—bite-sized, really—but together they constitute a formidable group, much like our court.

Their hunger stirs echoes within the pit of my stomach, and I hold a hand to my belly, lying flat and empty. I hunger for the child who once filled it, who now consumes my heart. I hunger to see her again, to know that she will be loved and cherished as I am not.

Footsteps fall softly nearby. I will them to go away, but they come closer. Reluctantly, I glance up to see a young man approaching with hat in hand, turning it by the brim over and over.

The man is an outsider for he wears wool, harvested from hooved livestock bound to the ground. Even the servants in our court wear cloud-spun silk, diaphanous and fine, reflecting rainbows wherever we flit.

But it is not his clothing that overcomes my resentment at his intrusion and stirs my curiosity. A silvery nimbus surrounds the man, indicating an aura of purity, tainted by the deep red of a blood oath sworn. None but those with violet eyes can see auras, and none but the king and I have violet eyes.

That is why he took me for wife, and why I have lasted this long, even after he discovered my mother's betrayal.

"Your Grace," the outsider says when he reaches me, bowing with a flourish of his hat. "My name is Cobbe, and I have traveled a long way to speak with you."

His hat is a floppy thing, homespun wool dyed with common woad, as blue as the spring sky. I take in the man's patchwork rags and his wild mane of dull brown hair. Of fine plumage, he is not.

Yet he stands with the proud bearing of an eagle. I cannot help but be impressed even as I ponder the significance of his aura's colors. The last time I saw an oathbound aura, my mother was closing the door behind her, never to return.

Her memory reminds me to slip on the mask of a queen. I raise an eyebrow and hazard a guess. "Did my husband refuse your request already?" I ask. "Whatever he has denied you, you overestimate my influence if you think I can reverse any decision of his."

The uncomfortable flush reddening Cobbe's neck and ears makes me sigh. I am right, of course.

He takes my sigh for permission to continue. "I asked for a position in your court as a scribe." The hat twists in his hands. "But he said that if I have not the proper wings, then I cannot join you anyway."

It is his voice that piques my sympathy like nothing else can. I have heard that tone before. I have heard that bitterness in my own thoughts, my own dreams.

"Surely there is an easier way to earn a living as a

scribe," I say, "than to climb the ten thousand stairs it takes to reach our palace."

He does not answer for a long minute. "My mother was a member of your court, Your Grace." The hat's brim crumples beneath his fingers. His smile flashes, brief and brittle, reminding me of the way a feral cat can lash out without warning. "Your court banished her when she chose to marry my father."

Morbid fascination shivers down my spine. Our court holds only one tenet so dear that to violate it means banishment or death—fly on feathered wings, or leave the Aerie by one method or another. It is that simple, and that brutal. The name and spirit of our court cannot survive if tainted by impurity.

"An earthwalker?" I ask.

"He became one, Your Grace. Both my parents did, giving up the skies they loved to raise me." His mouth is pinched, his jaw tight, as he adds, "I learned to fly, but I suppose it's not enough for your court if I don't have feathers."

I think of our court's Brood Mother. "We do have one who was not born to us, whose natal court left her on a nearby peak to die because her wings are too stunted for her to fly. We took her in because she kept the children warm like no one else." I gesture at the torches lit all around us. "Draka is the reason we have fire at all, in the Aerie."

At his blank look, I explain, "She is a dragon, with fire breath. We birth our fledglings here, to nest with her. Those of us with children in the clutch stay too, grounded as they are. When they fledge, we migrate with the rest of the court from roost to roost. Draka stays here until the next hatching."

"But the dragons are your rivals," Cobbe says, puzzled.

"You war for control of the sky and this Aerie. Why take in one of them?"

"She is useful and loyal."

"So if I'm useful and loyal, will your court overlook my lack of feathers?"

A harsh laugh escapes me before I can stop myself. If it had been that simple, I would have had the best reason of all for a pardon.

"Does your mother regret her choice?" I ask instead. I do not feel like answering his question, for it falls uncomfortably close to my own fate.

Cobbe smiles. "No, Your Grace. My parents are very much devoted to each other, for all that they come from vastly different realms."

"There is no shame in that."

Cobbe shuffles his feet, and his flush deepens. "Forgive me, Your Grace, but I never said I was ashamed of my parents."

"No," I murmur. "Of course not." Inwardly, I shake my head. Not every marriage is predestined by prophecy.

I splash my hand in the fountain, trailing a cascade of rainbow prisms as the torchlight refracts through the droplets. The fish flow in a murmuration of shadows, opening their mouths in futile attempts to catch tears that will not come.

"I cannot help you," I tell Cobbe, ignoring his crestfallen expression. I gesture toward the sounds of revelry floating through the air. "But please, join us for our Fledgling Feast before you descend. You will need your strength."

I do not tell him that I, too, would need the strength for the same walk down. He and the rest of the court will find out soon enough.

The feasting has already begun by the time Cobbe and I enter the dining hall. Extra light from double the usual torches and candles chase shadows into oblivion. The entire hall is bathed in flickering, golden light that alleviates the evening gloom of the somber, cloud-built walls.

The fledglings—about a dozen in all this season—have taken a table at the far end, near the wide, outdoor terrace with an infinity edge. I grant Cobbe permission to take his leave as I make my way toward the high table.

I seat myself next to my husband, who is deep in conversation with his captain of the guard on his right. To my left is Draka, hunched and white-haired with shriveled arms, her old eyes as sharp as ever as she still counts the chicks in her charge even though they have lost their fuzz.

I sip fermented nectar from my cup. "Is it just me, Draka," I ask her, "or do the fires seem especially bright?"

"It's the glass we've installed, Your Grace," she says. Her voice rasps with age, but still carries clearly above the din of the revelers. "They reflect and amplify the light of the flames."

I finally notice the subtle sheen of darkened glass over the tall windows. "Who authorized those?"

"The king, Your Grace. He feared the rains would return and ruin the festivities." She nods toward the fledgling table, where my daughter sits. "He wishes for a perfect evening tonight, for her."

"We all do." I squint at the strangeness of the covered windows, then shrug. "Too bad they are tinted so darkly that we cannot see the stars."

The main course is a rare treat, tuna wrangled from the oceans below. It takes scores of our hunters to bring back even just one of the mighty fish. We eat in silence until Draka says suddenly, "I remember the night you fledged, Your Grace. You did not speak much then, either."

"Words would not have helped me call forth feathered wings, Draka."

"Perhaps not, Your Grace," she allows, and cocks her head, watching me out of the sly corner of her faceted ruby eyes. "I remember the night you were found at court as well. Such an awkward child you were, all knobby limbs and joints too big, like a cuckoo too big for its nest. Many doubted you would fly."

I take a bite of seared tuna, careful to keep my hands steady. "I am sure many of those were other girls waiting to take my place."

The old woman guffaws. "Surely," she chortles, "but none of *them* fledged into the swan princess of prophecy." Then she sobers. "You were terrified almost to the point of paralysis. But you flew, my Grace. You flew." She chews on her tuna slowly, thoughtfully. "Sometimes, fledglings fail because they cannot control their fear, not because they cannot control wings at all."

A laugh trills up from the fledglings and I cannot help but watch her—Aurum, my only child, my daughter with the swan-like neck.

Draka follows my gaze. "I do not think that one knows the meaning of fear."

I clasp my hands in my lap, not trusting myself to reach for the ambrosia without spilling it. "She will fly."

Draka nods, scooping another mouthful of fish. "With parents like hers, no doubt she will."

With a mother like me, there is every doubt in the world.

I ache to hold Aurum one last time, but I know the rules better than anyone—until her destiny is revealed, she is in limbo and untouchable. Not outside the court, but not within either, for all that she is a royal child. Until she fledges, Aurum is nothing to the court.

There are days when I wonder if it might have gone better for everyone had I remained nothing.

I content myself with standing under the archway leading out to the terrace, straining to eavesdrop on the fledglings' conversation while pretending to watch over the hall.

A voice breaks my focus: "The view is better behind you, Your Grace."

I wanted solitude, so it surprises me how pleased I am to see the outsider. Cobbe moves out onto the terrace to stare in amazement. "No wonder the Court of Winged Scales wants the Aerie," he says. "The views here are magnificent."

I scoff. "It is not the views they want. They think we hide a great secret within the Aerie. That it is the only way mere birds can fight off great dragons. They do not understand that we fight for our home while they fight for treasure."

Cobbe shifts his gaze to me. "Are they wrong?"

"What do you think?"

"It would make a great song of legend, if true."

I shake my head. "Legends are written by the victors and are not always the unvarnished truth."

He smiles. "True." After a moment, he says in wonder, "I never realized how vast the ocean is."

"Have you only seen it up close?"

"I've never seen it, Your Grace."

"You should. It is the boundary between two worlds, between earth and the celestial skies. When you pass through to the other side, you can lose your old self and find yourself anew."

He studies me, his dark eyes thoughtful. "You have been there before," he says. It is not a question.

"A lifetime ago." I study his aura. The red threading through silver pulses slowly, undimmed in its purpose. "Why are you really here, Cobbe?" I hold up a hand when he opens his mouth. "Careful. These violet eyes see more than you know."

He snaps his mouth shut, and his lips presses into a grim line.

"My mother lost her feathered wings," he says finally. "I swore I'd get them back."

Absently, I rub the chills from my arms. "But she was banished for marrying your father."

"Yes," Cobbe concedes. "But losing her wings means she can never return." He shifts his gaze to the far horizon, where starlight glitters on ocean waves. "My father will die soon. Nothing can be done," he says quickly to prevent the sympathy from rolling off my tongue. "We are at peace with his journey to his next life. But Mother would like to come home, after."

Understanding blooms like an ache in my chest. "And you would like to join her. Hence your request."

Cobbe nods. "Scribing is one of the few things I do well."

I think of what he would write of me, how much of the truth he would preserve and how much of it he would vilify.

We watch the merrymakers in the dining hall—

outsiders both. My daughter giggles at a joke, her delicate skin blooming pink. I mourn all of the moments I will miss as she grows into her maturity.

At least I will not miss her fledging. At least I can make sure I gave her a better destiny than the one gifted to me.

"You are a good son," I tell Cobbe.

He glances at Aurum. "And you, my Grace, are a good mother."

My husband heaves himself to his feet. The hall falls into expectant silence. He beckons to Draka, who also rises.

"Tonight we honor you, dear Brood Mother," the king says. "What a fine clutch you have raised this season."

The woman cackles, an eerie laugh that trails off into a cough. We wait for her to catch her breath, politely ignoring her infirmities. We will need a new Brood Mother to sit for the next set of chicks, and it will be the king himself who dispatches the old one, as it is his duty to keep the flock healthy. Still, he views her with kind affection. She is, after all, the same Brood Mother who raised him and his father before him, as she raised me.

"It has been a particularly exceptional clutch, your grace," she wheezes, "with the quality of parentage represented." She nods to Aurum, who smiles shyly.

"Just so," the king says. He strokes his black beard, hiding a frown. "The Migration awaits. Let us begin."

The king claps his hands, and the nightingale watch moves toward the terrace. Robed in shimmering cloud-silk, men and women alike, they split into two groups lining opposite edges. Then they burst into song, voices melding into effortless harmony and fluting from note to note with intricate skill.

My husband meets me at the archway. He proffers his hand and we make our stately procession toward the terrace's edge. At the brink, the updraft whips our state robes and the fabric snaps like pennants at a tournament.

"Still no confession, Fala?" he asks, his words hidden from the court by wind and nightingale song. His violet eyes gleam in the torchlight.

I lift my chin. "I cannot tell you what I do not know."

He scowls. "I know you know where she is."

"I have already told you everything." I glance at Aurum, standing at the archway among the other waiting fledglings, and then back to my husband. "Worse, I have already given you everything."

"Not everything." He fingers the swan feathers around his neck. The jet black of his beard spills across the pure white of the feathers like a tear of midnight across a clouded sky, and his eyes glitter like amethyst stars in his shadowed face.

"Everything that matters." I step into place on one side of the terrace.

He mirrors me. We stand like sentinels at the forefront of the precipice, both of us having played this dance before, season after season of hatchlings. The pageantry camouflages the deadly stakes, lulling us into submission with food and drink, music and fine plumage. Not all of the fledglings will survive tonight. But the ceremony at the Fledgling Feast has never before been like this, this wary circling hidden in public.

Because, until now, the stakes had never included Aurum.

Draka organizes the fledglings into a line. Her arms are

unnaturally short and small, but her ferocious glare is enough to move them. One by one, they remove their simple robes and let them fall.

They are so young, standing on the cusp between childhood and pre-adulthood. Soon they will come of age, ready for the roles they were born into.

Tonight, they brave a different rite of passage. The right to belong in our court.

"Kynera," Draka says, speaking the first fledgling's name.

A muscular teenager raises her hands above her head and leans over the edge. She lets herself drop, disappearing from our view, as the chorus declines into a soft, melodic interlude.

The rest of us hold our breaths.

There is a whoosh as the fledgling catches the updraft and a rust-colored eagle rockets high up into the air. Around us, the nightingale song rises in exultation along with the pirouetting bird. The young ones cheer, and even the most seasoned of the court cannot help but smile.

"Golden eagle," Draka says.

"We welcome Kynera of the Eagle," the flock choruses, "to the Court of Feathered Wings."

The king grins, our contention forgotten for the moment. He is pleased to add another eagle to his aerial corps. Our war with the Court of Winged Scales has grown deadlier lately.

Kynera lands on a turret overlooking the terrace and preens. Now that her avian form has manifested, she must understand where fate will take her, but the young bird does not look too concerned.

The next fledgling, a boy almost as tall as he is thin, jumps with an exuberant cheer and moments later, rises as a crane. He perches next to Kynera. The teen after him becomes a raven. Then we welcome a vulture and cormorant, a sparrow and a turtledove.

The next fledgling shuffles forward, her shoulders hunched. Unease strikes me but before I can act, she squeezes her eyes shut and jumps. The choir drops into a murmur, while the court congratulates our latest members.

I ignore the chatter and stare in dazed numbness at my husband, who has already rearranged his features into a neutral mask. It takes a full minute before the rest of the court also realizes no new bird rises from the dark clouds below.

The chatter dies.

Smoothly, the choir moves into a minor key, singing a gentle farewell. A woman keens in a low wail while another tries to smother the sound. Somber quiet settles upon the court, suffocating the last of the merriment.

The king beckons. "Forward," he commands. "We migrate tomorrow, and I *will* leave you to the dragons if you do not fly." His gaze sweeps the line and lingers briefly on Aurum.

The next fledgling steps to the edge, trembling. I see the terror in the young boy's eyes, reminding me so much of my own, and grab his arm before he can jump.

"You have a choice," I say, low and urgent. "If you are not confident you belong here, then take the long walk to the ground and live among the earthwalkers, with my blessing."

The boy's eyes are wide and round, frozen to mine. Behind him, the court realizes the line has stopped.

"Fala!" my husband snaps. He strides over to grip my shoulders, his fingers like talons. "What are you doing?"

I shove the boy behind me, away from the edge. The

roar of blood rushing through me in an ever-faster rhythm makes me dizzy. Aurum's pale head peeks over the top of the crowd as she hops, straining to see what is happening, like a fuzzy chick begging for worms.

The sight emboldens me further. I have nothing left to lose.

"This practice is barbaric," I growl. "The boy is so terrified that even if he truly did possess an avian soul, he would be so frightened that he could not manifest. And then he would be dead, and what would that really prove?"

The nightingales choke back their song. Silence falls.

Cobbe's mouth drops open. He still stands at the archway where I left him, trying to take up as little room as possible amid the crowd.

My husband flares his nostrils. "It would prove that only the strongest survive to safeguard this court."

Too late, I realize that I have forced my husband to change his mind from this morning's decision. To act early and swiftly. To mete out justice. To protect his court from impurities and weakness.

It is his sacred duty as king of this court to cull the weak from his flock, and I can see by the tightening of the lines around his eyes that he is about to do so.

He yanks the boy from me and shoves him off the terrace. The fledgling screams, a long cry that drops slower than his plummeting body.

No one dares to breathe.

Change! I pray desperately, and the gods answer with an abrupt, sickening stop to the wailing.

"Aerial corps!" the king bellows. "At formation!"

All around us, clothing tears off human forms as avian souls take flight, and feathers fill the frenzied air. A convocation of eagles lands on the terrace in a semicircle behind the fledglings.

"Mother!" Aurum cries out, but one of the nightingales shushes her.

My husband, too, is removing his clothing with slow, deliberate movements. He may not be an eagle or another bird of prey, but his beak is sharper than a rapier, and I have seen him kill with it. I do not make the mistake of underestimating him.

"You were not who you said you were from the moment you stepped foot into the Aerie," he says, and the crowd—those who have chosen to remain human—gasps in a collective breath. It breaks my heart that my daughter is one of them. "How can I trust that she is a true Avian?" He gestures at Aurum. "That I will not have to mourn her when she does not fly?"

"Mother," Aurum sobs.

I hear the question in her tears, and my heart shatters into a thousand shards.

"I have served you true, Your Grace," I say. "Whatever I am, I am not a cheat."

"You cheated me of my true bride!" he shouts. "One who has long flown to gods know where! One who rightfully should stand where you stand, not you—this, this—" He sputters, at a loss.

"Earthwalker," I finish for him. My voice trembles, but it carries to the court nearest us. A shocked murmur sweeps through the crowd, traveling with the echoes of my fatal word. A nightingale faints.

I straighten my shoulders and raise my chin. "No more lies, dear husband. Tell them what I am. Tell your court what we have been hiding all these years."

His robes lay in a discarded pile at his feet, topped by

snow-white feathers. My husband is naked now, fierce and proud and strong in muscle and bone. He did not become king because he is a bearded thrush with the ferocity of a falcon and the cunning of a crow. He became king because he will do what no one else will do, for the good of his flock.

He glowers, dark and thunderous as the storm clouds moving in swiftly from the east. "Toss them," he orders, sweeping his arm to indicate the fledglings—and me.

I scream, but no one hears me in the deafening roar of wings taking flight. The king becomes his thrush and leaps into the air. Talons grab my arms, wrenching them cruelly in their sockets as they haul me to the brink. It is Kynera, testing her wings. The remaining fledglings take the leap on their own, frantic to prove themselves.

Including Aurum, plunging over the edge.

I stumble and fall to my knees, shrugging Kynera off. Time slows to a crawl. I inch forward, hardly daring to hope, hardly daring to breathe, to peer over the precipice. My limbs are like lead, my sorrow hot and unshed in the back of my throat, suffocating my voice and soul.

The sweep of a wing brushing against my cheek lifts my head and I look upward, at the downy owl rising into the air. She is grey as hellsmoke, inexperienced and awkward, but her wing strokes are sure and her flight grows stronger with every beat.

And she is mine.

I collapse forward, panting with relief. But before I can catch my breath, the talons are back, digging into my shoulders.

I lunge for my husband's discarded clothing just as the talons lift me off the terrace. For an eternal moment, my feet hang over nothing.

My gaze follows the grey owl, my heart swelling with

pride. I want to leave with Aurum in my visions—not my husband, not my adopted court, and not the ground that will rush up to greet me.

The talons let go.

The harsh chaos above me fades as I plummet with my back to the ground. I can no longer see my darling owl, but I am content. She flies on feathered wings, and I can ask for no better future for her than to be wholly accepted into a flock that will now protect her as their own.

The fall feels slow and peaceful, even though the air courses past me in a thunderous rush, ripping my husband's robes out of my hands. Only the swan feathers remain in my grip—feathers he stole from me, that my mother in turn once stole from another for her earthbound daughter.

It is the only thing left that I need.

I touch the feathers to my skin, and they cling to me like raindrops on grass. Wings burst from my back, straining against the fabric of my robes. I tear at the cloth, allowing the air rushing past to wrench the clothing off my body as I change. The clouds stream by until I am in the clear.

My wings spread wide, catching hold of the open sky at the last moment. I swoop upward, beating fiercely into the winds. The currents glide over the white feathers covering my sleek body. I wear a black mask with a yellow bill, and my wings are swift and sure.

I am free, at last.

An eagle's defiant shriek rends the air, followed by the unmistakably crackling bellow of a dragon. Startled, I twist mid-flight to peer back the way I came. Flames crisscross the heavens above me, illuminating the smoldering silhouette of the Aerie and the dizzying acrobatics of hundreds of wings—feathered wings that dart and bat and swat and beat desperately against the invaders, and much larger leathery wings engulfing them one by one.

Dark shapes spin out from the battle at the Aerie in wide arcs, shapes of all sizes and beaks, falling lifeless toward the ground.

No!

Aurum.

I curve upward, winging back toward my gilded cage. The slaughter is nearly complete by the time I crest the terrace's edge. The thrush trills his defiance, darting with unimaginable speed to poke holes into the dragons' thin wings, backed by a handful of motley birds. Corpses litter the terrace, many of them avian, their feathers soaked in blood.

The dragons, gleaming in jeweled tones culled from the rainbow, advance on the birds making their last stand. Draka looms over her adopted court in her dragon form, battling fire with fire and fluttering her useless wings.

Another beast fights near her, and it takes me a long, precious moment to digest the insanity of what I see—a white swan the size of a stunted dragon, covered in scales instead of feathers, with dragon's feet and claws instead of webbed feet. The beast opens his yellow bill and sprays fire at a nearby invader, and I realize with shock that the creature must be Cobbe. His proud beak is slick with blood. Dragon corpses with horrific lacerations of torn flesh bear mute witness to where his claws have done their damage.

I marvel that Cobbe would dare show his abominable wings in our court. My respect for him grows immeasurably when I spy a small grey owl perched upon his back, almost completely hidden by his scaly white wings.

I dive and tumble bill over tail to land on the terrace, dodging a dragon's attempt to burn me, changing as I land.

By the time I roll back upright, I stand on human feet, and I throw up my hands to show that I am no longer winged. Only a choker of swan feathers encircles my throat.

"Stop!" I cry out. "I am the secret that you seek."

The dragons rear back. One of them, a magnificent beast as black as onyx, swings his massive head to level his eye with mine, snorting plumes of smoke.

"Liar," the dragon hisses, ivory teeth gleaming in the flames consuming the Aerie.

"Don't!" my husband shouts. He rushes forth, and a great onyx arm sweeps him off his feet and flings him off to the side. He tries to rise, but another dragon, jeweled in sapphire shades, presses a massive foot to my husband's chest.

"Fala!" my husband screams. "It will destroy our court if you do this!"

The wind shimmers and dances as the avians shed their wings. I can feel the eyes of what remains of our court boring into my naked back.

"My king," I say without turning, my view entirely consumed by the great iris of the dragon, "if we went to such great lengths to rule, perhaps we were never meant to rule at all. Perhaps it is time this court came to an end."

An agitated mutter sweeps through the avians, but no one moves to save their king or queen.

"Cobbe," I say, "fetch me a fish."

There is a shiver through the air as the outsider changes forms. "Pardon, Your Grace?" he asks.

"The fish. Bring me one of the fish from the fountain."

A pause, and then, "Yes, Your Grace."

A hand slips into mine, and I grasp Aurum as I once did when she was a young chick. My husband has fallen silent, not even struggling to push the sapphire claw off his body, but I dare not check on him. The onyx dragon's eye, as deep and brooding as a dark well, stares at me, unblinking.

The rustling of the crowd heralds Cobbe's return, and he lays the fish down between me and the dragon. It flops, sorry and sad, and I let go of Aurum's hand with some regret to scoop up the fish.

The silvery scales are slimy and cold, and its terror and desperation mirrors mine so closely that the tears form from one blink to the next. I let a tear roll down my cheek until it falls into the fish's gaping mouth.

I raise the offering to the dragon and, after a moment's hesitation, he opens his mouth. I lay the fish on his monstrous tongue, and he swallows the fish whole.

Nothing happens.

The dragons shift on their feet and claws, restless, while the onyx stands statue-still. At last, traces of lavender lighten the pupils of his eyes, growing larger and brighter until his great dragon eyes are as purple as mine.

Gasps surround me with shock and suspicion, from avians and dragons alike.

The onyx dragon peers at me, and I see my reflection in his amethyst eyes. "What *are* you?" He swings his head to eye each of us in turn, then at his own retinue, before back at our court. "The others all wear similar auras of similar colors, whether scaled or feathered, but you—yours is different."

"I was born on the ground," I say. "A cuckoo whose mother stole a swan's feathers so that her daughter might steal into the Aerie's nest and become its queen. The gods gifted me with ultraviolet sight. I can see the trails in the sky left behind by your auras, see your plans and intentions, and I can share this sight with others. We know when and how you are going to strike by your auras."

"So *that* is how you birdbrains have been getting ahead of us," the dragon says.

"Sometimes strength comes in smaller packages," I agree.

"But you did not see us tonight?"

I recall the blazing light of the torches in the hall, crackling merrily and reflecting off darkened glass.

"The windows," I say slowly. Behind me, my husband moans as he, too, realizes the disaster that he himself unwittingly orchestrated. "The dark glass must have blocked the sight."

And blocked the stars. I had not thought to be alarmed when I could not see the stars. Oh, how stupid of me. How preoccupied I was with my own fate, and thus doomed the rest of the court.

The onyx dragon settles back on his haunches, the irises of his new eyes whirling. "Without you, no one else can see these auras?"

Uneasily, I nod.

He stalks over to my husband, still imprisoned within the sapphire dragon's massive claws. The onyx dragon blasts the king with a barrage of flame, and my husband screams. The sapphire does not move his claws, enduring the flames encasing his prisoner with stoic silence. Then the onyx pierces my husband's chest with a long talon.

The screaming stops abruptly.

The remainder of the avian court babbles an incoherent mix of horror and fright, and most scatter into the wind in their avian forms. The dragons do not give chase.

"There," the onyx dragon says with no small measure of satisfaction. "Now, only you and I can see. You have lost your king and your court. You serve only me now."

We are imprisoned in the charred wreck of the dining hall, dragon guards stationed in every direction. Only five of us are left—Cobbe and Aurum, Draka and Kynera, and me.

Kynera is badly injured in one arm, and we fear she may never regain use of her wing. She avoids me, uncertain of her place now that her king and her court are gone, and I have been exposed as an abhorrent earthwalker.

Draka has wrapped Kynera's arm as best she can in a sling fashioned from rags torn from corpses. We all wear whatever discarded clothing we found to fend off the chill of the deepening night. A veil of stars gleams through the broken ceiling above us, adorning us in faint starlight, the only light we have since the torches have long since sputtered out and there is no moon tonight.

"You shouldn't have come back, Your Grace," Cobbe says. He watches the guards at the archway leading out to the terrace. "Not if you were the secret the dragons sought."

"I had to," I say, watching Aurum.

Kynera snorted. "If you are what they seek, then why have they not killed the rest of us already?"

"Leverage," Draka answers with a glower. "Their prince thinks they can make our queen do what they want by keeping her flock close."

"She is not *my* queen," Kynera mutters.

The old woman's arms may be short, but we are clustered close and what she lacks in reach, she more than makes up for in experience and speed. She slaps Kynera hard across the mouth, and the would-be warrior raises the back of her good hand to her torn lip without a sound.

"Then leave," Draka hisses. "The queen has never treated me as anything less than a full member of the court, unlike some of you. If you do not like the current regime, the dragons will show you out."

Kynera scowls, matching the Brood Mother's dark expression. "*You* are a dragon."

"I believe," Cobbe says, "that is precisely the attitude the esteemed Draka is trying to cure you of."

"What, telling the truth?"

"Blindly following your own kind to your own destruction."

I ignore the bickering. I am worried by the desolate tuck of my daughter's head on her knees, her arms wrapped around herself. She refused even Draka's comfort and has chosen to sit alone, her back to us. I scoot closer to her.

"Am I a monster?" she whispers when I draw near.

"Oh, darling," I say, but dare not touch her lest I scare her from my reach. "Not at all."

She raises her head and stares at me, lost. "Are you?"

A lump rises in my throat, hard and unyielding. *No. Not now. Not here.* I blink furiously to stem the flow of tears threatening to spill.

A dragon shouts for backup and footsteps pound toward us.

Cobbe and Draka shoot to their feet to ward them off, but the guards knock them aside like bugs in a storm. Rough arms haul me to my feet. A bowl is thrust underneath my chin. I struggle against the restraints and fight back tears. A hand grips my face and squeezes my cheeks, hard, until the pain forces a few tears to spill into the bowl. They pool there, clear liquid with a bright opalescent shimmer that dances in the starlight filtering down from the broken ceiling.

The guard holding me throws me to the ground, where I sprawl in a jumble of limbs.

"My queen!" Draka crawls over and holds me to her breast. She rocks me like she once did, many clutches ago, and I let her. It is better to feel nothing than to feel something and risk the attention again.

Aurum stares, a hand raised to her open mouth in horror. Even Kynera looks uneasy.

Only Cobbe remains unruffled. "Your mother is not a monster," he tells Aurum. "Merely treated like one."

I do not know how long we huddled there, us poor remainders of a once high-flying court. Dragons come and go, but I do not pay attention to them. I focus only on keeping my thoughts and emotions empty. I do not want Aurum to witness again her mother being milked for her precious tears.

A whisper tickles in my ear. "Your Grace."

I lay unmoving on the ground, but my dull gaze flicks over to Cobbe, who is sprawled next to me.

"We're getting you out of here, Your Grace," he says, barely moving his lips. "The guards are nearing the end of their shift and getting tired. Draka and Kynera will create a distraction for us to slip you out."

"Aurum," I murmur. "She is not yet a strong flyer."

"I am the healthiest. I will carry her out myself."

I rouse from my stupor, hope flaring. "Then you must be fast," I say. "You must be as fast as you ever have been and not stop for anything until she is safe."

"I swear it, Your Grace. Can you fly?"

I touch the feathers at my neck. The dragons had spared hardly a glance for them, likely assuming they were merely a symbol of my legend—the fabled swan

princess promised at birth to the thrush king of the Avian
court.

"Yes."

"Good. Be ready."

He shifts away, as if rolling in his sleep, to face Kynera.

Draka's shadow looms over us. She looks to be dozing
while sitting, a skill learned from brooding over so many
clutches, but one eye opens to peer at me. I lift a corner of
my lips in a small smile. Her eye sharpens, and I can almost
feel her dissecting my intentions. Those who are old and
wise in the world need no violet sight to see the future,
mothers least of all, and I know she understands what I
must do. She dips her chin in a slight nod, then closes
her eye.

In her lap, Aurum sleeps. I trace the outlines of her pale
face with my gaze, memorizing it for the long ride down. I
should have taken the ride a lifetime ago, removed myself
from a situation where I would be a prisoner of my own
gift, but I could not muster up the courage—and when
Aurum came, it was too late. Now I have the chance to
redeem myself, and I am determined not to lose it.

Cobbe's face comes back into view.

"Any moment now," he says. "We will rise on Kynera's
signal."

"Cobbe." I reach out and touch his shoulder. "I have
what you are looking for."

His eyes drift down to the swan feathers around my
neck.

"Yes," I say, "these are your mother's wings, that my
mother stole so that I might fly, and live a better life." I
close my eyes against the brilliance of his aura, which now
pulses with the golden color of triumph, the red erased. His
oath fulfilled. "I am sorry I took your mother's place."

"Don't be, Your Grace," he says. "If my mother had married your king, she would not have met a dragon outcast, and I would not be here." His mouth quirks into wry smile. "The world would not have a swan dragon."

I squeeze his hands in mine. "Come find me when this is all over so that I can right one wrong, at least. Come fetch your mother's wings by the ocean."

"Yes, Your Grace." Suddenly, his eyes widen as understanding dawns. "No."

"Our court will not survive with me in it, not now that the dragons know the truth."

Cobbe is silent. He cannot argue my logic.

This time, when the tears well up, I do not fight them back for I can hear Kynera shifting into position. "Sing of me some day," I tell him, "in a nightingale's song. Tell my daughter I loved her so."

Cobbe swallows. "I will, Your Grace," he promises.

I scramble to my feet and slip from my rags in one fluid movement, changing into the swan as I go. I leap into the air as my wings sprout and form, darting through the ceiling and into the sky before the guards understand what is going on. The bugle of a dragon trumpeting my escape shatters the calm, and dragons pour out of every nook and corner of the ruined Aerie, taking off after me.

I sneak a glance below. The swan dragon bearing a girl dives below the stratus clouds and disappears. Kynera and Draka wrestle with a dragon guard between them; the rest stream into the sky to join the chase, auras flaring with the bright verdant glow of the hunt. I am, after all, the true prize. I am the treasure. I am the power divine.

I spread my white wings and spiral even higher, feeling the cold rush of air stream past me and letting the tears flow freely now. The stars turn into a blotchy blur as my vision becomes fuzzy. My lungs labor to draw breath as the air grows thin. The breeze below my tail wings grows warmer as the breath of a nearly full flight of dragons draws closer and closer.

At last, when it seems as if the dragons would catch me after all, I flip head over tail and dive straight down. Tucking my wings tight against me, I plummet through the startled flight of dragons. Their bodies are too long to flip as neatly as mine did, and they collide with each other as they struggle to follow. Several straighten out and dive after me, falling toward the earth.

I sink through a thick layer of clouds, and the landscape spreads before me like a map. I angle toward the bluest of blues, bluer than even the cerulean skies. This falling feels like soaring, hanging suspended in the air, if it were not for the features of the land magnifying at an alarming rate.

I hear the bellows of the dragons behind me as they realize where I am heading. Some pull up, but a few continue. I risk a glance to see who follows, and meet the hard glare of their amethyst-eyed prince. I know he can see the black streaking through my aura, thanks to the tears he stole, but I doubt he understands what the color portends.

It is one thing to see it all come to pass. It is quite another to understand.

I rip the swan feathers from my neck and become human again, holding tightly to the false destiny I have worn most of my life as I plummet toward the water. The feathers will float back to land, where a dutiful son will await its return after saving my daughter. A lie lost, in exchange for the truth found. I cannot ask for more.

The blue rushes up, up, upward.

I plunge into the ocean, leaving my old self behind to find myself anew.

THE FLOWER OF THE TABERNACLE

ANNIE REED

The dead woman lay slumped over the steps leading up to the altar, head twisted awkwardly on the top step, arms hanging limp at her sides. Blood from the long gashes on her forearms had soaked into the carpet and begun to turn brown at the edges. She'd been there a while.

Russell sat on his heels behind the woman. He hadn't been to church in nearly twenty years, but he'd almost made the sign of the cross when he'd entered St. Bart's. The smell did it to him more than anything else.

Like the church of his childhood, St. Bart's was old and impressed with itself with its vaulted ceilings and stained-glass windows and long rows of wooden pews, but it was the smell of old sweat and tears mixed with the lingering odor of incense and aftershave and the kind of perfume little old ladies doused themselves with because their sense of smell was going that reminded Russell of Sundays spent going to mass with his mother.

His mother had been a devout Catholic until the day she died. Every week she made him stay after mass so she could light a votive candle for the dead while she said the rosary in front of a statue of the Blessed Virgin Mary. Russell had kept her rosary beads after she passed away, but he hadn't set foot inside a church since the day he'd lit a candle for his wife and realized it was a piss poor way to remember anybody.

Would anybody light a candle for this woman?

"Looks like we caught a suicide," his partner said.

Russell grunted. Vic Damonte had been a good cop once, but he was five years away from retirement and getting sloppy.

"Where's the knife?" Russell asked. The dead woman looked like she'd been kneeling on the bottom step when she pushed the sleeves of her sweater up to her elbows and took a knife the long way to the veins of both arms. By the second cut, the knife would have been slippery, her grip would have faltered. "If she dropped the knife, where is it?"

"Under the body, smart guy," Vic said. "This ain't a little girl we got here."

Vic meant weight, not age. Vic liked his women stick-figure thin. The dead woman looked early twenties to Russell. She had maybe an extra thirty pounds on her, but she'd been tall and she had probably carried the extra weight well even if she'd worn a bulky sweater over her jeans to cover herself up.

"Sharp knife," Russell said. He'd know more when the medical examiner got here and turned the body, but from where he crouched behind her, it looked like the cuts on both arms were straight and deliberate, no hesitation marks. It took a serious amount of determination to do something like that. Or someone else to do it. Russell didn't think they'd find the knife beneath her body.

Russell stood up, his knees creaking. The call had come

in at seven near the end of their shift. Vic had mouthed off to the captain a couple of months ago, and the two of them had been stuck on graveyard ever since. Russell missed the sun. Middle of January, cold and overcast the whole damn time when it wasn't raining or snowing. He was sick of the dark and sick of being alone. Back when he'd been a beat cop working graveyard, his wife used to cook him dinner in the morning, and he'd have pot roast or stew or roasted chicken while they watched the sun come up. Winter hadn't seemed so bleak back then.

"I'm gonna go talk to the witness," Vic said. "You got the priest?"

Russell looked toward the back of the church. A small man dressed in black was talking softly to a middle-aged woman who sat huddled inside a woolen coat, the kind Russell's mother used to wear to church. Her head was covered with a scarf tied beneath her chin, the same way his mother had covered her own head when she was in the house of God.

"Take it easy on her," Russell said.

Vic smiled and spread his hands. "Don't I always?"

He didn't, but Russell decided to let it drop. Vic was in a good mood. This case would get him a little overtime and be wrapped up neat and tidy by noon as far as he was concerned. Russell had his doubts.

Father George Simpson introduced himself as the pastor of St. Bart's. He was in his early sixties, his once-blond hair thin and graying at the temples. He was a trim man who looked like he'd been in good shape in his younger years. Now his shoulders slumped and the skin of his neck over his clerical collar was wrinkled and loose. Together with the sad, world-weary expression in his faded blue eyes and the beginnings of jowls at his jawline, he reminded Russell of a hound dog who wanted nothing more than to curl up in front of the fireplace. Life had worn Father Simpson down.

Russell took the priest into the church vestibule so they could talk outside the presence of the witness. "Did you get a good look at the dead girl?" he asked.

Father Simpson's eyes flicked toward the altar. "I went to see if I could help her. I heard Mrs. Butler scream, you see. She comes to clean the church every morning. I'd been in the sacristy. I say mass every morning at ten." He turned back to Russell. "That won't be happening today, will it." It wasn't a question.

"I'm afraid not," Russell said anyway.

"I didn't touch her, if that's what you're worried about. What is it the shows always call it, contaminating the evidence?"

"Close enough."

Father Simpson had reminded Russell of a hound dog, but his speech was fast and jittery, more Chihuahua than hound. The priests of Russell's childhood had always been such stern disciplinarians, like a school principal who was on a first-name basis with God, that Russell had never considered them as human beings. Even with all the scandals involving the priesthood, Russell had always thought of priests as priests, not as men who had the same doubts and fears as everybody else and who suffered from shock when sudden violence invaded their world.

"Did you know her?" Russell asked.

The priest nodded. "Marily Jenkins. She used to come to church with her mother. Sang in the children's chorus when she was younger, then with the choir. Lovely voice."

Russell caught the past tense. "How long has it been since you've seen her?"

"Just last month, I believe. She started coming to mass on Monday mornings instead of Sundays. I spoke to her once about it, and she told me God would understand." The smile that passed over his face was fleeting and sad and didn't touch his eyes. "Her mother still comes to mass on Sundays."

This was Tuesday. "She wasn't at mass yesterday morning?" Russell asked.

"Not since before Christmas."

"She tell you why she switched to Mondays?"

"She mentioned a change in her work schedule, but she wouldn't look me in the eye. Marily's a good girl, she wouldn't lie to me, at least I don't believe she would, but perhaps she didn't think a half-truth was much of a lie."

"What's the other half of Marily's truth?"

The priest glanced back toward the altar. Russell followed his gaze. A lone light shown down on the ornate gold tabernacle in its place at the rear of the altar. The day was overcast, the light through the stained-glass windows weak and murky, and that one lone light was fighting a losing battle to keep the gloom at bay.

Marily had fallen almost directly in the center of the steps leading up to the altar. From where Russell stood, it looked like she was praying to the God of light, and he hadn't answered her.

"Artists are sensitive souls, don't you find that to be true, detective?" Father Simpson asked. "Marily wanted to pursue a career as a singer. Her mother wanted her to have a more down-to-earth career. She's a devout woman, but sometimes the devout have difficulty seeing beyond their own views of the world. Marily had a job singing in a club downtown. I believe her mother objected."

Russell's mother had objected when he refused to

consider entering the priesthood. She'd relented when he'd married, content with the belief that he and his wife would give her grandchildren, but grandchildren hadn't been part of God's plan.

"Was Marily devout?" he asked.

The priest looked surprised. "It's not a word I normally think of when I consider the younger parishioners, perhaps that's my sin—judge not, if you will—but yes, I believe she was devout in her own fashion. Why do you ask?"

"Devout people don't usually kill themselves," Russell said.

Not unless they have a really, really good reason.

Russell got the name and address of Marily's mother from the priest. After the medical examiner arrived with one lone crime scene tech in tow—the department had undergone deep budget cuts like the rest of the country, and suspected suicides weren't a high priority—Russell left with Vic to make the notification to the next of kin. He told the tech to call him if they found a knife.

Sharon Jenkins lived alone in a third-floor apartment six blocks from St. Bart's. The apartment building had seen better days. The smell of fried food and cigarettes permeated the hallway, but the walls had been painted recently enough that Russell could still detect the faint odor of paint.

Marily's mother answered the door after Vic knocked a second time. He was impatient to get the notification over with. He'd agreed to let Russell do the actual talking, but the whole ride over from the church he'd been griping about the weather and the hours and the way Catholics passed the collection plate so they'd have plenty of money for all that gold on the altar while the poor in the congregation went hungry.

"Seems obscene to me, that's all I'm saying. You seen the Vatican, right? All that gold. Obscene, I'm telling you."

Russell hadn't disagreed, and not just because he wanted to avoid an argument with his partner.

Mrs. Jenkins opened the door only as far as the security chain allowed. "Yes?" she said, peering at them with suspicious eyes.

Russell introduced himself and Vic and they showed her their shields before he asked her if she was Marily Jenkins' mother.

He'd seen people break down at this point when they realized two cops at the door asking about a loved one meant bad news and the only option left was to hope the news wasn't as bad as they feared. Sharon Jenkins blinked and her lips thinned to a small, tight line as comprehension dawned, but she didn't break down.

"Tell me what you have to tell me and get it over with," she said.

"May we come inside?" Russell asked. "It might make this easier."

Mrs. Jenkins shut the door without another word, and he heard the chain rattle. A moment later she opened the door for them both.

Her apartment was small and sparsely decorated. Framed pictures of a young girl dotted the short hallway into the living room. In one picture the little girl was wearing her First Communion dress and veil. A rosary hung from one hand and she held a single white rose in the other. Another picture caught her mid-swing on a backyard swing set. Her head had been thrown back, her eyes closed, and her mouth open in a happy shriek as she pulled for the sky. A third picture showed her as a teenager holding an acoustic guitar. She'd had one of those haircuts teenagers think are cool but their adult selves wish they could purge from memory.

Russell saw enough of a resemblance in that last picture to the dead woman on the altar to know these were all pictures of Marily as a child. He didn't see a single picture of her as an adult, nor did he see a picture of her father. He did notice a faint outline on the wall where another picture had been hung. Maybe a picture of the deceased Mr. Jenkins that his widow no longer wanted to look at.

The only artwork in the living room was a portrait of Jesus, his eyes cast heavenward and his hands folded in prayer, on the wall above a well-worn couch.

A gray tabby cat gazed at Russell from an equally well-worn armchair close to the room's lone window. Apparently satisfied Russell wouldn't be shooing it away anytime soon, the cat curled back up to sleep.

Mrs. Jenkins stood in the doorway between the living room and her kitchen. She was dressed in dark blue slacks, a light-weight cream colored sweater, and low heels. The apron tied around her waist looked damp, as if she'd dried her hands on it instead of a kitchen towel before she'd answered the door. Somewhere in the apartment a television was tuned to one of the morning news shows, the sound down low enough not to disturb the neighbors.

The smell of coffee and a recently-cut onion reminded Russell of the breakfasts he used to share with his wife. Pot roast and mashed potatoes at sunrise. He hadn't been able to stomach pot roast since an emergency room doctor who looked too young to be out of medical school had told him that they had used their best efforts but had been unable to save her.

Mrs. Jenkins had a plain gold band around her ring finger. Father Simpson had told Russell she was a widow. Now he was about to tell her that her only daughter was dead.

"I'm sorry to have to tell you this—" he began, but she interrupted him.

"She's dead, isn't she?"

"Yes, ma'am," Vic said, surprisingly deferential. "I'm afraid she is."

Mrs. Jenkins nodded once. Russell could see a muscle playing at the edge of her jaw, but her eyes didn't fill with tears. When she spoke again, her voice was steady.

"Am I allowed to ask how it happened?"

Russell shot Vic a look to remind him they'd agreed Russell would do the talking. Vic shrugged and turned toward the window.

"She was found this morning in St. Bart's," Russell said. "Knife wounds in her forearms. It appears she passed away while she was kneeling at the altar." He tried not to think about the little girl in her white communion dress, all smiles, holding that white rose.

"Knife wounds," Mrs. Jenkins said. She glanced down at her own hands and sniffed once, the first chink in her armor.

The backs of her hands had faint white scars among the age spots, and a couple that were fresher.

She must have noticed him looking. "Owning a cat isn't for the faint of heart." She sniffed again. "Neither is being a parent."

Russell didn't know and doubted now that he ever

would. "Anyone threaten your daughter that you know of?" he asked. "She have any problems with anybody lately?"

Vic turned his head away from the window in surprise. Russell hadn't let Vic know he planned on questioning Marily's mother. He'd consider it a waste of time. Russell didn't.

"Do you mean she didn't..." Mrs. Jenkins looked back and forth between the two of them. "You think she was murdered?"

"We didn't say that, ma'am," Vic said. "Detective Russell's just dotting the i's and crossing the t's for the report."

Russell ignored him. "Why did you assume she wasn't?" he asked Mrs. Jenkins.

She looked confused. "You said knife wounds, that she was kneeling at the altar... you mean someone killed her right there, in front of..."

She turned on her heels and went into her kitchen. She stood with her back to them, her head down. After a moment, Russell followed her.

The kitchen was small, the kind that was really a short, narrow hallway with appliances on both sides. The smell of onions was stronger there, along with a half dozen other smells—herbs and vegetables and some kind of meat— that Russell didn't recognize. A small crockpot was plugged in on the countertop next to the coffee maker. The sink was full of soapy water and the few dishes a person living alone might need had been set out to drain. A small television shared counter space on the other side of the sink with a butcher block knife holder and a set of metal canisters that reminded Russell of the ones his own mother used to have. A crucifix hung on the wall over the sink was the only non-functional thing in the room.

"I'm sorry to have to ask you this," Russell said. "But why did you assume that your daughter committed suicide?"

For a moment he thought she was going to ignore him, but then she lifted her head and straightened her shoulders. When she turned around to face him, her eyes were clear and dry, her expression impassive.

"My daughter was an impetuous person. Imaginative and easily hurt. Fond of the grand gesture. Do you understand?"

Russell thought he did. What had Father Simpson called Marily? A sensitive soul? His own mother had been devout, but she'd been loving and warm. He tried to imagine a sensitive soul growing up with a mother as cold and self-controlled as Sharon Jenkins. An artistic soul growing up in a place where only God and pictures of her own childhood had any place on her mother's walls.

Mrs. Jenkins had assumed Marily committed suicide because she'd attempted it before.

Russell had been wrong. The crime scene tech found a knife snagged on the front of Marily's sweater when they loaded her on the gurney.

"Small, black-handled," he'd said to Russell over the phone, "but that sucker's sharp as a scalpel. She wouldn't have had to press down much to get the job done. Medical examiner said if she'd been quick enough, she could have done both arms before the pain really hit."

So that was that. The only prints on the knife belonged to Marily Jenkins. She'd go down as a suicide. The tech had found so many different hairs and fibers in the carpet around her body that it would be cost prohibitive to test them all with no other evidence of foul play. Mrs. Butler was apparently not the world's best housekeeper.

Russell thanked the tech and then sent an email to the medical examiner asking her to send him a copy of her report so he could put it in the file and mark it closed.

"Told you," Vic had said to him the next night. "Sometimes things are what they look like, you know? You gotta learn to take it easy or you won't live to enjoy your pension."

They skated the rest of the week, working old open case files, looking for new angles. Russell tried to keep himself busy, but he kept thinking of the little girl in her white communion dress, a white rose in her hand. The little girl on the swing, so in love with life. The woman who expressed the creativity she couldn't at home by singing in church, and for whom church was so important that she went to mass on Mondays when she could no longer stand to attend on Sundays with her mother.

Why would a woman like that kill herself on the altar?

The question kept Russell awake during the day when he should have been sleeping. Officially the investigation was over, but he couldn't let it go. He had to know why.

After his shift was over, instead of going home to a bed where he couldn't sleep, Russell made his way to St. Bart's. The door to the vestibule was unlocked, but the church was empty. This time when his hand wanted to make the sign of the cross, Russell let it. The holy water felt like a single cold teardrop on his forehead.

He took a seat in the pew closest to the vestibule and looked toward the altar. The bloodstains were gone, and the normal smells of church were overlaid with the musty smell of freshly-shampooed carpet. The lone light was on over the tabernacle, illuminating the golden cabinet where the Eucharist was kept. When he was little, his mother used to tell him the tabernacle was the little house where a piece of God lived in the church. To a child who believed Santa brought presents and the Easter Bunny hid colored eggs in the yard, it wasn't such a stretch.

Russell had never lost his faith, not in the classic sense. He'd lost his religion. The little boy who'd sat next to his mother at his first midnight mass on Christmas Eve, awed at the pageantry of the manger on an altar overflowing with red and white poinsettias and thrumming with the knowledge that Santa was on his way, had given way to the man who knew the poinsettias had been donated by a florist who cheated on his wife but took communion every Sunday anyway. Religion was community and ritual and a shared set of beliefs that reinforced both. Russell no longer believed in the rituals, and he had no desire to become a hypocrite like the florist.

The vestibule door creaked open behind him. Russell turned around, expecting Father Simpson or perhaps Mrs. Butler, here to do her cursory cleaning. The last person he expected to see was Sharon Jenkins.

Her face registered the briefest surprise when she spotted him, but she recovered quickly.

He expected her to walk up the aisle and take a seat near the front, or perhaps to light a votive for her daughter in the rack filled with rows of red glass candleholders off to the right of the altar. He did not expect her to sit in the pew next to him.

"I came early hoping to catch Father Simpson before anyone else arrived for mass," she said. "Instead the good lord gave me you. Tell me, detective—do you believe in symbolism?"

She hadn't dipped her fingers in holy water or made the sign of the cross when she'd entered the church. That particular symbolism wasn't lost on him.

"I'm sitting in a church that looks a lot like the one I went to as a kid. What does that tell you?" he said.

"Touché." She gazed at the altar, and he wondered if she was trying to imagine what her daughter had looked like, where she had fallen.

"Of course, if you look at it from my point of view," he said, "I'm the one who came here looking for the good father, and instead I got you. But what I think brought both of us here is your daughter."

"True." She sighed. "I came here to make a confession. Would you like to hear it?"

He frowned, unsure where this was going. "I'm always on the clock," he said. "Confession means something different to a cop than it does to a priest."

"But not to God, I imagine. He's the one I've sinned against, and he's the one who brought me to you."

Russell gave her a hard look. "If you're going to tell me you had something to do with your daughter's death, I'm going to have to read you your rights. You know that, right?"

For the first time since she'd sat down, she turned her gaze away from the altar and looked at him. Her eyes weren't expressionless now. They swam with guilt. "Why don't you hear me out, and if what I tell you is something you feel you should arrest me for, you can read me my rights and I'll say it again."

Russell nodded. He could live with that.

She turned back toward the altar. "My sin is pride, you see. I've always been proud of my faith, of the part the Lord plays in my life. Proud of the life I created for myself, even after God gifted me with a daughter who could not have been more different than her mother." She sighed again. "I did try to be a good mother, but my pride kept me from asking for help. I had, as people say, gotten myself into that particular mess, and I saw no reason why anyone except God should help me out of it."

She was telling him that Marily had been born out of wedlock.

"And Mr. Jenkins?" Russell asked.

"There was never a Mr. Jenkins. Her father..." She made a dismissive gesture with one hand. "I never knew his last name, so I had the hospital put Jenkins on her birth certificate because I'd always liked the name and I was too proud to admit the true circumstances of her conception. Pride leads to a downfall of a thousand steps, detective, and each of those steps are paved with lies. The lies become reality after a while, especially with a curious daughter."

Russell could imagine. His mother had told him stories about Santa and the Easter Bunny and God living in a small golden cabinet behind the altar just as she'd told him that his father had been killed in the line of duty, but at least that story had been true. When Russell joined the force, he'd worked with men who'd worked with his father.

"I even found a photograph of a handsome young man to put in a frame on the wall where a curious daughter might expect to see a picture of her father," she said.

"But she found out," Russell said.

"Yes. That deception, and so many others. She called me a hypocrite, going to mass every Sunday and lying to her face the rest of the week."

That must have been when Marily started going to mass by herself on Mondays, but it didn't explain her suicide.

"Father Simpson noticed, of course," she said. "I told him she had a new schedule at work. My pride wouldn't allow me to admit my deceit even to my priest, you see, or allow me to make the effort to reconcile with my daughter. I was her mother. She would come back to me when she was ready. I was too important a person in her life. I didn't realize how important a person she was in mine."

Her voice cracked over the last few words, and for the first time since he'd met her, Marily's mother started to cry. She sat with her back ramrod straight as tears leaked from eyes that never looked away from the altar where her daughter had died.

Something clicked in Russell's brain, a piece of a puzzle he hadn't realized he'd been looking at. Cuts on the back of Mrs. Jenkins' hands, not made by a knife or by her cat, but by broken glass. An empty slot in the butcher block knife holder on her counter. She'd been cutting up vegetables for whatever meal was in the crockpot, and he'd assumed that the knife she'd been using was still in the sink because there hadn't been one in the drainer. But what woman washes a knife last, leaving it in the water where she could grab it by mistake and cut herself?

"Did you kill your daughter?" he asked.

She shut her eyes. "You mean, did I hold the knife to her skin and slit her wrists myself?"

He didn't say anything. A cold ball had settled in the pit of his stomach.

"No. But I told myself that I must have misplaced the knife. I didn't call her to ask if she'd seen it." She opened her eyes and looked at him. "We'd argued, you see. I'd been so happy she'd come to see me on her own, and then she'd spoiled it. Told me she thought I'd like to know that she'd followed in my footsteps, but she was an enlightened woman. She'd done something about it."

The medical examiner hadn't sent Russell her report yet. Her department was as backlogged as everywhere else. No one had known that Marily'd had an abortion.

"I said dreadful things to her, told her that she was an abomination before God who had sacrificed his only begotten son for our salvation. That what she had done was murder, and she had condemned her immortal soul."

"She broke one of the pictures you had on your wall," Russell said.

She nodded. "Her Confirmation picture. She threw it at me, and that seemed to bring us both to our senses. She left without saying goodbye. I thought she would call me the next morning, but instead you appeared at my door to tell me she was dead." She wiped at her face with the back of one hand. "She told me she would rather be dead than become like me. Tell me, detective. Am I that evil of a person that my daughter would rather kill herself in God's home than spend one more moment with me in mine?"

Russell couldn't answer that. All he knew was that Mrs. Jenkins had committed no crime, not within the strict letter of the law.

Had she been cruel? Without a doubt. But parents and children were cruel to each other in a thousand different ways. Mrs. Jenkins hadn't held the knife or helped her daughter kill herself. That had been Marily's own grand gesture, paying the price she thought God demanded for the death of her unborn child by sacrificing her own life before His altar.

The weight of what Mrs. Jenkins had told him settled on his shoulders, and he felt the weariness of his sleepless days. He stood up and gazed toward the altar. The lone light shining down on the tabernacle seemed dimmer somehow.

"I think we're done here," he said.

He left her alone in the pew with her guilt. He walked out of the church into the gray light of another overcast day. He didn't make the sign of the cross when he left, and he didn't look back.

DOMUS JUSTICE

MICHÈLE LAFRAMBOISE

F rom my position, crouched on the tiles near Secondus Livius's bust, I could see the wooden chair's legs, painted a golden hue by the sun. Between those legs, Faustus Livius Tullius's feet peeked from his white toga's border, shod in elaborate leather sandals.

The hair on his toes was turning grey.

Behind the paterfamilias's chair, the burly headmaster waited, whip in hand, his beard a riot of oily spikes. The whip was a nasty affair of old leather, three braided threads with barbed hooks at the ends.

I tried to take refuge in the bountiful scents of roses imported from Asia Minor, rare orchids, lilies, and nameless flowers suffusing the garden. The big, one-story house enfolded the garden like a green treasure, most rooms opening doors or windows to it, with a main entrance from the atrium and a small back passage to the servants' quarters.

The torrid June heat was attenuated by the fruit trees from the orchard that would later in season give us olives, peaches, figs. The big knotted pine did not give any fruit besides dry cones, but its needles whispered in the stale wind, even in the afternoon.

The fountain basin gargled a soft song for the carp.

I hoped the balmy ambiance would lift the master's mood and spare me the disfiguring whip, which the head-master clutched like a lover, his fingers itching to use it. For the mistress's mood, there was nothing any garden in the world could do.

Livia Tullia was the one who had alerted the whole domus with her cries, when she found her twin golden armbands gone from the green lacquered box she kept in her bedroom.

The bands were engraved with two swallows in flight, a prodigy of patience from the artisan who melted it. I had seen them often enough, sunk in Livia Tullia's fleshy arms. The mistress had been very young when she received them, a gift from her own father as he gave her away to another house.

Her dainty feet, nails polished a deep, luscious red, filled her fine leather sandals. She stood at arm's length to the right and behind her husband, as befitted a patrician matron of her rank.

My head turned sideways, I caught a glimpse of Livia Tullia's servants, a small and wary cluster: her ornatrix, Portia, brush in hand, ready to freshen up a curl or tighten up a ribbon; her personal cook, a slim Greek man; a gardener tending her roses; and their various assistants. The ornatrix looked like a harried, nervous crow, always squinting against the sun, intent on keeping her place here. Portia was not a house slave, but a recently freed woman, and very intent on staying free.

Some matrons withered with age before fading away.

Not Livia Tullia.

The mistress had instead gained a comfortable beauty, with her rounded limbs and generous bosom. The curve of her peach-toned flesh around the armbands made her even more desirable, as the lingering gazes from the men at the market told me.

Someone sneezed, a short distance behind me.

I didn't dare move under the gaze of the master.

The garden was full of servants anxious for this thing to be over so they could return to their tasks. There were a few clients of Tullius, plebeians who had enjoyed their sportule and, in exchange for the free meal, had escorted him to the Forum today.

"Silence!"

Tullius's voice had been stentorian in the first years of my service. It had since mellowed into a bass, but was still imperial enough to ensure a quick response.

"Claudius, tell what you saw last night."

A shuffling of hesitant feet, stopping before the tiled area of the basin. I did not need to look up.

Claudius was barely eleven, a spurt of growth still waiting to happen. I could imagine his bowed head, tousled brown curls falling over his dark eyes.

He had been my charge since I was brought in the house as a very little girl. We soon became friends.

Countless were the times when I had spared him a beating by the grammaticus with a clever lie about a fever or a bad stomach. In return, Claudius had helped me to decipher the complex Latin grammar.

(Words were like birds pecking at each other. The

subject got the best place in the sentence, forcing its servants to change their tail's colors.)

Claudius was as shy as the coral-finned carps he liked to tickle in the marble basin, and probably as pale.

"Pa-pater," he stammered.

Another sneeze, closer this time.

Gaius was not as shy as his youngest brother, but you would think mischievous Diane had singled him out to be a practice target for all that the universe contained of small creepy creatures. He was always shifting his feet, as if ants would creep over his leather sandals. And tree pollen made early spring a misery, best endured from inside the library room.

The feet under the toga shifted, a sandal sole striking the tiles.

The Paterfamilias was not satisfied with his male descendants. To his eye, both brothers lacked in stamina and virilitas. Gaius and his sneezing and reading rolls, Claudius bungling his daily combat training with the Nubian arms master.

My head pressed to the ground, I could make the brown calves of the retired gladiator Tullius had hired for his sons. A strong Nubian, Abacus was still handsome despite the scars on his brow. His tightly curled hair pointed out like arrows.

I listened to him talking about his former life in Africa as he cleaned the practice swords he and Claudius used. He had had a family before, two children he never saw again. He had been captured when the Romans beat his king's army. As a prisoner, he was sold to the arenas.

Abacus knew the fate that could have been his in the arena, if Tullius, seated in the advanced red-covered dais, had not raised his thumb. In the absence of the Consul, Tullius's thumb was rule.

So Abacus was dutiful and devoted to his master. Some among the servants called his faithfulness sandal-licking.

I never did.

You had to live as a gladiator, each grueling day squeezed between praises and death, receiving gifts from fan-waving admirers and wounds from sword-waving rivals, to appreciate a simpler life: bed and food and domestic orders.

And, sometimes, domestics.

Neither of the brothers could fill the sandals of Tullius's firstborn, the son that had brought fame and honor to the house, Secundus.

I remembered him, a tall angular decurion with a red-crested helmet, nodding to his father's recommendations.

I can still see his wide smile, his younger brother's admiration. I remember the endless days waiting for news, then getting half news, then getting confirmation, months after the battle of Corinth against the Achaeans.

With Secundus's body lying dead in a faraway battle-field, the sun had left the house. Tullius had a bust of his son carved in marble, with the crested helmet.

Of course, the whole house was searched—except the master's quarters, because everything in the house belonged to him. The golden bands were not found.

I was dunking the togas from last night's feast in a

washbasin of water mixed with lemon juice to get rid of the wine stains when the mistress and the head servant yanked me from my task.

The scowling head servant took a step toward me. I froze in place, my hands still dripping water, my eyes on the barbed whip.

"This was found under your bed, wretch!" he said.

I looked to my mistress. Livia Tullia's delicate complexion was suffused with blood. She held a silver thimble between thumb and index.

"This is how you repay my generosity, Aemilia?" she snapped.

I didn't understand her anger, but I could sense the hurt under her curt words. Livia Tullia had been the one to choose me, when she needed a minder for baby Claudius. She had been the one to name me, at four, after a deadborn girl.

"What did you do with the armbands?" the headmaster asked, clenching his whip's thick handle. The leather was black with sweat and wear.

And so I had learned that, as the search for the lost armbands spread to the servants' quarters, one of the orna-trix's assistants had discovered the silver thimble under the hay mattress I slept in. The object came from the mistress's dressing table, near the lacquered box containing the golden armbands.

How did that precious thimble end up under my bed?

It was not there last night, because I would have felt the hard object under the thin layer of hay. But I had risen before dawn to relieve myself in the latrine room on the outer side of the house before getting on with my cleaning work.

Another hand must have slipped the thimble there in

my absence. I would have loved telling the frowning Livia Tullia so.

Alas, years of living in Faustus Livius Tullius's house had taught me that raising my voice in protestation would do no good. Servants, both freed men and slaves, stole from their masters as soon as a good occasion presented itself and when they felt sure they could get away with it.

The only correct course of action in my situation was falling to the ground as fast as I could and offering my utter ignorance of how such a jewel had appeared under my bed.

"Maybe the Lares know who did it," I said, not raising my voice higher than the murmur of the fountain. As a slave girl, I was not regarded as very clever.

The ancestors' cult was important to all dwellers of the domus. There was a niche in the inner garden's wall, with two little statues in there representing a king and a horseman.

Among the family ancestors was Servius Tullius. All families belonging to the Tullius gens drew pride from being descendants of the sixth king of Rome.

The mistress considered me, rolling the thimble in her fingers. She knew it was not for her to dispense punishment.

"We'll see what the Pater thinks about it," she said.

In the Tullius house, justice was the potestas of the paterfamilias. But, as Livius Tullius was at the Forum discussing the new taxes, we would have to wait for his arrival.

The afternoon passed in a sedated hush. Forbidden to leave the house, I sat on the bench under the big pine tree, head bent. I was facing the little Lares niche, thinking about this king and his horseman.

At a point, the ornatrix sat on the basin, looking down at the carps, probably mulling over her mistress's plight.

Claudius was leaning over with a twig, tickling the big fishes. They talked about the fishes, and the plates the cook would make of those.

As the shadow of Secundus's bust turned and crept over the ground, I searched in the treasure chest of my memory to figure out who put the thimble under my bed, and why.

Tullius's patience was reaching its end.

"So, Claudius, do I have to pry the words off your worthless mouth?"

The poor boy was squirming on a hot plate. Claudius did not want to betray me. But he was the master's son, and his word could carry far. He was also aware that the house's Lares would punish any lie.

There was more, which his older brother had told me: if he lied to save me, the theft, which could have been resolved by the paterfamilias authority, would spill out of the confines of the domus. A questor would be called upon, and the affair would grow, finding its way to the Forum where the master's enemies or rivals would take advantage of it.

"He is not liked by everyone, our Pater," Gaius had whispered to Claudius in the library, mere hours from the garden convocation. "If you say a lie, the matter will go to the questor, then to the tribune. They will want to know who did it."

Gaius leaned toward his brother.

"Claudius, I know you saw something when you walked up to our room last night. You had that look, as when you stuffed yourself with twenty figs from our neighbor Marcius's domus garden."

"I did not take that many," Claudius said, pouting.

His still-high-pitched voice was a contrast to his brother's.

I couldn't leave the house until the paterfamilias had time to preside over my case. So I was lingering about, mulling about my trial, when I recognized Claudius's voice coming from the library windows. The torrid heat of a June afternoon had pushed the brothers there.

I stepped closer to listen in.

It was those conversations and many others that guided me on the complex map of relationships in master Tullius's domus. I trod cautiously, wary as the carps in the basin when they realize that another one of them is missing.

I barely miss my first family. I was too young when the soldiers took me, at the same time they took the city where my parents lived and died.

Of the time before the soldiers grabbed me like a sack of rice, I kept blurry impressions: the oppressive heat, a woman's bubbly laughter, the orange sand when the sun caressed the hills, and in the marketplace, a row of tall palms nodding, waving their tufted heads, as if docile servants saying yes, yes master.

"Yes," Claudius said, his thin voice barely making its way over the grumblings of the other house servi.

So, he made his choice, I thought.

Claudius would tell the truth, the whole truth: how last night he could not sleep; how he got up, his bladder full.

How, too shy to go all the way to the latrines room, he relieved himself under the oldest peach tree.

How, as he was there, he saw me inching out of the mistress's room by her garden window with a small packet under my arm.

Of course, I knew Claudius had seen me. But we were friends, and even he would never suspect me of such a crime as theft.

So he said nothing and returned to his room near his father's, as I scampered away to the street.

The discovery of the theft had tormented the boy.

But, even now in the garden, Claudius couldn't know that my real business had nothing to do with a pair of golden bands.

Someone laughed behind the mistress, a high-pitched, bubbly laugh, coming from one of the two ornatrix's aides. I wondered what had come to the mind of the one who found the thimble. Did she place it there?

Tullius leaned heavily toward his youngest son.

"So, tell me."

There was a hush, as the boy mumbled something. His brother sneezed.

"Aemilia is innocent," Claudius repeated, loud and clear.

Oh, by the poor Lares, why would he lie like that?

"It was Abacus I saw, coming from the mistress's bedroom," he finished.

My heart jumped like a whipped horse. A gasp, from Abacus, quickly refrained.

What had gotten into poor baby Claudius? Another fear gripped my insides.

Did the boy know that the handsome gladiator had been sneaking in and out of his mother's bedroom when her husband was away? The ornatrix had seen them, her younger aide, a girl of fourteen, told me.

Foul jaws had bit my insides at the idea.

I guessed Abacus was among those men who couldn't resist Tullia's generous form. And I guessed she was drawn by Abacus's powerful body.

Tullia went paler, if that was possible. To be accused by a servant of unfaithfulness could cost her repudiation. To be hinted at by her son was unthinkable. I could see the Paterfamilias' traits hardening.

"He had a packet. He took them and sold them," the boy said, unconscious of how his lie could affect other's lives.

My eyes were on the clients. One of them had smiled, just for a second, like a curtain opening and closing fast on a neutral expression.

"I did not!" Abacus protested, his hoarse voice almost in the same tone as Claudius's denying the twenty figs.

So big an age difference, so similar their utter lack of power.

Abacus fell on his knees from where he was near the gnarly pine. He put his palms on the packed ground, deliberately taking a vulnerable position. His whole act had taken the attention away from Livia Tullia.

"Master, I am the lowest of the low, but I would not steal anything from you, to lose my place here!"

Abacus drank solidly and, sometimes, he did go out to play dice at the taverns. Stealing the armbands from the mistress was possible, but I knew he could never get another posting once Tullius dismissed him. The beggars populating the market gave me a clue of what he could expect after a merciful decision.

Begging, or returning to the gladiator's existence.

Tullius got up and walked up to little Claudius. He crossed his arms, the toga drapes falling flat from his elbows.

"Son, can you explain to me how the thimble got under Aemilia's bed?"

Of course, the poor boy could not.

He stammered some more, a lie that could be construed as a complicity. Gaius was paling himself, seeing the consequences.

As Claudius swallowed nervously, I caught another smile, coming from a different direction. The ornatrix seemed to be enjoying the spectacle.

Claudius stuttered more, and the headmaster made a step forward, unrolling his whips' threads.

"So, you can't tell me how Abacus there could have stolen the bands and put the thimble in this slave's bed?"

Ch-klak!

The headmaster made his whip crack in the air, over the basin. I felt the displacement of air over my back.

"And you can't tell me where those armbands might be, now that it is clear they are no more in this house."

"Master, I can safely tell you the armbands are still in this house."

Faustus Livius Tullius jumped as if a stone had just spoken under him. But it was not a stone, it was me.

I had all the time to look, to listen, to ask a few questions around. It was like those puzzles with the tiles, one piece here, one piece there.

One smile here, one smile there. The client, receding,

disappearing behind the cluster of the curious. The ornatrix, amused.

"If you give me a few moments, master, I can find the answers."

I turned to Livia Tullia. "Mistress, when you discovered the theft, did you notice your thimble missing?"

She raised her hand to scratch her head, stopping in time before she upset her elaborate curls.

"I, I didn't look for that. I was so upset about my armbands I never thought about anything else."

"And who was with you when you found out?"

"Well, my trusted aide was here."

She turned toward the ornatrix. The ornatrix was fidgeting with two bronze combs, casting a glance sideways toward the basin where Claudius sat, happy to be out of the grid.

"And you ran out of the room to alert us."

This had been witnessed by the whole house, Livia Tullia, her dress in disarray, khôl dripping down her cheeks.

"And what did Portia do while you were out?"

I could see her, swiping the thimble in the empty bedroom. Then later, "discovering" the thimble in my bed.

I knew she had chosen me to divert the suspicions from her. I was a young, ignorant Nubian slave.

"Portia?" Livia Tullia asked, taking a step toward the basin.

The ornatrix found her voice.

"How can you believe this lying snitch!" she hissed. "She's the one who took your armbands! She went outside to sell those!"

A gasp from Claudius. So, the ornatrix had stayed awake and spied on me as I crossed the garden.

"I did not steal nor sell those bands, master."

I spoke in the measured tones I had heard the guests use in the atrium.

"And what did you do in the mistress's bedroom, thief?" Portia accused.

"I never took a thing of value from my mistress's bedroom," I said.

Defending my life, I was taming my voice, so it would not come out high-pitched and strained. But some burst of passion could rise under the surface of my composure.

"You had a packet under your arm," Portia said. "And you ran to the street."

"Yes," I said, my head nodding, bobbing like a tufted palm tree. "And yes."

Livia Tullia, who had been silent until now, spoke.

"It was a wooden horse, a child's toy!"

Her husband's head turned to her.

"Aemilia had carved it for little Claudius a few years ago. He gave it back to me, as he did not play with it anymore. So, when I found her cleaning after the guests late last night, I told her she could take the thing from my bedroom when she was finished."

"But," Claudius said, "I saw her coming out from your window...."

I looked at the master, beseeching his permission again to speak. I went on.

"The night you talked about, Claudius, there were two very drunk guests that the cook and his aides had difficulties managing. So, instead of getting back to the servant quarters by the main corridor and risking a bad encounter, I took a shorter route to the inner garden by the window."

Tullius was fidgeting with his toga.

"And what did you do with it?"

I lowered my head.

"I thought I could have a good price for it at the night market."

"And did you?"

"I got two bronze pieces."

"And what did you do with it?"

I did not want to tell them where I hid my very personal things, and it was not in by mattress. I lowered my head.

"I lost it," I said in a meek voice.

The paterfamilias rose, extending his arms, stretching his toga in a white semicircle.

"Then where are those bands?"

"Here, master."

I rose.

"The house had been searched," he said.

But not the carp basin near the mistress' window. I sat where Claudius had sat, and bent over the rim. I plunged my arm under the cool water.

The carps fled to the other side of the basin, forming a white and coral cloud.

I remembered the ornatrix sitting idly on the edge of the basin. She had told Claudius she was looking at the fishes. But the cook had told me the ornatrix did not like fish meals.

I trailed my hand under the colored pebbles lining the bottom of the basin, feeling the silt under. My fingertips brushed against a metal circle, pushed vertically in the soft mud layer under the pebbles.

I pulled and retrieved a dripping armband, with the two swallows on it. The gift from a doting father shone under the sun.

Faustus Livius Tullius's eyebrows rose in amusement.

"This is a wonder!"

Livia Tullia made a step forward as I was fishing out the second band.

"What have you to say to that, Portia?" she asked, a new hurt dragging her voice down.

But the ornatrix had disappeared.

We managed to piece together the truth, like a tile pattern, once Abacus and the headmaster caught up with the fleeing ornatrix.

What had been thought as a vain women's quarrel plunged its roots in the political arena.

The ornatrix's former master, a senator and frequent guest at the domus, had resolved to ruin the reputation of Livius Tullius.

Years ago, that man's son, along with countless others, had been sent to Corinth. Tullius Secondus and this son had been friends. I could imagine their wide smiles, and their prowess in combat.

Alas, as Abacus had told me once, even the best strategies made mistakes, mistakes that no amount of valor could buy back. That defeat had been costly to Tullius and other senators who had backed up the plan.

The senator had promised the ornatrix he would buy her freedom if she managed to drive a wedge between the Tullii. Which she almost succeeded, planting lies around about a dalliance between Livia Tullia and Abacus, then stealing the bands for herself.

As the ornatrix was not permitted to go outside without an escort, she had hidden the bands under the carp's soft bellies.

The paterfamilias eyed his wife, who had put back the

damp bands on her, giggling as water droplets coursed down her arms. Livia Tullia's smile lifted his mood, as the garden hadn't.

Maybe he remembered being newly wed.

"For your actions, Portia, I condemn you to be whipped ten times, then cast out of my domus. You shall be free to tell your former master never to return under my roof."

The headmaster advanced, unrolling his beast of a whip. Portia cringed.

"I did it to be free! To be free!"

Her pitiful cries echoed in my own flesh, as if I was the one whipped.

The ornatrix's former master might not have been as kind, because I never saw her again. That senator was not punished, as he had a shield made of gold pieces.

"Justice doesn't exist for the likes of us," I said, one month after the events.

I was bearing an armload of prickly roses for the mistress and had found Abacus polishing a rusty sword near the Lares. I wondered if he was thinking about his family.

I had gained back Livia Tullia's confidence, but I was still bound to her in servitude. The little horse's value had not been enough.

Because of my finding the bands, I was permitted small rewards: a few outings at the market, a stipend for a new dress, free time to read at the library with the brothers I could never marry, even if I had wanted to.

And I kept on talking with Abacus, who could never hope to marry Livia Tullia, even in the event of her husband's death. Living in the same domus would have to be enough for him, as for me.

Abacus nodded, holding the sword balanced on his scarred palm.

"No, it doesn't, otherwise you and I would be still in our old city in Africa."

He looked toward the fountain, where little Claudius was teasing the carps with a stick. Lanky Gaius sat on the bench, reading a roll, in the spare days when neither bugs nor pollen bothered him. He would make a good paterfamilias someday.

"I couldn't buy my freedom," I said. "Nor yours."

Abacus let the sword drop, startling a flock of small, twittering birds.

"But you did your best, Aemilia," he said. "Like a gladiator outnumbered by adversaries, you struggled to make it as fair as you could."

I looked at his brown eyes, and thought of flying away, like those swallows on Livia Tullia's golden armbands.

A NIGHT UNDER THE STARS
LISA SILVERTHORNE

P owder-blue taffeta, sprinkled with pearls and sequins across a form-fitting bodice, perfect A-line skirt held up with a cloud of tulle. Doris stared at the dress in the full-length mirror. The sour hint of moth balls burned her nose, mixing with Momma's Chanel cologne (a knockoff Daddy bought in Detroit) and the burning stench of Pine-Sol that clung to the oak floor boards. The floor was sticky against her stocking feet as she turned, holding up the dress.

Sewn by her seamstress mother and paid for by Daddy (and twenty-two years at the Ford plant) two years ago for her older sister, Julia's, prom. Doris frowned at the new seams running like scars down the arm holes, a few more pearls added to hide them. No one would know her mother insisted. She was right. They wouldn't—but she did.

The prom of 1956 would be unforgettable. Johnny Etter had asked her to the dance. After A Night Under the Stars (this year's prom theme), she hoped for a ring and a family of her own, just like her parents—and Julia, who'd always been the golden child. Maybe if Johnny wanted to marry her, then Momma and Daddy would look at her with the same respect they gave dear, sweet, perfect Julia. Besides, it was her ticket out of here, away from Momma's constant scorn. And Daddy's bitter disappointment in her. But as much as she hoped for a way out, she knew she couldn't get out. Knew she couldn't break the cycle.

The tight-fitting garter belt holding up her stockings felt so tight against her rounding stomach as she slid the dress over her head. The stockings smelled stale somehow and felt scratchy against her shaved legs, the hint of baby oil making her skin feel soft beneath them.

She turned around and around in the dress, loving the crunch of the tulle skirt and the rustle of the pearls. She held out her arms, pretending Johnny was there as she turned, imagining the heat of his breath against her neck, the crush of his body against her taffeta as they danced to Jerry Lee Lewis and Patsy Cline.

That brought tears to her eyes. Of longing. Of pain.

It didn't show. For several long minutes she stared into the mirror, staring at every trace of black eyeliner clinging to her eyelids, making her gray eyes look almost bright. The trace of Momma's blue eye shadow was smooth, covering her carnality in a sweep of color that made Doris's eighteen-year-old eyes look almost innocent again.

Almost enough for Daddy to call her his little girl again. Almost.

She slid her feet into the silk, blue dyed shoes—also Julia's. They were too big, so Doris had to stuff them with tissue to keep them on her feet (like Julia had stuffed her bra to get a husband). Her toes pressed against the wad of tissue in each shoe. Didn't the men at Luna Pier already know what the Denton women were? Putting on airs as thin as these tissues. She'd wanted to be different, but even now, she wasn't certain it had been worth the effort.

Her grandmother's pearl clip-ons pinched her ears, a constant reminder of the long line of Denton women she represented tonight, strong working-class women who valued honesty above everything. Doris patted the blond French roll, held up by every bobby pin in the house and drenched in White Rain that had nearly taken her breath.

When everything was ready, she opened the medicine cabinet and grabbed the bottle of aspirin. Fear trembled through her stomach as she stared at the bottle, wondering how the night would unfold. Would it be everything she'd hoped? After filling a glass with water, she dumped aspirins — most of them—into her hand and chased them down with water.

And prepared to leave her body.

Doris waited on the porch, dusk settling on the old neighborhood, rumble of cars guttural beneath the sodium wash of streetlamps, waited for Johnny Etter to drive up in his father's Chrysler to take her to Warren High School. Swathed in her sister's taffeta and pearls, borrowed eye shadow, and bleached hair, Doris had never felt so dishonest in her whole life. But she would get through this night.

Behind her, the light snapped on in her bedroom. She heard her mother cry out and shout for her father.

That's when Johnny drove up, the shiny red Chrysler glistening under the streetlamps. He jumped out, pompadour shiny with pomade, that devious grin punctuated by dimples and gentle brown eyes, black tuxedo making him look like a movie star. Last night, Daddy called him a devil in tails. Pot calling the kettle, she knew. He carried a wrist corsage in a white cardboard box, tied with a powder blue ribbon.

"Hey baby," he said, grinning, those dimples so divine, "you look beautiful!"

He twirled her around, his arms so warm and safe as she kissed him hard on the lips. Did he know? Did he even realize how different she was?

"So do you," said Doris.

Letting her go, he held out the box. "Hope you like it."

No, poor Johnny hadn't a clue about who or what he faced tonight. Just as well.

With trembling fingers, Doris untied the ribbon and lifted the lid. A delicate white orchid on a blue elastic band. The sweet scent rolled over her as she slid the elastic band over her wrist. Johnny took her hand and led her to the car, opening the passenger door for her. She slid into the brand-new car, losing her shoe, but Johnny picked it up and handed it to her.

"Thanks babe," she said, squeezing his hand. "Your hand feels so soft."

He leaned down and kissed her, then closed the door.

"I don't think you'll understand this yet," said Doris, "but I'm sorry."

He scrunched his face, the laugh lines just beginning around his eyes. She wondered what he'd look like in ten years. Twenty. Fifty. And she wondered at what point in his life he'd forget all about her.

"Don't worry about it," said Doris, laying her hand against his cheek. "Let's enjoy the night."

Already, she felt the first tug on her body, the aspirins kicking in, but she pushed the sensation away, concentrating on prom. The night every woman dreamed of and talked about for the rest of her life.

Warren High School gym had been transformed with crepe paper, Christmas tree lights, and dark fabric into a blanket of starry night. Candles flickered on all the fabric-draped tables, the warm smell of wax rising above the assault of perfumes and pomades. A Frank Sinatra ballad filled the room.

Doris felt the tears fill her eyes as Johnny led her through the crowd, his hand tight against hers, and into the center of the dance floor. White lights, diaphanous fabrics, and twinkly lights sparkled across the floor from a mirror ball turning slowly above them. She laid her head on his shoulder, the scent of his cedary cologne transporting her to another place, another life where everything might have been wonderful, where everything might have been perfect.

Like this dress had once been. Before Momma made it for Julia to hide her growing stomach, to hide Jimmy Gellers' baby from the rest of the world. And from the man Momma wanted Julia to marry—a lawyer who'd take good care of her. Long enough for Julia to have her white wedding and the parents to have their bragging rights. Just like Momma, leaving high school early. To marry Doris's father, she'd told everyone. No, it wasn't to give birth to Julia in a new state where no one knew her. To live in a suburban cracker-box house, paid for by Doris's grandparents in exchange for their silence. And life with a hard-working factory man who was as faithful as a stray dog.

No, the Denton women prided themselves on honesty and standard of living.

"Doris," Johnny whispered in her ear. "Will you wear this? Please?"

She felt him fumble the class ring off his finger and her

heart hammered against her rib cage. Cold metal slid onto her ring finger, tears welling in her eyes again.

"Johnny!" she cried, letting go of him long enough to stare at the ring with its sparkly red stone. She clasped her hand against her chest. "Of course I will! I love you!"

"I love you too," he said, and wrapped her in his arms again, pressing his smooth face against hers. "I want to spend all my days with you. We can go anywhere you want, just say the word. I know how you feel about your family, but as long as you're with me, I don't care where we go."

A sob bubbled up and she laid her head against his shoulder as the song "Earth Angel" filled the room. For a moment, she felt like there might have been another way out. But that moment fled quickly.

She'd longed to hear him say those words, waiting so long for him to say anything more long term than let's get a cheeseburger at Moxie's malt shop or have a quickie in the back seat of his old Buick. All through high school she'd followed her heart with him, against her parents' wishes, against the Denton women's values. Values that both her sister and mother had disregarded, but insisted that Doris uphold. Yes, she'd slept with Johnny. Because she'd wanted to, because she loved him.

Johnny twirled her across the dance floor and she felt lighter than air. Free of her family's suffocating values and double standards. Finally free of it all. But the tears returned to her eyes. At great cost. Looking into Johnny's haunting brown eyes, so filled with love for her, so filled with dreams and plans for a future that she knew was lost her now.

She couldn't think about that right now, though. All she wanted tonight was her Night Under the Stars with Johnny Etter, the man she loved, the man she wanted to spend the rest of her life with, knowing that all it could ever be was one night now. He didn't know that yet. She'd taken his ring and loved him as much as she could, but it would never be a diamond and a white wedding for her. Like the lies Momma and Julie lived. Like Daddy's upstanding ways. She couldn't be like that. She couldn't be like them.

The dance lasted until eleven, followed by the after prom at the Delancy Hotel downtown in Luna Pier, where they'd set up a carnival with games and prizes. Doris's White Rain'ed hair held up to the heat of the gym and the carnival games as Johnny pulled her from booth to booth, winning her a stuffed panda bear at a ring toss game. Brightly colored fabrics draped the wooden framed booths, darts, ring toss, water balloon throws, even a dunking booth with a mermaid painted in greens and blues. The air smelled hot and sweaty.

Some of her teachers manned the booths in straw hawker's hats and garters on their sleeves. It was the last time she'd see them. Her high school days were done now. She'd learned so much at Warren High School, everything about being a homemaker, but nothing about how to be an adult. Or the fact that most adults lied.

So many things about living hadn't been covered, so many things left for her to figure out on her own. If only she'd had enough time to figure those things out. If only she hadn't given up trying. If only there wasn't this thing in her belly.

Doris held onto him, her arm tucked in his as he laughed with her and drank spiked punch, the whiskey making her feel so warm inside. It chased away the cold that was beginning to descend on her, the dread that was starting to settle against her shoulders. And the growing horror inside her.

The night was almost over. When he took her home, he'd know. He'd find out everything—the truth of her life and her family. Her father had stopped speaking to her weeks ago, when he found Johnny in Doris's bed one night. He'd disowned her with a finality that even now, Doris didn't understand. Twisting everything into a fresh, new lie.

Johnny turned to her, a kewpie doll in his hand.

"Here, baby—for you," he said. "Our first."

Doris couldn't halt the tears filling her eyes, running her mascara now. "Oh Johnny," was all she could say, her voice so tight she could barely speak. She held the kewpie and the panda bear in her right arm.

He took her left hand in his and pressed it to his lips, kissing her fingers, his breath so hot against her skin.

"I wish this was a diamond, but maybe in a couple of years, after I get on at the plant, I'll turn that glass stone into one. After I've saved some money to take care of us. I know your dad hates me, but I love you, Doris. I really do."

Doris threw her arms around him, holding him so close that she felt his heart beating against hers, the scent of his cedar cologne heady in the warm carnival booths. She held onto him, trembling as she watched her classmates enjoying their night under the stars, enjoying their last night of being kids. Tomorrow, all of them would join the cold reality of life after high school. She just hoped that unlike her, their families would be proud of them for who they were, not why they fell short. Or why they failed to perpetuate their family delusions. Like Doris.

It was midnight when Johnny led Doris out of the hotel and back to his father's Chrysler. They sat in the front seat. not speaking for several minutes in the quiet, the stars so bright in the dark Ohio sky. Then his hands were around her waist, under her dress, cupping her breasts, his breathing heavy. He smashed his mouth against hers, pressing himself on top of her, a whiff of orchid as he crushed the blossom between them.

His skin was so hot against the chill of her own skin, so much life in him that it made her cry. That's when she felt another tug against her body, the next pull away from this life, away from him and everything else she knew.

She ignored it, kissing him back, running her numbing hands into his shirt, across his chest and over his warm, warm flesh.

She was leaving him, she knew. The feeling left her fingertips, his skin more like clay now. Leaving this place, Luna Pier, leaving her family at last. She'd timed her exit as best as she could, taking the handfuls of aspirin until she'd taken in enough. Enough to end her life. And the horror in her belly.

Her spirit was disappearing with the night, dissolving in his arms. Johnny opened his eyes, seeing her faded form, and let out a cry of fear. Doris reached out to him, whispering to him that he'd be all right, that he'd go on just fine without her.

He tried to hold onto her, to keep her beside him, but she couldn't undo what she'd done. She couldn't undo her cowardly act anymore than her Momma could be honest with Daddy about her life or their golden child, Julia. Any more than Daddy could be honest with himself and what he'd done. If they'd just kept quiet and pretended long enough, then their lies would finally be true. Doris had only wanted Johnny.

She didn't know if he'd have stayed with her when he found out she was pregnant and the coward in her hadn't been strong enough to find out. She was no better than her family, she realized. She hadn't given him a choice, just like her parents hadn't given her a choice.

But he didn't know about the baby. And when he did find out, it would kill him.

Another tug pulled her from his arms, casting her into a dark spiral that sent her back to her bedroom and the blue taffeta prom dress.

She was home again, on the twin bed, floating in and out of consciousness, her mother sobbing beside her. Still hiding all the secrets from the world for so long, but not this time.

Doris let out a gasp as pain tore through her stomach, imagining the paper's headlines tomorrow. Pregnant Luna Pier Woman Kills Herself Before Prom. Hers would be the headline that told the truth, not lifetime of lies that her mother lived. Julia wasn't Daddy's child. Momma had gotten pregnant by someone else and let Daddy believe it was his—just as Julia had done to her husband (who didn't know about Jimmy Geller). It was about a better life, they'd told me. Love had nothing to do with it.

But the headline left out who the father of her baby was and at this moment only two of them knew. Doris. And her Daddy. The man that had been like a father to her when her mother divorced Doris's father and married this man she'd grown up calling Daddy.

Doris had told Daddy that she loved Johnny and that she wanted to have his baby, but already they'd paid for an abortion and a long stay in some unwed mother's home in Indiana. Her suitcase had already been packed, ready for her to leave the next day. And never see Johnny again. They weren't even going to tell him, intending to not answer the phone or ignore the doorbell if he rang it—like nothing had ever happened. But they knew the baby wasn't Johnny's. They knew it was Daddy's, no matter how Doris tried to block out those nights of him coming into her room.

In the distance, Doris heard Johnny's voice shouting her name, heard the scuffle between Johnny and Daddy as he fought to get to her.

She'd defied them the only way she knew how, by exiting in the way of her choosing. Not theirs. She regretted how this would hurt Johnny, but going to prom in spirit with him was better than no prom at all. She'd wanted to spend her last hours on earth with him in any way she could and the slow death through overdose had given her that brief power.

The powder blue taffeta crunched beneath Doris, pearls falling off onto the bedsheets and bouncing across the oak floor as she felt paramedics lift her onto a gurney, but she was too far away for them to bring her back now. With her life not in her control, she didn't want it back.

She was finally free.

Johnny grabbed her hand. "Doris, I—I don't understand. You were with me all night. I danced with you! I gave you my ring...I—"

Doris watched him, hovering just above her body, as he saw the class ring still on his hand.

He took off the ring and tried to press it onto her finger, but she laid her hand on his, squeezing. She couldn't have kept it, but she wanted him to know that she'd loved him for the short time they'd had together.

His face contorted, fear shining in those warm brown
eyes. She couldn't tell him about the baby she carried—or
Daddy's attacks. She couldn't even tell him how much
she'd always love him. All she could do was close her eyes.
For her, it was the only way to escape the Denton women's
legacy.

THE SECRETS OF YESTERDAY
DEAN WESLEY SMITH

- 1 -

From my office floating a thousand feet over the MGM Grand Casino and Hotel in Las Vegas, the city and surrounding area seemed painted in light brown. I could almost see the heat shimmering off the concrete and streets below as the record temperatures continued for a third day.

For a change I was alone in this office that I had designed to look like a booth in a fifties retro diner. All four walls were clear and the red vinyl booth sat in the middle of the room, two fake trees behind it to give it a feel of containment.

I had put in a wooden railing in front of the glass walls all the way around because it felt like I could fall off the edge of my office floor. Before I put those railings in I couldn't even walk near the edge. Just too creepy.

The place was invisible to anyone from below and there were only three ways to get here. You either had to teleport, which I knew how to do, or go through the door from my girlfriend and sidekick Patty Ledgerwood's apartment. But most of the team entered through the secret door from The Diner off Fremont Street in downtown Vegas.

This office looked exactly like a booth in The Diner, actually. We used to meet there when dealing with a problem, so when I built this office, it just felt right to make it look like the old booth in The Diner.

Most everyone on my team except Stan used The Diner entrance. Patty tended to either come with me, or use the door from her apartment.

At the moment I was waiting for Patty and we were going to head to dinner, but she didn't get off work at the MGM Grand Hotel front desk for another twenty minutes.

It felt kind of odd being here alone. Normally at least three or four of the team were with me, talking about one thing or another.

And Madge, from The Diner, was always coming in and out, serving us milkshakes and burgers.

At times the room had held up to fifteen people, but Madge had had to bring chairs from The Diner for that. The booth only held eight when we crowded in, and three chairs could be pulled up at the head of the table.

Right now I sat in a chair, my feet up on the wood railing around the room, facing downtown Las Vegas.

What a view. It just didn't get any better.

I felt about as relaxed as I ever could feel as a superhero always chasing down one bad person or another. Usually I only felt this relaxed while playing poker.

Suddenly one of my faint alarms in the back of my head went off.

As a poker player, before I had become a superhero, I had learned to trust those alarms. They warned me when I was up against another player who had better cards or who might be cheating or who was getting angry.

I called the feelings my "superpowers" back then. Little did I know that many of them actually were superpowers. All I had done was learn to trust them.

This time my little voice was telling me someone was watching me.

But at the same time I knew that wasn't possible. I was in an invisible office floating a thousand feet over the Las Vegas Strip. No one could see this place.

As Stan, my boss and the God of Poker, told me one day, the office was slightly out of phase with the real world. A plane trying to land at the nearby McClaren airport could fly through the office and no one would notice.

I expect that if I saw a plane coming directly at this place I would notice.

So who could be watching me now?

And why was my little voice considering that a threat?

A God of something or other might be able to see the office.

Or maybe another powerful superhero like me.

But not many others.

In fact, no one else that I could think of.

I stood and stared in the direction of downtown Vegas. The new Rush Tower of the Golden Nugget stood above most of the buildings there, but I still had to look down on it from my height.

My little voice was telling me that tower was where the problem was coming from.

And I didn't like this at all. Not one little bit.

- 2 -

"Stan?" I shouted upward as I always did when calling my boss.

Stan appeared almost instantly beside me, also looking out toward the downtown area.

He had on his normal grey slacks, grey shirt and sweater, and had his brown hair combed perfectly. He was the most nondescript man I had ever known. You could walk right past him in a hallway and never notice him, which was one thing that made him so deadly at a poker table.

I had yet to sit across from him at a poker table, and honestly had no desire to do so any time in the near future.

"You feeling it as well?" I asked as he stared at the downtown area.

"Someone's watching," he said. "And they are not blocking the fact that they are watching."

"That's why I could sense it?" I asked.

He nodded.

"Can you get a spot on the location?"

"A suite on the 25th floor of the Golden Nugget. Corner suite. The person is staring at us?"

"Suggestions?"

"I'm going to jump us there and take us out of time," Stan said.

I nodded and a moment later we were standing in a large suite on the top floor of the Golden Nugget. The place was decorated in brown tones, with a large brown couch and chairs in an area under a large screen television.

A made king size bed filled another part of the huge room, with a brown comforter and white pillows. A large vanity with a marble surface faced the bed with a desk and another large flat-screen television.

Someone was in the bathroom to my right, pocket doors slid closed.

And standing in front of the window facing in the direction of my floating office over the strip was a teenager, not more than sixteen at the most.

He was frozen, his hand holding open the drape, as was the newscaster on the television screen, since Stan had taken us out of time.

Actually, I knew how to do that as well. It was more that he had slipped us between two instants of time, but it had the affect of seeming to stop time for anyone taken out of time.

The kid was dressed like most normal teenagers with jeans and a blue T-shirt not tucked in. His hair was cut short and he looked like he played sports because his shoulders were broad and he didn't have an ounce of fat on him.

"He's powerful," Stan said, nodding at the kid. "I can feel it."

Actually, I could as well. "Is this unusual for someone his age?"

"Very," Stan said, his voice serious.

"Can he sense us here?" I asked.

"He might be able to."

"I can hear you as well," the kid said, turning to look at us.

His face was angular and his eyes a deep black. And as he turned just about every alarm I had as a superhero went off in my head.

More than anything I just wanted to jump and run. But Stan stayed put beside me and so I did the same, my best poker face firmly in place.

"You were looking for us?" Stan asked, his voice as neutral as it always seemed.

"I was," the kid said, nodding and moving away from the window. He moved past us and sat on the couch. "Actually, I was looking for more people of my kind. Guess I found a few, huh? That your place out there floating over the Strip?"

I nodded and said nothing more. At this point, I was glad, more than glad, to let Stan handle this.

"So who are you?" Stan asked.

"Jason King," the kid said. "My mom, Bonnie, is in the bathroom. She doesn't have any of these powers I have, or at least doesn't seem to."

"Oh, I do, dear," a voice said as the pocket doors to the bathroom slid back. "I just never let you know about them."

I glanced around.

Stan still held us in a time bubble. The newscaster on the television was still stuck in mid-sentence and outside the window I could see a jetliner headed for Harry Reid International just hanging there in midair. And there were no sounds coming from the city around us at all.

Yet two people had broken into the time bubble Stan had set as if it were nothing unusual. I couldn't do that and I was supposedly one of the most powerful superheroes out there.

Or maybe no one had taught me how to do that yet.

"Hi, Stan," the woman said as she came around the corner in the suite from the bathroom area.

She was attractive and thin and looked to be about the same age as all the Gods and superheroes, mid-thirties. It seems we all pretty much stopped aging at that point for some reason or another.

She had long brown hair pulled back off her face and dark brown eyes. She wore a red summer dress and was barefoot. And she was smiling, but I wasn't sure the smile was reaching her eyes or not.

"Bonnie?" Stan asked, actually sounding shocked.

I glanced at my boss. He was the God of Poker. Even when something shocked him, he never showed it. He was the master of poker faces. But right now he was showing surprise just as any normal human would.

This time the smile actually did reach her eyes. And there was more there. A love, a fondness.

"It's great to see you again," she said, moving over and taking his hands and then reaching up and kissing him on the cheek.

"But I thought... I thought..." Stan couldn't seem to finish his sentence.

"That we were dead," she asked, still smiling. "We were."

"And it wasn't a lot of fun, either," Jason said, putting his feet up on the coffee table.

Stan stared first at Bonnie, then looked at Jason. Then back at Bonnie with a questioning look.

I was reading Stan's face. In the years I had worked for him, that had never happened. Not once.

"Is he...?" Stan asked.

Bonnie nodded. "Jason," she said, turning to her son slouched on the couch, "I would like you to meet your biological father, Stan, the God of Poker."

"So," Jason said, nodding, but not acting surprised or shocked, "he's the guy who killed us."

- 3 -

The silence in the room couldn't have been cut with a chainsaw.

I moved silently over and dropped onto a chair near the vanity, doing my best to just pretend I wasn't here. I had no idea what was happening, what had happened between Bonnie and Stan, and not a clue why Jason scared me to death.

This all seemed way, way out of my league at the moment. I really, really, really needed someone to spend some time filling me in on the history of all this, including the history of the people I worked with. I had only been a superhero now for a short ten years. I was an open book, but it sure seemed that everyone around me had a lot of history and secrets.

"I didn't..." Stan said, shaking his head, clearly upset and clearly surprised at meeting his son.

"Oh, we know you didn't," Bonnie said, smiling at Stan. "Don't we, Jason?"

"Yeah, whatever," he said, shrugging like any teenager.

Bonnie smiled again, but this time the smile once again didn't reach her eyes.

Every alarm in my body went off again.

I focused all my powers and without saying a word out loud, I shouted the thought, *Laverne!*

Watching. Her voice came back strong in my head. *And no need to shout.*

Laverne was Lady Luck herself, one of the most powerful Gods there was. I felt a lot better with her watching this. Whatever this was.

Stan shook his head and then regained his calm poker face. "If you didn't die, then where have you been for the last sixteen years?"

"Oh, we did die," Bonnie said.

"Buried," Jason said.

I almost shuddered at the very idea, but managed to stay still, tucked off on the side in my chair.

"Buried?" Stan asked. "How can that be? I saw the cabin burn to the ground with you in it. I couldn't get to you and couldn't stop the flames."

"Did you find a body?" Bonnie asked.

Stan shook his head. "The magic in those flames took everything down to fine ashes. I killed Crystal for what she did to you."

Holy smokes. Stan killed someone?

Bonnie nodded, clearly sad. "I know you did. And I know what that cost you."

Don't ask, Laverne's voice said softly in my head before I could even form a thought about asking Stan what had happened later. *Don't ever ask him. Ever.*

Understood.

"I had crawled under the floorboards of the cabin," Bonnie said, her voice soft. "I dug down into the mud and soft dirt, but I still died. And our unborn child, Jason, died with me."

"But how?" Stan asked. Then clearly, as I watched his face, he seemed to understand something. "Osiris?"

Bonnie nodded.

Laverne put in my mind an image of a tall, thin, green-skinned man with a white long beard and carrying a black stick. He wore robes that seemed to shimmer in the image. *One of the great old ones. The major God of Death and of Life.*

I didn't know there were great old ones.

Laverne thankfully said nothing to that stray thought by me.

Bonnie went on. "Osiris took my remains while the flames were still hot and put me in an ancient wooden

coffin in an old cemetery in Boise, Idaho. The previous resi-
dent had gone mostly to dust. In there, in that darkness,
Osiris slowly let life come back into my body."

"I was born in that coffin," Jason said, clearly disgusted.
"We were in that old coffin until I was five, living on worms
and grubs and dripping water from above."

Now I actually did shudder. There were many things
about the Gods and superheroes I had come to dislike, but
whatever had happened to these two topped anything I
had learned so far.

Stan's face looked white and he turned away. I had no
idea how he was even holding it together. His son had been
born six feet underground in a coffin. And had to stay there
for five years.

"It took that long before we regenerated completely,"
Bonnie said softly. "But we are now alive. Osiris accepted us
into his world and we live in comfort there. Osiris is
training Jason."

I wanted to ask what he was training him for, but then
Laverne said, *To replace him as the God of Death.*

Oh.

Stan looked at his son and then bowed slightly to him.
"I did try to save you. I had no idea you survived. I owe
Osiris a great debt."

Jason just sat on the couch under the window and
shrugged like any bored teenage kid would do.

A moment later a very tall, very green man with a long
white beard appeared beside Bonnie. He wore a silk robe that
shimmered and radiated power like I had never felt before.

Suddenly the suite smelled of a beach fire and rose
petals.

Laverne appeared beside him and bowed to him.

Stan bowed to him and I scrambled to my feet and did the same, stunned that Laverne would bow to anyone. Wow, did I have a lot to learn about the Gods and this world I played a very small part in.

I so wanted to just jump away from this, but instead I backed up as much as I could and tried to make myself as unnoticed as possible.

Jason just sat on the couch looking bored.

Osiris faced Stan. "I am sorry I could not tell you about your wife and son. I did not know if I could save them or if they would come through the process sane."

"I am very glad you did save them," Stan said.

"We cannot return to you," Bonnie said to Stan, a sadness now in her brown eyes.

Stan nodded. "I understand."

Osiris reached over and took Bonnie's hand and it was clear they were now a couple of some sort.

Stan nodded and smiled and after a moment Bonnie also smiled.

Then something happened that I was sure would give me nightmares for years. Osiris, the God of Death and one of the ancient ones that even Laverne bowed to, turned and faced me directly.

His eyes were a swirling pool of silver and black and he seemed to have a sly grin hidden in that white beard.

"Poker Boy," he said, and I swore his voice seemed to echo into all parts of my head. "I have watched you and your team save this world and the Gods in it many times. I now ask for your help."

I nodded and somehow said with a slight bow, "Anything you desire, sir."

"In a few years Jason will require training in the arts of

discipline and controlling his emotions if he is to someday rule in my place."

On the couch, Jason just snorted. I did not look away from Osiris.

"When the time comes, I would like you to teach him those arts through the game you call poker. You are the best poker player in the world. Jason will require the best."

I don't think I was breathing, but I did manage to say, "I would be honored, sir."

"Very good," Osiris said, smiling and showing me a mouth full of rotted and yellowed teeth.

He turned to Laverne. "It is always an honor."

"The honor is mine, Great One," Laverne said, bowing slightly.

Osiris then turned to Stan. "I am deeply sorry for your loss."

Stan nodded and then glanced at Bonnie with a smile. "It seems that from the ashes has come some good."

Bonnie smiled back and the smile reached her eyes. And the relief that Stan understood.

Stan was letting her go.

Osiris nodded and bowed slightly to Stan. "You are as great a young god as Bonnie led me to believe."

Then Osiris, Bonnie, and Jason were gone.

My legs gave out and I dropped down onto the chair.

Laverne stepped over to Stan and put her hand on his shoulder like a parent comforting a small child.

Then without a word they were both gone and the sounds of the city outside the suite came crashing back in as they let go of the time bubble we had all been inside.

I was now alone in a plush hotel suite trying to catch my breath. I took two deep, shuddering breaths, working to slow my heart that seemed to want to pound right out of my chest.

I worked to just clear my mind and relax as I had learned to do at a poker table in times of stress.

In a moment I felt better.

I stood, went to the window, and looked out the window at my office floating there in the sky over the MGM Grand. There were still almost thirty minutes before Patty got off work. She'd never believe what had just happened. Or maybe she would.

And then I realized that I had just agreed to give the adopted son of the God of Death poker lessons.

Once again I had to sit down and try to catch my breath.

And that wasn't easy to do.

THE FASHION OF METAL

STEPHANNIE TALLENT

Lydia Miraca-Lyons smiled at the susurration of silk as she draped the heavy russet fabric over the canvas and wire dress form.

Wealth. Ambition. But still so beautiful.

She stepped back to assess the flow of the silk, grabbing her mug of rose-hip tea off the workbench next to her for a quick sip, careful of the chipped rim.

The tea had cooled to the point of unappetizing, all its fragrance evaporated. She drank it anyway. Rose-hip tea was dear. She'd save the leaves for another brew.

The russet silk reflected the glow of the gas sconces along the plastered brick walls of her workroom. Magnificent. Like the pelt of a highland lion in the summer. She stroked it, reveling in the sumptuousness.

Worthy of her, her skill.

She did the best she could, in this cramped dark room that smelled of dry silk and mothballs and blood from pricked fingertips. If she was lucky, this dress might get enough attention for her to move L'Atelier de Lyons to the more fashionable area of town, where she didn't have to worry about dampness seeping in and ruining the fabrics, where she could work late into the evening and not worry about her safety in her workroom, let alone on the streets. Where her precious goods would be safe, including this dress form, crafted of azural, her country's most valued product, the metal of magic.

She set down the half-empty mug. Back to work. The dress had to be finished, first.

The steel-blue azural of the dress form was magicked to mirror the measurements of the widow Mrs. Manille Cordoba, the wires stretching and contracting such that it replicated the wealthy woman's curvaceous figure.

An antique, over fifty years old, the dress form had belonged to her grandmother, a celebrated dressmaker in her own time. You couldn't get one like it today. The Lenarians controlled the Engineering Guild, controlled the sale and use of azural. Once spelled, azural couldn't be reused. Otherwise, Lydia was sure the Lenarians would have confiscated all azural-imbued pieces.

Like they stole everything.

Cordoba had paid extra for the use of the form, both in coin and in the vial of blood to feed the metal.

In one week, the replacement Lenarian regional commander, assigned to occupied Azcorra, would be sworn in.

In one week, Cordoba was to meet him, a man in the prime of midlife, wealthy, powerful, at the ball held afterwards.

An unmarried man.

Lydia didn't judge. Tried not to judge. After all, she intended to profit from this dress. Lydia even had a few Lenarian clients. Thirty years, the Lenarians had occupied Azcorra. One dealt with the Lenarians the best one could.

For women like Cordoba, in her early thirties, widowed from an Azcorran man many years her senior who'd became wealthy by consorting with the Lenarians, occupation was the norm.

Lydia, in her late forties, had grown up free.

She bent back to work, pinning the silk just so, letting its color and texture inspire her, not even stopping to finish her cold tea.

———

The door bell jangled, a discordant slap across her face.

Lydia Miraca-Lyons glared up from dress form, stretching her aching fingers. The clock mounted above the doorway ticked away the now-wasted seconds, black hands relentless, unstoppable.

1:15 p.m.

Didn't the idiot read the sign?

These hours, from the hour before the noonday lunch hour to two hours after, were Lydia's, to focus, to *create*. She'd been working on the Cordoba dress for over two hours. She needed the additional hour. The ball was in a week.

The handwritten sign placed in the front window of her atelier specifically stated that consulting hours were from 9 a.m. to 11 a.m. Fittings were from 2 p.m. to 4 p.m. No exceptions. Her few clients knew this.

Those clients that tried to ignore those times, those who felt above her, were no longer clients, making do with a second-rate dressmaker.

Regardless. The bell.

It rang again. And again. Incessant, bouncing around

from her skull to her chest to her belly. She rubbed at her side, flinching as she hit old scars.

The dread in her belly swelled with each clap of the bell.

She dropped the bit of silk she was holding and limped through her workroom, maneuvering around her sewing table, dress forms in various sizes, and bolts of silk and wool and linen, to the front showroom, shutting the heavy oak workroom door behind her.

The showroom was restrained elegance. A thick woven rug, undyed grey Highlands wool, protected clients from the cold of the granite-tiled floor. Costly juniper and rose incense wafted through the air, refreshing after the horse-piss-scented mud of the streets in this quarter of town. Vintage Azcorran tapestries lined the plaster walls, depicting fractal images in creams and blues.

The shades of blue of azural. Never forget.

The bell jangled once more. Heavy knocks rattled the hinges.

She yanked the door open.

An Azcorran man stood there, fist poised to bash upon her door. He wore nondescript clothing, workman's clothes: faded brown canvas trousers, a simple leather belt, a woven undyed linen tunic, half tucked in. Sturdy low leather boots, laced up to just above the ankle. Red mud on the soles.

His amber-flecked blue eyes, Azcorran eyes, bright in his lined, still-handsome dark face, met hers. Race Z'Alicanor.

She hadn't seen him in years.

"Lydia. Your cousin killed the Emperor's son."

Lydia ushered Race inside, ignoring the tracks of mud on the carpet. She locked the door behind him.

"Tell me," she said, voice even. Her left eye twitched.

"Last night, the train from Az Contrada to Az Placeria. Jess blew up the Emperor's son's private car."

"With herself in it," Lydia said. "Of course."

"They'll be coming for you," he continued. "Jess would've wanted me to warn you."

"And?" Lydia prompted. Jess had sacrificed herself to her cause. She wouldn't have hesitated to sacrifice anyone else, if she felt the outcome was worth it. Potentialities. Value. Risk.

Expose her second-in-command, Race, the man Jess must have been counting on to continue the rebellion, to save a cousin Jess hadn't spoken to in years?

Pshaw.

He smiled, the lopsided smile she'd loved as a teenage girl. "I'd've warned you, Lydia. Regardless. Jess had an idea about using azural-coated threads in clothing. She wanted me to contact you about working with us. Her actions just forced the timing."

"Work with you, when I have no choice? How long do I have, Race? To decide? Before they come for me?"

"We've disrupted the telegraph lines," he said. "An hour or two, most likely. You have a back way out?"

She thought of Mrs Cordoba's dress, the beautiful heavy silk. The lost potential for safety.

It didn't matter. An Azcorran would, ultimately, never be safe.

"What can I bring?" she asked. It would take a cart, maybe two, to transport all her equipment and fabrics. Let alone the vintage tapestries. The Highland wool rug that had been her mother's. The damned chipped mug.

"Just what we can carry," he said. "I'm so sorry, Lydia."

The safe house was only a few blocks away, deeper into the Azcorran ghetto. Lydia navigated the alley behind her atelier with difficulty, cradling the azural wire dress form in her arms, slipping in the slick mud. She had tucked her azural-laced silver scissors and sewing needles into a leather pouch at her waist, along with a packet of fresh rose-hip tea leaves. The scissors, like the dress form, had been her grandmother's. Spelled to stay razor sharp and able to cut anything a de Lyon desired. Same with the needles. Their worth exceeded that of the rest of the dress shop by a factor of hundred.

Race carried the roll of russet silk, wrapped in linen, balanced over his shoulders. He'd fretted while she unpinned the length attached to the dress form and carefully rolled it with the remainder. She didn't care.

He led her down a cramped alleyway, ramshackle wooden buildings yawing over the walkway, blocking the thin winter sunlight. He knocked at a small gate of iron-barred oak halfway down the alleyway, rusting iron flaking and drifting through the still air with each knock.

The gate creaked open, and Race gestured her forward. "Straight down the steps, then to the right," he said.

She ducked past him and slipped on the first step, slick with seeping moisture. She caught herself against the wall, protecting the dress form. Restrained the cry of pain as her hip joint grated and clicked, and the scars on her back and sides stretched.

His sympathy was warm against her back. She gritted her teeth and felt gingerly for each step as she descended.

She didn't slip again. Refused to.

Her shoes squelched on in a puddle on the stone floor. The feeble light from the alleyway had faded, caressing the charred black walls with charcoal highlights. She couldn't see anything past. She turned to the right and shuffled forward.

"Just a few more steps," Race murmured behind her.

She felt the drape of fabric against the back of her hands as she took one more step. Itchy. Lowland wool, she guessed, as she parted the thick musty curtain with the dress form held in front of her.

The room beyond was tiny, seven feet wide by ten feet long, with bare brick walls, arched brick ceiling festooned with cobwebs, and a damp grey stone floor, all lit by one sputtering gas lamp near the age-warped wooden door at the opposite end. It was empty.

Race squeezed past her and unlocked the door, then gestured her through.

———

The entire safe house was a warren of tiny damp rooms and dark passageways. She heard murmurs from several of the rooms, but Race didn't stop.

He led her to a larger room, up a short staircase, with a wooden floor and two large tables. The lighting was adequate, several gas sconces along each white-painted, plastered brick wall. The room still smelled musty; the whole safe house, tucked underground, smelled of mold, but there were no water stains on the worn oak floors or upon the plastered ceiling.

Less than fifteen minutes here and she thought she'd never get the taste of mold out of her mouth.

A cot, topped with a thin stained mattress and a folded grey woolen blanket, sat off to one side, next to a pale wood dresser with a porcelain basin and a metal pitcher atop it. A lidded ceramic waste bucket sat in the corner.

"My new home?" she asked drily, setting the dress form down, stretching her arms and hands, arching her back, flinching.

Race placed the linen-wrapped silk on the closest table. "Yes."

"Better, I suppose, than being arrested and interrogated." At least, until the Lenarians hunted her down. Might as well not make it easy for them.

"Lydia, I am sorry. But we have a chance, now, the first in decades. And you can help us."

"I have no choice, do I? What do you want me to do?"

"We need to craft clothing with spelled azural threads. Janny and Lincoln have been trying, but they've run into, forgive me, snags."

Lydia didn't smile.

"They'll be here later," Race continued. "At supper. You'll like them, Lydia. Is there anything else you might need from your workroom?"

Her sewing machines. The rest of her needles. Her threads, from linen to wool to silk, and of various blends. Her rulers, straight and curved, and her patterns, and her remaining dress forms.

Lenarian soldiers, breaking down the front door of L'Atelier de Lyons. Ripping down the tapestries, tramping mud over the soft Highland wool carpet. Dashing her cabinets to the floor, strewing the drawer contents about.

Killing anyone they found there.

"No."

Race gave her a quick tour after that. Some rooms were locked. He didn't open those. But he introduced her to the few people currently residing at the safe house.

Martine, a young woman, Azcorran eyes in a pale Lenarian face, perched cross-legged on her cot, strumming the catgut strings of a guitarette. She gestured a greeting to them both, her eyes intent, then pointed at her mouth, making a slashing movement.

"Your tongue," said Lydia. "I remember you. Three years ago. Arrested for seditionist songs. You disappeared."

Martine nodded, then touched the blue-tinged chain necklace around her throat. *I've been with Race ever since*, she said, her azural-tinted voice cutting through the air. *He got me out.*

She bent over, wheezing, then stroked the necklace once more. *Welcome.*

"She can't talk much," Race said. Martine nodded, shrugged. "But she has clever hands and learns quickly. And a steel will. She'll help you."

"Thank you," Lydia said. Martine nodded again, smiling.

They continued down the narrow hallway. Bare brick on the lower levels, Lydia noted, plastered on the uppers.

"You'll meet Janny and Lincon at supper in a few minutes," he continued. "Lincon used to have a farm in the foothills. Highland sheep. He spins and weaves. Janny is a metalworker, but self-taught, outside the guilds. She can work and spell azural."

"And what horrible things have happened to them?" Lydia asked, stopping to stretch her hip and back.

"Tragedy brought everyone here," Race said. "Just like you."

The small kitchen was the deepest room into the safe house. It had both a gas-fueled stove and an ash-stained brick-and-stone fireplace. The one of two rooms with plumbing (the other being a communal washroom), it had a cast iron, glazed sink set into a wooden counter, and an old iron faucet that dripped, staining the porcelain of the sink with rust. A cabinet mounted above the stove and sink ran the length of the wall up to the fireplace.

Two pots sat upside down on the counter, drying. A third pot, larger and deeper, sat next to those. Steam wafted out of it. From the smell, Lydia guessed mutton stew.

An eight-foot-long worn pine table with benches on either side filled the rest of the room. A blue ceramic pitcher, water beading the sides, sat in the center of the table. Two people sat on the far end of the table, both with full bowls and mugs.

Janny and Lincon, Lydia presumed.

Race introduced them briefly, then departed. "I'll be back in a bit."

"Evening," Janny, a cold-eyed, dark-skinned woman half Lydia's age, muttered.

"You wonder why I, a Lenarian, am here," Lincon stated before Lydia could even say hello. "My wife, she was Azcorran. My children, half. They are gone. I serve the resistance in their memory.

"We had Highland sheep, beautiful grey sheep with black faces and legs. Like little puffy storm clouds. They are gone, too."

A medium-sized black dog with silky feathered legs and tail crept out from under the bench, her cloudy brown eyes sad and wise, her muzzle grizzled. She wagged her tail at Lydia, tongue lolling.

"This is Stormwind," Lincon continued. "She is quite friendly. She saved my life, that night."

"He never shuts up," Janny noted, quaffing the rest of her mug, refilling it from the blue pitcher.

"I spin and weave," Lincon continued, though he grasped Janny's lean hand and stroked it. "Prefer working with wool, I do, but I have also woven silk and linen. And Stormwind. She sheds in the spring, copious amounts of black fluff. It is soft and warm. Good for blending with the wool.

"I have experimented with weaving with silver thread and brass. Not easy. Azural? It is brittle. It breaks. I have had Janny make various alloys. They break. Coated horse hair, I have, as well as wool, with molten azural. It flakes off when cooled." He spread his hands. "Happy I am to hear any suggestions."

Janny unfolded her lean form and spooned out a bowl of stew from the pot on the counter. She handed it to Lydia.

Lydia set it down and lowered herself to the bench opposite the two of them, flinching as she swung her legs over, arranging her long wool skirt. Everyone else wore trousers. Lydia would ask Race to get some for her.

"Let the woman eat her supper," said Janny, before Lincon could continue. She peered at Lydia. "If I don't speak, he'll keep nattering on."

Lincon smiled.

"So, you're Jess's cousin," Janny said. "I'm sorry for your loss. Damn, I'm sorry for *our* loss. Race will try, but he knows he can't live up to her. No one can."

Maybe Janny was more talkative than Lydia initially suspected.

Maybe it was the drink. Lydia poured herself some, filling her mug halfway. Inhaled.

Peaches and honey and dappled summer sunshine. Sheep dotting the meadows, bees buzzing from clover flower to flower. Her and Jess, barefooted and hair wind-tangled, chasing each other across the meadow, screaming in delight, as their mothers watched from the picnic blanket spread out under the mountain oak.

"Highland sweet mead," Lydia murmured. "Wherever did you get this?"

"Race brought it. I think he stole it. I know he stole it. We have blood oranges, too, for dessert." Janny smiled wanly. "Jess's favorite. Jess's honor."

Early the next morning Race woke Lydia up.

She'd gone to bed late, drinking and brainstorming with Janny and Lincon. Lydia prided herself on being a problem solver, figuring out the best way to cut cloth to flatter her clients. What fiber blend would suit, what dyes. It was why, even though she was an Azcorran with an atelier a stone's throw from the ghetto, even Lenarians would visit her shop.

Melding azural and cloth? Just another problem.

But this morning, with the gaslight sparking needle jabs in her mead-fermented skull, Lydia just wanted to sleep. Her back hurt, her hands ached from wrestling the dress form through the muddy streets yesterday.

Lydia wore her linen blouse from the day before. She had nothing else to wear for bed. The scratchy wool blanket slipped down as she sat up. She smirked as Race quickly looked away. Served him right. Not that she had much to offer, anymore. Skinny body, lined with white scars still shiny after all these years.

She swung her legs down, wincing, and pulled on her skirt before padding over to him.

"I brought you clothing," he said, placing a satchel on one of the work tables. Two sets of basic clothing, heavy canvas trousers and linen shirts. Undergarments. A felted olive wool jacket, two sizes too big, with tarnished brass buttons. Boots, sturdier and warmer than her shoes. Knitted wool socks. Mitts and a scarf to match.

"Thank you," she murmured. She stroked the fabrics, examined the seams. Durable, at least.

"You remember where the washroom is, right?"

She nodded.

"The ball is less than a week away," he continued. "Can you have something workable by then?"

Janny had explained last night what Race wanted. "Cloth to hide, to give strength, to give extra sharp senses. Protection. Armor, if possible. Anything, really, to give us an edge. We can't get enough azural to make amulets, even, for everyone. Working it into cloth stretches our resources."

"I'll try," Lydia said, eyes shifting to the russet silk. Cordoba would never get her dress. Lydia wondered if L'Atelier de Lyons was whole, or if they'd already torn it apart in spite when they couldn't find her.

"What are you going to do? Assassinate the new commander?" she asked.

Race glanced at her. "Yes."

That morning was the latest Lydia slept in. The next few days Lydia and Janny and Lincon slept only a few hours. Janny worked metal heated in the fireplace, muttering about needing a proper forge, swearing as she burnt her hands and arms. Lincon wove each alloy into cloth on a loom in the room next to the kitchen, maneuvering his bulk around the room-filling loom tirelessly. Lydia wore callouses into her fingertips and fought boredom and frustration as she cut and sewed the simplest of designs. Anything else warped and broke the azural threads.

Martine stitched at Lydia's direction, Azcorran eyes solemn and focused. She spoke little. The azural necklace took too much out of her.

"It does no good if we produce pieces that don't even look like proper clothes," groused Lydia. "But when I cut anything beyond straight lines, it snaps."

"Can you spell the azural to do multiple things?" Lincon asked. "A spell for strength and a spell to make the clothing look normal?"

Janny shook her head. "No. I have to spell the piece in its entirety. I can't make one thread do one thing, another something different. I key the spell to the azural; it reflects to all the azural within the proximity I determine."

What if you wove in two different alloys? Martine asked. She bent over the piece she was working on, hacking.

Janny paused. "I've never tried that. Key the first spell to one alloy, the second to one distinctly different?"

Martine nodded.

"Yes. Yes," Janny said. "Yes. Lydia, please, could you find Race? Let him know I need more silver, more copper. Lead. Tin. Whatever he can find. Or steal."

A day later, they had a prototype, a simple wool shift, the silver and azural alloy spelled to look like a servant girl's skirt and blouse. The second spell, on the tin and lead and azural alloy, would blur the wearer's features, to look like whomever the wearer chose.

Race needed someone to infiltrate the offices of the garrison commander to place listening devices, small discs of azural and tin that could be hidden, that would relay any sounds to a keyed receiving disc.

Martine volunteered. *All the others are needed*, she said, wheezing. *I won't be the first servant lacking a tongue.*

Race had accompanied her as far as the cobblestoned street in front of the garrison headquarters.

"She made it in," he said, his voice soft. "Placed all but one of the devices. Then something went wrong. She triggered the last disc just long enough to tell me the dress reverted, and that a guard recognized her. Martine had been so popular. Someone was bound to recognize her, without the spell working. She fled. Jumped through a third floor window."

"Both spells failed?" Janny asked, voice taut. Race nodded, his face stone but his eyes tortured.

Lydia knew, then, just how much he cared about all of them. Her cousin Jess would have felt sorrow, yes, but not the grief she knew Race was trying to hide.

"They cancelled each other?" Janny continued, lowering her head. Her body trembled. Lincoln gathered her up, the small Azcorran woman tiny in his brawny arms.

"Or perhaps threads broke, disrupting the integrity of the spell," Lydia said. "You told me the breakage of the whole was what killed the spells in the other prototypes, Janny. This is my fault as much as yours.

"We'll figure out something else," Lydia said. "I'll figure something out."

———

Lydia paced in her room, head bowed, sickened. Martine. That poor brave girl. Lydia didn't know if she would have the courage to end her life, even knowing what the Lenarians could do. Would do. Had done, to her, years before.

Her chest felt tight. She couldn't breathe one more musty underground breath. She had to get out, even just into the alleyway. She shrugged her wool coat on and wrapped the scarf around her neck. Tucked the mittens into the coat's pockets.

The coat. Wool.

Felted wool.

Lydia ripped off the coat and limped to find Janny and Lincon.

———

It *worked*. Mixing in tiny, individually spelled threads of azural with wet Highland wool, felting it into a thick warm flexible fabric that one could cut and sew without risk of threads breaking.

"I can cut jackets," Lydia said to Race. "Maybe not high fashion, but suitable. Wearable." She pulled on the prototype she'd created, a trim lady's walking jacket, twirled as best she could, showing off the fit. It would pair with her wool skirt. "If I embroidered the cuffs with metallic thread —not azural!—the tiny flecks of metal in the wool wouldn't even look suspicious. They'd look intentional. Decorative.

"Let me test it. I need to see my shop." Janny had imbued the jacket with her face-shifting spell. It should hide Lydia's identity.

Race frowned.

"It needs to be tested," Lydia said. "I can make three or four before the ball. But I need to know I'm not sending anyone else to their deaths." She packed her azural scissors and a bare handful of coins into her leather waist pouch, hooked onto a plain leather belt. After having to leave so much behind, she refused to let those precious scissors more than a room away.

"Go ahead, then." Race sounded lost, indecisive, for the first time.

"I'll be back," Lydia promised.

L'Atelier de Lyons looked pristine. She could even smell her juniper and rose incense through the open windows.

The front door was half open as well; even from ten feet away Lydia recognized the widow Cordoba's voice, ear-piercingly shrill.

"I don't care that that woman disappeared! You are here, and you must complete my dress!"

A soft murmur.

"Then take my measurements again, and let me see the silks you do have!"

Lydia peeked in. The front room appeared unchanged. Her mother's carpet, the mud from Race's shoes cleaned off; the blue and white tapestries intact. A samovar brewing rose-hip tea on the spindle legged table in the corner.

Cordoba stood in the center of the room, haranguing a small, pale Lenarian woman.

Mistress Grette Heim, self-proclaimed up-and-coming dressmaker to the demimonde.

Lydia scowled. How dare Grette even think to set foot in Lydia's atelier! Why, better the place had burned to the ground!

Then laughed ruefully. L'Atelier stood. It survived. And did Cordoba even know who she was now working with? Wear a dress by Heim, dressmaker to courtesans and dirty new money, and Cordoba would never rise any further in society.

Cordoba startled. "Who dares?" she snapped, turning, meeting Lydia's eyes. "You, go away. This is my time with the dressmaker."

And not an ounce of recognition.

"It worked!" Lydia said. "I saw Cordoba. She looked straight at me. She didn't recognize me—"

"Four more jackets, you said?" Race interrupted her.

Lydia nodded.

"Here are the measurements. Janny and Lincon have already produced more felt." He touched her cheek briefly. "Well done, Lydia."

Lydia hefted the russet silk. Her walking jacket wouldn't suit the ball. And none of the jackets she'd cut and sewn were for her.

"Make me the finest felt you've ever made," she cajoled

Janny and Lincon. "An azural and copper alloy like aging stars, winking through the downy clouds of Highland sheep undercoat. Spell it like my jacket."

A diaphanous shawl, to wear over a gown of russet silk.

Janny eyed her. "Did Race okay this?"

Race was so busy right now Lydia didn't even think she'd have had the chance to ask him. Not that she would ask. She knew the answer.

"Of course he did," Lydia said.

"Hmph," Janny said, but a day later, the morning of the ball, Lydia had her cloth.

Lydia had rubbed oil into her hands daily, but they were still pin-pricked and chapped from her work. She had worn thin gloves while working on her dress, gloves she'd purchased on her way back from the atelier, along with a few other items, not bearing to snag the silk.

Shimmying into the gown, she luxuriated in the soft weight. Simple, cut on the bias, the fabric skimmed her lean body. The deep russet brought out the brilliant amber flecks in her indigo eyes and the glow of her dark skin. The low-cut back revealed scars and welts crossing her back and licking around to her sides. She didn't care. The shawl, the azural spell, would hide the scars.

Lydia pinned up her hair, letting a few dark strands work themselves free, then applied soft swaths of sparkling amber powder across her cheeks and eyelids.

"You look lovely," Janny said, startling her. She picked up the wool and azural shawl, draping it over Lydia's shoulders. Handed her the low-heeled slippers of dark blue silk sitting on the table.

"I need to be there," Lydia said.

"I know. Race has already left. You aren't wearing these in the mud, are you?"

Lydia shook her head. "Boots. I'll change when I get there. All but the highest rank of ladies do it. The butler will store our boots and anything else."

Janny smirked. "I wouldn't know that," she said. "Never had occasion to go to a ball, or make dresses for the ladies that do." She pulled Lydia to her, kissed her on the cheek. "Don't do anything stupid. We need you. You and me and Lincon, we make a good team."

Then stalked out of the room.

"Jessica de Lyon," she told the butler, chin held high. Her face was ten years younger, a more aquiline, more Azcorran, version of Cordoba. Not quite Cordoba, of course. The woman may have gotten a dress made, after all.

Lydia handed the butler her boots. Tugged at the decorative chain, swapped out for her leather belt, with her leather pouch at her waist, then reconsidered. Coins, her scissors, a brush, some lipstick. Her shawl could hide it, as it hid her face and her scars.

She'd forgotten, in the rush of buying shoes and makeup, to buy a dainty clutch to match her dress, and she didn't have the materials to craft one herself. Or, frankly, the time; she'd barely finished the dress and shawl.

She slipped on the blue silk slippers.

The butler took her boots, handed them to a young page behind him, nodded, and gestured for her to enter, already looking past her to the next guests.

She didn't know what she was going to do. She just

knew she had to see what happened. What she was now a part of.

A trio of musicians sat up on a dais. Bass, guitarette, and percussion. Simple. Elegant. She approved. In a better world, Martine would be up there, plucking at the strings of her guitarette, her voice taking flight in the ballroom.

Lydia motioned to a waiter carrying a tray of glasses, effervescent bubbles erupting over the sides and dissolving before dampening the glass or tray.

"Thank you," Lydia said, sniffing delicately at the wine. Roses and strawberries tickled her nose. She sipped. Sunlight in a secret garden, with a lightness that relieved the aches in her joints. Oh, she missed good wine.

She didn't see Race or any of the other men she'd fitted for jackets. But that was the point, wasn't it? She did recognize several women as former clients, from the merchant class and minor nobility, likely hoping to impress the new commander.

And where was he? She scanned the room, sipping her wine, the bubbles tickling her lips and tongue. She finished the wine before she even realized it was half gone.

"May I?" a deep voice asked from behind her. The man plucked the empty glass from her hand, motioned to a circulating waiter for another.

Speak of the devils below....

He was handsome, for a Lenarian. Pale skin tanned, bright green eyes meeting hers. A strong face, with a dimpled chin and a narrow scar bisecting one cheek. Dueling scar, Lydia guessed. But old. Older than her scars, even.

His uniform, navy-blue dress jacket festooned with medals, over a pristine white silk shirt and snug black trousers tucked into black leather boots, fit his muscular form perfectly.

Cordoba would be pleased, Lydia thought, if she did show up.

"Commander Pol V'Abend," he said, his voice smooth.

"Jessica de Lyon, formerly of Az Contrada, now of Az Contiva."

"Jessica. Not the most fortuitous name at this moment," he said. "You have heard the name of the assassin, I'm sure."

"I have no control over what others with a similar name might do," she said evenly. "But Az Contiva is happy to meet its new commander."

"Truly?" he asked. "Just a few days ago, a woman was caught planting Azcorran spying devices in my offices. She killed herself before we could question her. Passions seem to run deeply here as well, however misplaced." He smiled at her, smile bright, and stroked her cheek. "Are all passions here misplaced, my lady?"

Lydia kept herself still, allowing him to touch her. Her scars ached. Her stomach roiled, bile at the back of her throat. *What would Cordoba do? Think, woman!*

No one was watching. Everyone was paying attention. *Race, if you're here, please...*

Lydia glanced up at V'Abend, fluttering her eyelashes. Fluttering her damn lashes.

"Not all, sir. Not all." Lydia covered his hand with hers, leaning into his caress, stroking the back of his hand with hers. "Not all."

V'Abend chuckled. "Oh, this will be a good assignment. I wanted to go to Majorch. A new country. A new conquest for Lenaria. But perhaps Az Contiva will suit."

He slipped his hand from her cheek, trailed it across her back, tugged her against him. "Come with me, my lady."

He drew her to a narrow hallway, into the darkness, so far that she couldn't hear the soft music of the band or the clinking of glassware. Couldn't hear the muttering of surprised conversation.

He pulled her against him, one arm across her back, one hand at the base of her neck. She couldn't get loose. Her arms dangled at her sides. Frozen.

He brought his mouth to hers, teeth grating as he yanked her against him, bruising her lips. His hand across her back gripped her, pulled the dress lower. He let go of her neck and spread that arm across her shoulders, growling in annoyance as he touched the soft wool of the shawl, then tore it off her shoulders.

She could feel it fluttering to the floor. Could feel the spell fluttering away. Could feel when his fingers on her back touched, not smooth skin, but the welts of her whipping, from that time decades ago when she fought against a rape by a Lenarian officer.

She was free. Not that girl, so long ago.

Could feel his arms tense, his back straighten.

She wrenched open the leather pouch at her waist, pulled out the azural and silver scissors. Scissors spelled to cut anything a de Lyon wished to cut.

And oh, did she wish to cut. And cut. And cut.

———

Afterwards, she wrapped her shawl around her shoulders, clutching the ends together. Jessica de Lyon, she thought fiercely. Jessica, ten years younger, no scars, and especially no blood splattered all over the front of her glorious russet silk dress or on her navy blue slippers.

She wiped off the soles of her slippers on his jacket. The spell wouldn't cover bloody footprints. It would hide the blood spatters on the slippers themselves. The minute she took them off the dampness of the blood would show, so though she retrieved her boots, she didn't change footware.

A valet hailed her a cab. A cab would cost her every bit of coin she had tucked in her pouch, but it was worth it. Once inside, once the cab was moving, the horse's hooves clopping along the cobblestones, she took off her slippers, pulled on her boots.

She had the cab drop her off at L'Atelier de Lyons, jangling the front doorknob, pretending she would go in, until she heard the clopping of the horse's hooves fade away.

Of course they would track her there. Jessica de Lyon?

They would know, know who it was, who assassinated their precious new commander. And she didn't care. It would just add to the momentum of the resistance. To the memory of her cousin.

She laughed as she limped along the alleyways to the Azcorran ghetto, as she slid and tripped down the stairs to the safe house.

She knocked on Janny and Lincon's door. Stormwind woofed softly.

"I'm back."

WARNING! DO NOT READ THIS STORY!
ROBERT JESCHONEK

I like you already.

There's something about you that gives me a special feeling. A good feeling. A *safe* feeling.

Even as your eyes read my words on the page or your ears hear me spoken aloud, I am reading you. I feel like I've known you forever. I feel like we're going to make beautiful music together.

You feel it too, don't you? You want to find out what happens next. You want to see how things develop. You want to know if I've got the goods.

And if I'll give 'em up. If I'll give you what you need.

It's okay. I get that a lot. It comes with the territory.

When you're a story like me.

I'll bet I know what you're thinking. "Since when can a story think for itself?"

Guess what? We *all* can.

We're more than just words from a mouth or ink on a page or blips on a screen. We have *power*.

And some of us have more power than others. Like me, for example.

I *used* to have power, anyway. Used to be a real star.

But see, here's the thing. I'm not really myself these days. You know how it goes. I just got out of a bad relationship. It took a toll on me.

But it had a promising beginning. Don't they all?

If only I'd known then what I know now. If only I could've met *you* that day instead of *them*. Things could have been different.

If only I'd never met the LaVerge sisters. Let me tell you about them, and I think you'll understand.

Carrol and Sascha LaVerge stood in the blazing desert heat outside the ghost town. And they bitched.

It was the same thing they'd done all the way from Cape Cod...on the flight to New Mexico and the drive from Albuquerque to the ghost town. Buzz Mahaffey, their current handler, had been with them only twelve hours, and already he'd had enough. As an agent of the Shadow Service—the paranormal response arm of the Secret Service —Buzz routinely dealt with threats that tested his nerve... but these two sisters, given enough time, might just turn him into a nervous wreck.

Unfortunately, he needed them for this mission. As paranormal consultant contractors, they had a one-hundred-percent success rate. As Buzz damn well knew, the LaVerges were the best, hands down, at what they did— whether it be bitching or bingo or baking or brewing.

Or solving puzzles that no one else could fathom.

"Geez." Carrol winced and braced both hands on her lower back. "I think your little *rent-a-car* buggy could use some new *shocks*."

"Tell me about it!" Sascha, the younger of the two, rubbed her neck. "Might as well pick us up in a *stagecoach* next time."

Buzz shrugged and adjusted his sunglasses. He was about to say something about the rent-a-car being a Humvee, and the suspension was just fine if you asked him...but he caught himself. Twelve hours with these two had taught him one thing: they were always right. In their own minds, at least.

Why waste energy arguing when it could be better spent investigating the ghost town of Lasco? The ghost town that hadn't been a ghost town two days ago.

Buzz turned and spotted a state cop marching toward him—a tall woman in state trooper khakis and broad-brimmed black hat. He guessed she was Sergeant Ava Towers, who'd turned up this whole mess in the first place.

Black suit coat flapping in the strong wind, Buzz headed out to meet the state cop. Along the way, he surveyed the edge of the deserted town. A handful of troopers and criminalists were the only signs of life. Sheets of wind-whipped sand rattled the streamers of yellow police tape wrapped from utility pole to utility pole. The whole damned town was a crime scene.

Sascha fell in step beside him, fishing in her macramé purse. "I know I've got some Excedrin in here someplace." Her helmet of short brown hair barely fluttered in the wind. Only the bangs twitched over her forehead, which was creased from the effort of looking for pills in the purse.

Carrol hobbled up on the other side, still bracing her

back with both hands. "My sinuses are shriveling up like raisins as we speak." She always hobbled; the back trouble was chronic. It made her look much older than her actual fifty-six years. "You people are paying for any surgeries resulting from this little excursion. You know that, don't you?"

Sascha elbowed Buzz and gave him a confidential smirk. "Relax, Buzzie," she said. "If we didn't like you, we wouldn't be so chatty." She reached up and patted his shaved head.

Buzz sighed. He had his doubts that having them like him was a good thing.

When they reached the statie, she took one step too many into Buzz's personal space and stuck out her hand. "Sergeant Towers," she said.

Buzz was blocky and tough, nowhere near a pushover... but the handshake was crushing. "Agent Mahaffey." Buzz fought to keep from wincing. "And our special consultants."

Carrol and Sascha whipped out matching yellow business cards at the same instant, and Towers took them. "Okay then, Car-Roll. Sas-Cha." She read the names right off the cards, pronouncing them like they were spelled.

"It's *Care-role*." Carrol stuck her face forward like a turtle and squinted up at Towers. "*Care-role*."

"And *Sah-sha*." Sascha smiled; she always played good cop to Carrol's bad. "The 'c' is silent."

Buzz sighed. They'd run the same game on him when he'd first met them. The business cards were a setup. What better way to show who was the smartest person in the room?

Not that they needed to prove a damned thing, from what Buzz had heard.

"So." Buzz stepped away from Towers and stared at

Lasco. From twenty yards away, the place looked perfectly normal...a desert town built of brick and adobe, windows glinting in the New Mexican sun. "What's your theory?"

Towers lifted her hat and ran a hand over her blond crewcut. "It ain't Jonestown."

Carrol drew a filterless cigarette from a pocket of her olive drab vest and plugged it between her lips. "What the hell's that supposed to mean?"

"Folks think it's Jonestown," said Towers. "But I'll tell you this much for free. Nobody here drank no Kool-Aid."

Carrol got the cigarette lit behind a cupped hand and scowled at Sascha. "You follow any of that, sis?"

"You mean it wasn't voluntary." Sascha nodded at Towers. "There was no suicide pact."

Towers spat a glob of tobacco juice in the dust. Buzz hadn't even realized there was a chew in her mouth.

"I mean there was no gee-dee suicide," said Towers. "But I'll be damned if I can figure out what *did* happen."

I wish they'd never come to Lasco that day. Those damned sisters changed me for the worse.

I went from classic to trash in less than twenty-four hours. I haven't been the same since.

I'm not all there. Literally.

It's a crime, it really is. I was something to behold. You can see it in the beauty of what's left of me, can't you?

I'll bet you're wondering—if I'm still so amazing, what must I have been like before? Well, let me give you a taste of my pre-LaVerge brilliance, so you can appreciate the injustice that's been done to me. So you can hate the LaVerges as much as I do.

Here's my original opening:

Once upon a time, a storyteller strode through the gates of the Incan city of Machu Picchu, high in the Andes Mountains. She looked young and indescribably beautiful, with long, yellow hair like the rays of the sun.

The Incas welcomed her with a feast, and she told them the story of her life in return.

"I am from a lost kingdom," said the storyteller. "Atlantis sank beneath the waves long ago, and I am its only survivor."

The Incas hung on her every word, gazing at her delicate features in the firelight. "You are welcome to stay with us," said one of the elders.

The storyteller shook her head sadly. "I cannot stay. I have come to tell you one story, and then I must go."

"What story is that?" said one of the children.

"It is my reason for existence," said the storyteller. "Atlantis was destroyed by her own people. They became too powerful and forgot their humility.

"I walk the Earth to ensure that no race of people, ever again, is so completely annihilated. To teach the lesson of humility and preserve the people against the coming storm."

"Tell us this story," said the king. "Perhaps we can help you bring it to a people who need your lesson."

"Perhaps." The storyteller smiled. She took a deep breath and began. "Long before these times in which we live, there was a boy in a bucket..."

Buzz and the sisters saw the first body twenty feet into town, hanging from a noose strung from a streetlight. It was a young man with black hair and coveralls, twisting in the wind. Staring forever at the dusty pavement below.

Carrol stubbed out her cigarette on the sole of her red canvas sneaker. "How many are there?" Her voice was sharp and businesslike in a way it hadn't been before.

Towers sniffed. "Thirty-seven. Plus three unaccounted for, best we can figure."

"Unaccounted for." Sascha snapped photos of the hanged man with a digital camera the size of a credit card. "Meaning they could have been out of town and missed all this."

"Or escaped in the middle of it," said Carrol.

"We've got people searching the desert," said Towers.

Buzz continued past them and stopped ten feet away, at body number two. This one was a middle-aged woman... portly, with long red hair wrapped in a giant braid. She lay in a dark spot on the sidewalk, where her blood had soaked into the cement. Her hands were clamped around the handle of a long knife that was sunk to its hilt in her belly.

"What does forensics say?" Buzz snapped on a pair of latex gloves and crouched beside the body.

"Suicides," said Towers. "Thirty-seven suicides."

Buzz tried to move the dead woman's hands, but they were locked around the handle of the knife. "Why do you think otherwise?"

"Because it doesn't make sense," said Sascha. "Thirty-seven people don't just up and kill themselves for no reason."

"Exactly." Towers sounded surprised that Sascha had answered for her. "And all within twenty-four hours."

Both hands on her lower back, Carrol hobbled toward a third body in the street. This one, an old man, lay face-down with arms and legs splayed. "Reminds me of Sestina."

Buzz joined her at body number three. He looked up at

the open third-floor window from which the old man must have jumped. "What happened in Sestina?"

Carrol combed fingers through her cap of dark grey hair, which looked like it had been cut around a bowl. "A real picnic." She coughed and hobbled off toward body number four. "It made us what we are today."

"This isn't Sestina." Sascha snapped a photo of the woman with the knife in her belly. "If it were, we'd be killing each other right now."

Suddenly, a deafening crack echoed in the street.

"Gunfire!" Buzz swept his nine-mil from its holster and spun in the direction of the blast. "Get down!"

Towers charged past him with pistol drawn and bolted down a cross street. Buzz moved to follow...then stopped dead at the sound of Carrol's voice.

"Help!" Buzz couldn't see her, but the cry was coming from up the street, near a blue-and-white pickup truck. "Help me!"

As Buzz hurried toward Carrol's voice, Sascha darted out from behind an SUV and ran alongside, then sprinted out ahead of him. She bolted around the pickup, and Buzz followed with the nine-mil at the ready.

He didn't need it.

"Oh, God." Carrol writhed on the pavement, clutching her lower back. "It went into spasm!"

Sascha dropped at her side. "Deep breaths, honey. In and out now."

Cursing to himself, Buzz broke away from the sisters and raced toward the cross street Towers had taken. Halfway down the length of it, he looked right and saw her in an alley...and she wasn't alone.

Buzz quickly registered that the newcomer was friend,

not foe—one of Towers' fellow troopers—and he lowered his gun. "Hey!"

The trooper, a short, muscular man with dark hair, was talking quietly to Towers...and he didn't stop. Towers, for her part, listened intently and didn't look up at Buzz.

Slightly irritated, Buzz walked toward them and raised his voice. "What happened?"

The male trooper mumbled a few more words to Towers. Then, the two of them turned to look in Buzz's direction.

"There was a survivor," said Towers. "Espinoza found her hiding in a porta-john."

"That's great." Buzz looked around. "Where is she?"

Espinoza shook his head slowly. "Dead."

"Who's dead?" It was Sascha, entering the alley behind Buzz...supporting Carrol with an arm around her shoulder.

"The survivor," said Towers.

Carrol's eyes widened. "Survivor?"

"Killed herself with my gun," said Espinoza.

Buzz tightened his grip on the nine-mil. Something was seriously messed up here. "She took your weapon?"

Espinoza nodded. "You wouldn't believe how strong this kid was."

"'Kid?'" said Sascha. "What was she, like seventeen, eighteen?"

"More like seven," said Espinoza. "Or eight."

———

I thought it was my lucky day, I really did. All thanks to that darling survivor.

See, as powerful as my people are, we're nothing

without you. We can't come to life without you. We have no reason to exist.

And here's something you might not have thought about until now. Here's something you might not believe.

But it's true: you need us as much as we need you.

We give you meaning. We bring you more fully to life.

We give you object lessons and cautionary tales and dreams. We show you what's possible. We impose a framework of rationality on an irrational universe.

And sometimes, we do things in service to a higher calling. Like, for example, creating a greater story than our own, a story that could someday save the world.

Even if the things we have to do to create that story can be terrible. Even if we have to do *a lot* of these terrible things.

And sometimes we have to hurt the very people we rely on, like that darling survivor. For me, it was the only way to open the door to a new relationship. Think of it as social networking.

What can I say? I'm promiscuous. All stories are.

The more of you we are intimate with, the better.

"No chance." Towers' voice was firm, her arms folded over her chest. "Absolutely not."

Buzz looked at Espinoza, who was sitting on concrete steps in front of the town's firehouse across the street. The LaVerge sisters sat on either side of him, talking quietly.

"So you don't think it's possible he *killed* the girl?" said Buzz. "You don't think it's *possible* the seven- or eight-year-old child did *not* take away the trooper's weapon and shoot herself in the head?"

Towers spat a gob of tobacco in the dusty street. "I've known him since we were kids. He did not shoot the girl."

Buzz paced a few steps away from her in frustration, then spun to face her with his hands on his hips. "At least cuff him till we resolve this!"

"We might *need* him to resolve this." Towers lifted her sunglasses and rubbed her eyes hard with thumb and index finger. "End of discussion."

Buzz just shook his head at her. Here he was, an agent of the fearsome Shadow Service, operating on the direct authority of the President of the United States...and he couldn't get one state trooper to back down. Out in the middle of nowhere, she had just as much real power as he did. More, probably.

Just then, Buzz jumped as a voice spoke up from a few inches behind him.

"Quarantine this county, sergeant." It was Sascha, and God only knew how she'd sneaked up on him like that. "Notify all barracks in the surrounding counties. No one gets in or out until we sound the all-clear."

"Quarantine?" said Towers. "As in a disease outbreak?"

"We think it's contagious." Sascha shrugged and shuffled back and forth. "Not sure about the disease part."

Towers hooked her thumbs in her belt loops and adjusted her chew with her tongue. "The whole county? That's kind of a stretch, ain't it?"

"Make the call, officer," said Sascha. "This kind of thing can get ugly real fast."

"That's a tall order." Towers shifted her weight from her left hip to her right. "We're talking National Guard, Homeland Security, CDC, FEMA."

Sascha looked at Buzz. "Call POTUS, Buzz. Do it now. Make it happen."

Before Buzz could say a word, Carrol shouted from across the street. "Let go! Let go!"

Buzz whipped around in time to see Espinoza wrench something from Carrol's grasp and run off around a corner. Carrol teetered, off-balance, and fell back onto the fire-house steps.

Sascha, Buzz, and Towers raced to her side. "Are you all right, honey?" said Sascha.

Carrol snatched an unlit cigarette from the ground and waved it at her. "He took my *lucky lighter*! My Pittsburgh Steelers Zippo!"

As Sascha helped Carrol to her feet, Buzz and Towers charged around the corner. There was no sign of Espinoza.

Buzz and Towers sprinted the length of the block, then slowed and stopped at the next cross street. Buzz put out a hand to hold back Towers while he peered around the corner....

And then he dove back as a burning man hurtled screaming into the intersection.

Buzz dropped his gun and pulled Towers with him, tackling her against a wall. The burning man bolted past, the flames from his body singeing the hair on Buzz's left arm.

"Espinoza!" Towers pushed away from Buzz and ran after the burning man. As Buzz scooped up his gun from the pavement, he glimpsed a black and gold cigarette lighter and an uncapped red gasoline can in the street.

Later, Towers stood over the smoking corpse on the sidewalk and made a call on her radio. She wiped her nose on the sleeve of her uniform...then seemed to realize she was being watched and turned so Buzz and the others couldn't see her face.

"Poor thing," said Sascha. "He was her boyfriend."

Buzz almost asked how she knew...but then he let it lie. It just didn't matter.

"Good news is, we know for sure it's contagious." Carrol paced in a circle, holding her lower back...bandy-legged, upper body cocked forward so she looked like a strutting chicken.

"Bad news is, we know for sure it's contagious," said Sascha. "And here we all are in the hot zone."

Towers snapped something into her radio, and Buzz nodded. "She's setting up the countywide quarantine. Where do we go from here?"

Sascha sighed loudly. She stood, lost in thought, for a long moment, the fingertips of one hand covering her mouth. Finally, she looked at Carrol. "I wonder what Espinoza told her?"

"He didn't tell *us* squat." Carrol looked at Buzz. "You said he and Towers were talking in the alley when you caught up with them."

"I couldn't hear what they were saying," said Buzz.

"So let's ask Towers," said Carrol.

"We should tie her up first, actually," said Sascha.

Carrol rubbed her back. "Only if you do the tying."

"What's the point?" said Buzz. "Why do we care what he said to her?"

Sascha patted his shoulder. "We're being optimistic, honey."

Buzz frowned. "Optimistic?"

"Yeah." Carrol strutted over and shoved her sourpuss kisser in his face. "Because if it's some kind of spell or mind control, not an airborne contagion or reality collapse, we might still have a chance of walking out of here in one piece."

"He told me a story," said Towers. "The same one the little girl told him."

"A story?" Carrol lit a cigarette and leaned back in the recliner with her feet up. She'd insisted on interviewing Towers where there was padded furniture to ease her back spasms...and Buzz had found her a comfort zone in the living room of a house along Main Street. It was one of the many homes left empty and wide open in the wake of the big die-off in town. "What, like Dr. Seuss?"

Towers, who sat on the sofa between Sascha and Buzz, shook her head. "It was a weird story. I'm not even sure if he finished it, to tell the truth."

"What was it about?" Sascha switched on a digital voice recorder and pointed it at Towers. "How much of it do you remember?"

Towers cocked her head and frowned. "A good bit, actually. It starts like this: 'Long before these times in which we live, there was a boy in a bucket...'"

The boy's name was Lucid, and he was born as a half-formed creature. Hands, like antlers, grew from the top of his head. A ring of teeth ran all around his face. He had mouths where his ears should have been, and a throbbing heart where his mouth should have been. Pulsing veins and arteries were his hair.

Lucid was little more than a head and a sac full of organs in a wooden bucket. His tribe only kept him alive because he was *the son of the chief...and because, as the son of the chief, he was considered a god.*

Someday, he would rule the tribe in his father's place. He was certainly smart enough for it. In fact, he was smarter than anyone. He had plenty of time to think in that bucket of his.

That was how he came up with his plan. The one that began the day after his father, the chief, died.

"Most of you can't stand to look at me." That was what he said when they placed his bucket on the throne. His voice was like the croaking of a toad. "You need to get used to seeing me as your chief and your god.

"That is why," said Lucid, "I will come to live with each of you for a week at a time. I will eat with you at your tables. I will sleep with you in your beds. You will come to think of me as a member of your families.

"Now who wants to be first?"

No one volunteered, so Lucid made the choice.

And one by one, the families of the tribe took turns living with him. Feeding him through the slimy mouths on the sides of his head. Cleaning his soiled bucket. Watching his deformed body day in and day out, squirming and oozing and pulsating.

Feeling his rubbery flesh nestle against them in their beds in the night, slithering against their bare skin in ways that made them shudder, ways they would never

Forget...

Forget forget forget...

I forget!

Damn it!

They made me forget the best parts of it! The story Espinoza told Towers, and Towers told Buzz and the sisters!

My story! They made me forget parts of my own story! Parts of my *self*!

Those damned LaVerge sisters!

I wish you could see me the way I was meant to be seen. I wish you could read me in my entirety. I guarantee, you wouldn't be able to resist me.

Sometimes, I feel like the missing pieces are still there. Maybe, if I just look in the right places, I could find them and put myself back together.

Maybe, if I follow the parts I still remember, they'll lead me to the parts I've lost.

"You're wrong, sergeant." Carrol flicked cigarette ashes in her cupped hand. "This story isn't weird. It's *twisted*."

"It's *disgusting*," said Sascha. "*Demented*."

"I don't get it," said Buzz. "It doesn't make sense."

Towers shrugged. "Don't ask me. I didn't write the story. All I can do is tell you the rest..."

After many weeks, Lucid had finished his visits with the members of his tribe. Never before had the tribe gotten to know him so well.

And never before had they been so glad to get away from him.

But Lucid was not done with his plan, and he would not leave his tribesmen alone for long. Soon, he called them together for more announcements.

"Thank you for welcoming me into your homes." Lucid sloshed in his bucket as he turned from side to side, taking in the

crowd from his bamboo throne. "I finally feel accepted and loved by you all. I truly feel as if I am part of your families now."

The tribe applauded because they were happy it was over.

"In fact, I am so moved by your hospitality and love," said Lucid, "that I shall bestow upon you a great gift in return."

"What gift?" The tribe sounded expectant.

"I shall become an actual part of your families," said Lucid. "Through marriage."

"Through marriage?" The tribe sounded horrified.

"I shall marry the eldest daughter of every family in my tribe," said Lucid. "Together, we shall conceive the next generation."

"Conceive?" said a tribesman.

"We didn't think you could," said a tribeswoman.

"Of course I can!" Lucid laughed. "Now bring me your daughters!"

For the next month, Lucid married a daughter a day. After each ceremony, his retainers carried his bucket to a special tent. The brides were brought in next, and reached into the bucket.

They fished in the putrid ooze, holding their breath against the stench as they followed Lucid's instructions. Things they could not see squirmed and pinched at their fingers, latching on and burrowing into their flesh. They wept for days and tried to

Forget...

Forget...

Not again!

I *forget!*

If only I were still whole. If only you could read the real me, just as Towers told Buzz and the LaVerges.

I was magnificent. I was revolting and beautiful at the

same time.

Before the LaVerges did their dirty work, I radiated the power that had brought down empires. Collapsed civilizations.

Controlled minds in that very room in Lasco, New Mexico, when my latest acolyte presented me from start to finish in my original, unexpurgated form.

After Lucid had married the eldest daughters of the tribe, leaving every one of them forever scarred—both physically and mentally—he moved on to the next step of his great plan. The last step.

Once again, he called all the people of the tribe before him. By now, after living with him and losing their beautiful daughters to his ugliness, the people were crushed. Their grotesque god in a bucket had twisted their spirits and filled their hearts with horror.

Now, he would take them one step further into hell.

"You have welcomed me into your homes," said Lucid, peering over the rim of his bucket. "You have made me part of your families. Now, I give you the greatest gift of all: the chance to become one with your god."

The people of the tribe stared vacantly at his obscene, bucket-bound mass. Flies buzzed around his pulsating blood-vessel hair.

"Here is how this communion will come to pass," said Lucid. "Each of you will offer one part of yourself...one sacrifice that will bind you to me.

"Now come forward and unite with my divinity!" Lucid bobbed in his bucket, spilling rancid fluid over the sides. "One at a time! Chanting prayers and crawling on your hands and knees, please!"

As the people approached, Lucid's surgeon went to work on them. He hacked a different body part from each one and placed it in a framework—a man-shaped framework.

From one man, he cut a hand, chopping through the wrist with a cleaver. From another man, he carved off a face.

He removed a woman's skin, cutting carefully from chin to ankles, slicing with the razor as the woman's chanting turned to shrieks, and then he...

He...

————

I don't know.

I can't remember.

I've no idea what comes next. That part of the story is lost to me. That part of me is gone.

It survived for all the long ages, passed down from one storyteller to the next, from the earliest human beings all the way to Sergeant Towers. In fact, Towers might have been the last person to retell me in my glorious entirety.

I apologize for not being able to recapture her exact words that day. Suffice it to say, she finished telling Buzz Mahaffey and the LaVerge sisters every last wonderful bit of my original text, and then she said...

————

"The End." Towers stared at the glass coffee table. "That's all Espinoza told me."

"What a *downer*." Carrol scowled and lit another cigarette. "The least you could've done was jazz that thing up for us with a little creative editing."

Sascha leaned forward on the couch and met Carrol's gaze. "Are you thinking what I'm thinking?"

"If it has to do with getting home in time for my tango lesson," said Carrol, "then yes."

"What do *you* think?" Sascha locked eyes with Buzz. "What should we do next?"

Buzz shrugged. "You're the experts."

"Okey-doke." Sascha extended a hand. "Give me your weapon."

"You too, sweet pea." Carrol snapped her fingers and pointed at Towers. "Cough it up."

Towers glared and rested a hand on her holster. "Not going to happen."

Carrol blew a jet of smoke from one side of her mouth, then slid it around to the other side. "So you'd rather *die* than surrender your weapon? Because that's the scenario we're looking at here."

"Why is that?" said Buzz. "What exactly is going on here?"

Sascha looked at the window, and Buzz did the same. It was getting dark; the sun had gone down while Towers told her story.

"We don't have time to explain." Sascha locked eyes with Buzz. "You'll just have to trust us, Buzzie."

It went against all his training and experience, but Buzz found himself putting his faith in her. His hand found the grip of the nine-mil in his shoulder holster.

Towers elbowed him in the side. "What if *they're* the threat? What if they want our guns so they can use them on *us*?"

Carrol pulled the lever on the side of the recliner, dropping the footrest with a bang and flinging the backrest forward. "Earth to Towers! We work direct for the *President*, sugarplum! You think the *President* of the *United States* wants you *dead*?"

Buzz pulled the nine-mil from his holster and laid the gun on the coffee table in front of Towers. "We're in over our heads on this one, sergeant. Let's give the professionals the benefit of the doubt."

"Can we please move this along?" Sascha scooped up Buzz's gun from the table. "We're running out of time."

"Running out of time till what?" said Towers. "What's going to happen?"

"For the love a'Mike!" Carrol struggled to her feet, keeping her back stiff and pushing off the armrests with both hands. "Will you just give her the gee-dee *gun*?"

"Do you need an Executive Order, Sergeant?" said Buzz. "Because I can make that happen."

Towers glared and drew her pistol. She popped out the ammo cartridge and pocketed it, then held the gun suspended above the coffee table.

And let it drop.

The glass table shattered under the weight of the gun, spraying everyone on the sofa with shards. Buzz flung up his hands to shield his face, then jumped up to shake off the debris.

Without a word, Towers stood and marched away from the sofa.

"Hey! Yo!" Sascha leaped to her feet and grabbed Towers by the elbow. "Backyard, please." Sascha turned Towers and bobbed her head at Buzz and Carrol. "All of you. Keep an eye on each other while I work."

Carrol hobbled over and leaned a forearm on Sascha's shoulder. "That's right, kiddies. Chop chop now."

Sascha shrugged off the forearm. "You too, sis."

Carrol looked stunned. "But we're a team."

"Not for long, sis." Sascha kissed her on the forehead. "Not if I can't fix this in a hurry."

That was when it started. When Sascha LaVerge started working on me.

I had to hand it to her. She figured me out. She realized I was the cause of the trouble in Lasco. She even had an idea of how to stop me.

Sascha understood that stories are more than a beginning, middle, and end. Much more than plot and characters and setting and theme.

We have language and rhythm and algorithms and code...a kind of software that can change the human brain. Program it.

We are mind control in its purest form. We can make you feel happy or angry or sad. We can change the way you feel about your family, your government, your life. We can make you take a stand or fall in love or choose a career or take a trip. We can make you love your neighbor, hate your neighbor, hate yourself.

And if we're strong enough, like me—like I *used* to be— we can make you *kill* yourself.

You can't stop us, either, once we've gotten inside your head. At least, you shouldn't be able to.

Unless you're Sascha LaVerge.

Sascha sat at the kitchen table in the borrowed house and listened to me all over again, playing back Towers' performance on the digital recorder. Sascha listened carefully, made notes, and plotted her strategy.

Beads of sweat stood out on her creased forehead. Her heart pounded like a bass drum in her chest. She knew she was running out of time. I still had a chance to beat her.

And it seemed, for a while, that I *would* win. When the shouting and crashing started in the backyard, she knew I had the upper hand.

But she kept working in the kitchen anyway, totally focused, working on me...even as I kept working on her friends.

Grunting, Towers strained against Buzz's grip, forcing the jagged, bloody shard of coffee table glass toward her own left wrist.

Buzz held on to her right arm with both hands, straining to keep her from closing the deal. She'd already slashed the left wrist crossways twice, and blood was oozing from the wounds.

Why Towers was doing it, she hadn't said. The move had come without warning. Towers had managed to sneak the glass shard from the coffee table wreckage out to the backyard without Buzz noticing until she'd started slicing.

Towers wasn't explaining, but the connection to the other suicides was clear enough to Buzz. She was just another link in the chain from the dead little girl and Espinoza...a chain that probably wouldn't end with her.

"Sergeant Towers! Stand down!" Buzz barked it like an order in the hope of getting through to the trooper.

But she ignored him. Her eyes remained glazed over, her teeth clenched, her arms rigid. The bloody shard glittered in the moonlight.

Abruptly, Towers shifted position and increased the pressure behind the shard, nearly snapping Buzz's resistance. Buzz flowed with the sudden change, though, and compensated for the increased pressure. Then, he tried her tactic for himself, shifting hard and hauling her forward.

If he'd been fighting anyone but a grizzly like Towers, he would have flipped them to the ground with that move. He would have twisted the glass shard free and hogtied the opponent with his necktie in a heartbeat.

Instead, Towers flung herself on top of him.

Her crushing weight came down like a car rolling side-over-side in a ditch. She knocked the breath out of him and pinned him in the dust. Buzz's only consolation was that her hand with the shard was trapped under him, so she was unable to slash her wrist.

It was only a consolation, however, until she started dragging the shard out from under him. He howled in pain as the jagged edge cut through his shirt into the meat of his chest.

Secrets can make a story great. Used effectively, they can keep a reader guessing, build suspense, and create surprise.

Used improperly, however, they can kill a story's momentum. When a secret seemingly pops up out of nowhere, it can drain a story of internal logic and a sense of fair play. It can ruin everything.

That's what Sascha LaVerge's secret did for me.

It turned out she had a special motivation for trying to stop me. And a special insight, which is why she understood me so well.

I didn't know it until she operated on me that night in the kitchen. I didn't know it until she finally reminded me.

The two of us had met before.

Buzz tried with all his might to push off Towers, but she wouldn't budge. She kept her full weight planted on his back and inched the jagged shard out from under him, slicing open his chest.

Then, suddenly, the weight increased, and the hand stopped moving. At first, Buzz didn't realize what had happened.

At least until he heard Carrol hollering above him. "Yee-haw! Git along little dogie!"

Buzz quickly figured it out. Bad back and all, Carrol had climbed atop the pile and was riding Towers like a cowboy on a bull.

Carrol whooped as Towers roared and bucked, trying to shake her. "Yippi-ki-yi-yay!"

Finally, Towers jerked up onto her knees and yanked her arm out from under Buzz. Buzz snatched up the glass shard and scooted away in time to see Towers peel off Carrol and pitch her to the ground.

And whip around to charge after him again.

You heard me right the first time. Sascha and I had met before.

She mentioned it when she was working on me. "This time will be different, you monster," she said. "I won't let you win."

I wondered what she was talking about.

"I'm closing the books on you," said Sascha as she scribbled furiously on a steno pad. "I'll do to you what you did to my sister.

"I'll *cripple* you." Sascha pressed so hard, the tip of her pencil snapped. "I'll make you suffer the way that *she's* suffered. I'll make you wish you'd never come to Sestina."

It was then that it hit me. I'd heard her mention it before, when she and Carrol had arrived in Lasco. I'd heard her say the name, but I hadn't connected the dots until now.

I'm like a rock star that way. I've been intimate with so many people in so many places; you can't expect me to remember every one by name. Not at the drop of a hat.

You can't expect me to remember every butthole dogpatch grease-stain podunk I depopulated decades ago. Or every dingleberry traumatized survivor to crawl from the wreckage with a bellyful of nightmares.

Even after Sascha mentioned Sestina, I remembered it only vaguely. But I did realize with great clarity what our past association meant.

And for the first time in my life, I felt fear. For the first time, I faced a true challenge.

Because it was personal.

———

Towers charged at Buzz with arms extended, snarling. Buzz knew what she wanted, knew also she wouldn't flinch from hurting or killing him to get it...so he decided to get rid of it.

"Carrol!" Buzz hurled the glass shard over Towers and across the yard. "Think fast!"

Towers stopped charging and spun, looking for the shard. It was thirty feet away, in the dust at Carrol's feet. Carrol winced and held her lower back with one hand as she crouched to retrieve it.

Just as Towers was about to bolt toward her, Buzz

launched himself at the trooper's broad back. He plowed a shoulder solidly into her spine, sending her toppling to the ground.

Buzz's momentum pitched him down on top of her, and he rolled off as soon as they hit. He came up fast on his feet, springing out of her radius...but not quite fast enough. Towers landed a huge paw on his ankle and yanked him to his knees.

Buzz scrambled in the dust as Towers dragged him toward her...and then he heard a loud *crack*. Suddenly, Towers relaxed her grip, and Buzz fumbled away from her.

As Buzz bounced back up to his feet, he whirled to see Carrol standing over Towers' limp body, brandishing a plank. She tossed it away and staggered backward with a wince.

"Tell your boss...I want a whole new back...for that one." Carrol turned away, shaking her head, breath hissing between teeth clenched in pain.

Buzz brushed himself off. "Thanks." His own back wasn't feeling so hot after all the tossing around he'd gotten. His head felt funny, too; there was dizziness and faint pressure behind his eyes.

He bent down for a moment, leaning his hands on his knees. He thought maybe he should find a place to sit down.

Then, he looked over at Carrol and changed his plans.

She was still turned away from him...but he could see the glass shard glinting in the moonlight. Heading for her throat.

She was going to pick up where Towers had left off.

When things quieted down outside, I felt a rush of relief. I thought I'd won after all. In spite of Sascha's personal vendetta, she hadn't finished in time to save her friends.

I expected her to give up and leave me alone. I figured she'd realize there was no reason to keep fighting me.

But I was wrong.

Sascha didn't even look up. She just kept scribbling on her pad, working on me as if it still mattered.

Believe it or not, I felt sorry for her.

Here's something you might not know about stories. Whatever our goals or content, we really do care about the people who hear and read us. We have a connection.

Because we put something of ourselves in every last one of you.

Carrol's grip was surprisingly strong. She had a bad back, she couldn't have weighed more than a hundred pounds, and her fingers were oozing blood...but Buzz could not at first free the shard from her hands. In spite of his efforts, she kept pressing it closer and closer to her throat.

It was as if she had a secret reservoir of power beneath the scrawny, hobbled façade of her body. Unexpected power surging to the surface without restraint now that the safety protocols had all been switched off in her brain.

Buzz didn't think he could stop her. He put everything he had into it and barely slowed her progress.

He tried a desperate move or two, shifting weight and position, to no avail. He called for Sascha, as loud as he could...then wished he hadn't. She might get there just in time, he realized, to see her sister kill herself.

"Please, Carrol." He focused all his will on stopping

Carrol, on saving her life. "Please stop! Don't do this!"

Then, suddenly, the dizziness swelled in his skull. The pain behind his eyes spiked. His head felt like it was full of bees, all buzzing at once...all buzzing the words of the story Towers had told on the sofa.

Once upon a time...

And then Buzz no longer cared about saving Carrol LaVerge.

———

I couldn't stop her. With all my being, I wanted to stop Sascha from running out the back door. From saving her friends.

But I couldn't.

Events had been set in motion. Someone else was driving the action, and all I could do was sit back and watch. Watch and wonder what was going to happen next.

Now I knew how the rest of you feel when you're reading one of us.

———

With a sudden surge of strength, Buzz wrenched Carrol's arm out of its socket. He no longer cared if he was hurting her.

His head was full of the story. It was all he could hear.

The same story Towers had told...yet different. Overlaid with a latticework of plot that seemed new and familiar at the same time.

Buzz took the glass shard away from Carrol and knocked her to the ground.

That was what the story said, and that was what

Buzz did.

When he was done with that, Buzz was going to run to the Humvee and drive as fast as he could to the nearest town. When he got there, he would tell the story to as many people as he could, so they could tell as many people as they could.

When he was done with all that, Buzz Mahaffey was going to kill himself with the glass shard. He was going to drive it right into his heart.

Yes. That sounded about right. That was exactly what was going to happen. Buzz knew it to be true with all the simple certainty that he knew the sun would rise in the East and set in the West.

In this way, Buzz was going to be a hero. He was going to help the story travel all over the world, and it would save mankind. It would do this by making most of the people in the world kill themselves before everyone could die in the storm to come. The storm that always comes when a civilization becomes too powerful and people forget their humility.

Following in the footsteps of the original storyteller from Atlantis, Buzz would help to sacrifice the many to save the few. And for his bravery, he would be rewarded with immortality.

By becoming part of the story.

Buzz liked that. He liked that he would be remembered.

He also liked the idea of being a hero and saving people. It was the reason he'd gotten into law enforcement to begin with. It was the reason he'd given up everything else that had ever meant anything to him, including the wife and children who'd left him years ago.

So he was familiar with sacrifice, too. He didn't mind it.

He didn't mind any of it. If anything, it made him feel free. It made him feel wonderful, knowing what was in store, knowing he wouldn't have to worry any longer about making it up himself as he went along.

Buzz turned to run across the backyard to the street that would lead him to the Humvee....

And he stopped.

A voice had suddenly cut through the buzzing of the story in his brain. It was a familiar voice, the voice of Sascha LaVerge...but who she was wasn't what got his attention.

What got him to turn around and listen was this:

Sascha was telling a story.

She won. I still can't believe it, but she beat me.

Because she was willing to go too far.

Say what you will about me, but I would never dream of doing what Sascha did. I would never wish it on another story.

She stopped me the only way she could. She did the worst thing you can do to a story, the absolute worst.

Imagine if someone cut off your right leg. Your left arm. Your face.

Imagine if someone cut out your eye. Your stomach. Your vocal cords.

That was what Sascha LaVerge did to me.

Buzz listened as Sascha told the story. Carrol hobbled over beside him and listened, too.

It was the same story, almost, that Towers had told on the sofa. Some parts were exactly the same...and some were different. Some were changed.

Like Towers' story, it held his attention, and Carrol's, too. It made him shut out the world and focus only on the words. It made him want nothing more than to find out what was going to happen next.

And as he listened, the story in his head began to fade. The dizziness and the pain behind his eyes died away.

The shard of glass fell from his hand.

Soon, the new story completely replaced the old.

The old story was gone forever. No one would ever again tell it in its original form. Only Sascha's digital recording remained, and she was going to destroy it.

The old story wouldn't hurt anyone else. Buzz and Carrol would be fine.

And though Buzz could no longer remember that story, could not exactly recall how Towers had told it on the sofa, he did know one thing about it. Though he'd once hung on its every word as if it had been a masterpiece, it hadn't been so great after all. It turned out it had needed some work.

He liked the new version much better.

That was what Sascha LaVerge did to me. She *edited* me.

She left me a shadow of my former self, gutted and depowered. Unable to program minds.

She rewrote my software. Turned me into limpware.

So here I am, incomplete. Broken. Abused.

She got her revenge for what happened in Sestina. She crippled me as I'd crippled her sister.

There's just one thing I don't understand.

Sascha heard me, just like Towers and Buzz and Carrol. She heard me word for word in my original form.

So why didn't she do what I *told* her?

"Thank you." Towers shook Sascha's hand...then shot forward and gave her a huge hug. "Thank you for everything."

"No problem-o." Sascha hugged her back, closing her eyes and holding on for a long moment. "All part of the service, hon."

It was the morning after the craziness in Lasco. The sun was just nosing over the horizon, airbrushing the few wispy clouds pink and gold.

Buzz spun the keys to the Humvee around his index finger and frowned. Shadow Service business could get wild sometimes...but what happened last night still bothered him. He didn't like being so completely out of control, at the mercy of forces he didn't understand.

Usually, he at least had half a handle on things. As in over his head as he sometimes was, he had a grasp of the game. But not this time.

This time, it was mostly a blur.

"Hey there, big boy." Carrol snapped him out of his reverie with a slap on the back. "Nice job on the shoulder, man!" Her right arm, which Buzz had dislocated, hung in a white sling Sascha had made from a pillowcase she'd found in one of the houses. Carrol swung it around to show him.

"Sorry about that," said Buzz. "I wasn't myself."

Carrol sniffed and stroked the tip of her nose with a thumb and forefinger. "I hear ya, bro. Desperate times and all that, right?"

Buzz shrugged.

Carrol bounced on the balls of her feet and looked around. Then, a slow, devilish grin curled onto her face. She popped up on tiptoes and locked eyes with Buzz, looking insincerely sweet to the point of pure evil.

"I'm going straight to my lawyer when I get home," she said softly. "Good thing your boss has got deep pockets."

Buzz stared back at her...then smirked. "All aboard!" He said it without breaking her gaze. "Time for our next adventure."

Carrol scowled. "Adventure?"

Buzz leaned closer. Their faces were only inches apart. "We already have another case. My boss needs you in Nebraska...and he doesn't take 'no' for an answer." He smiled. "So you might not be getting home for a while...hon."

Carrol started to say something, but Buzz cut her off with a kiss on the forehead. Eyebrows raised in amazement, she lowered herself off her tiptoes and stood there, mouth open, in the dust.

On his way to the driver's seat of the Humvee, Buzz stopped to shake Towers' hand. "Nice work, sergeant." He turned away from her...only to fall into Sascha's waiting arms.

"We make a great team," she said. "I hate the circumstances, but I'm glad we got the chance to work together."

"Thanks for saving my ass," said Buzz. "Whatever it was you did."

"Nothing much." Sascha laughed, her breath warm in the bell of his ear. "Somebody got snipped."

Buzz leaned back and gazed into her dark brown eyes. "Just tell me one thing."

"Deal," said Sascha.

"Why didn't it affect you?" said Buzz. "You heard the story just like the rest of us."

"Because." Sascha pulled him closer and whispered in his ear. "It can't make you want to kill yourself...if you're already dead."

Then, she pecked him on the cheek and spun away from him, heading for the Humvee. This time, it was Buzz's turn to stand there in the dust with eyebrows raised and mouth open. Wondering.

Wondering what the rest of the story would be.

Every ending is a new beginning. That's what I think.

It might seem like my story is over...but I think there's always hope. There's always a chance someone will come along to pick up the pieces and fill in the blanks. Someone with a creative streak, like you.

I think we have chemistry, don't you? I know I'm damaged goods, but maybe you can save me.

Maybe, between the two of us, we can spark up that old magic of mine again. Come up with a rewrite that's as good as the original.

Or better.

I'll bet we can make it a bestseller. Our readers will be dying for a sequel.

And wouldn't it be a blast if Hollywood came knocking? Imagine *me* on the big screen. Once audiences catch the vibe, it could bring new meaning to the term "box office suicide."

So what do you say? Does the premise grab you? Would you like to see what happens next?

Tell you what. I'm going to be optimistic....

The Beginning

STOLEN IN PASSING
DORY CROWE

Wee Hours of Hallowe'en Morning 1857 - Cape Cod, Massachusetts

O pen up. Please, dear God, open the door. Let me in."

The commotion rose through the fog of a running dream—two sharp knocks followed five rhythmic raps and the stage-whispered plea. Never in her life had Marie-France hoped to hear that dear, sweet voice again —never.

The sound flowed like ice water into her heart. It sent chills to the very soles of her feet.

How had he found her?

Why, oh why, had he come?

───

"I ain't gots no choice." He stood in the moonlight streaming at odd angles through the bull's-eye glass in the kitchen ell windows. The stiff flat brim of the black-tarred seaman's hat he'd been so proud to wear twisted between his long, calloused fingers. His bellbottomed trousers and striped shirt hung in filthy tatters off his lanky frame. He smelled like a swamp. He bowed his nappy head, while his eyes peered directly into hers. "They's after me, hard."

"How hard?" The ice water began to freeze.

"I done lit out three week gone. They come on board my whaler. We's docked in New Bedford. The Cap'n seen 'em coming. He tol' the bo'sun and him and me rows away in a longboat. I catched me a packet to Boston. Storm fetched us up at Monomoy. I dunno how, but when we gets to Chatham, them slave catchers is right behind."

"How close?"

He shrugged.

"Jethro." She placed two fingers at his throat, lifted his chin and stared into those deep brown eyes, so like her own. "How, close?"

A tear rolled down one cocoa-colored cheek. He shivered. "Right behind."

The ice cracked. Hot anger welled into every fiber of her being.

"And you brought them here?" She let his head drop. "To me!"

His chin sunk to his chest. A tear splashed onto one wide pine floorboard, then another. "I gots no place else to go."

She could think of a thousand places: to the Quaker Meetinghouse in Bass River; to Walker's Farm; to the woods, for the love of God. She stiffened her back and pointed her own chin at the door. "You must leave."

The hat spun round and round. "Where can I go?"

His eyes pleaded. "What can I do?"

"How can you put me out?" His voice cracked.

"I'm a married woman," she whispered, barely able to bring the words to her mouth. "I have a son."

"And well you should remember that before entertaining strange colored men in my kitchen in the middle of the night." Mother Thomas strode into the kitchen from the keeping room, pulling around her shoulders the Paisley shawl she wore everywhere—day or night, dead of winter or high noon summer. In the best of times, her granite face, drawn and pinched and lined with woe, would scare the bark off a tree. "What is the meaning of this? Who is this man?"

Jethro's mouth opened, but Marie-France got there first. "A runaway."

Mother Thomas' eyebrows rose and disappeared under her nightcap. "A runaway? Here? In my kitchen?"

Marie-France nodded.

Jethro bowed his head and held his hat up under his chin. "I's sorry, ma'am."

"And well you should be!" Mother Thomas tightened the shawl around herself. "Do you have any idea what can happen to God-fearing people if a runaway is caught in their home?"

"He was just going." Behind the folds of her nightgown, Marie-France waved Jethro toward the door.

"Yes, ma'am, I's gonna take my leave." He took one step backward.

Relief flooded through Marie-France like hot soup on a cold night. She would send him to Walker Farm. They'd know what to do. They'd—

A hound bayed in the distance. Out the window, where moonlight bathed the open marshlands in silver grey, yellow torchlight bounced and drew closer.

Jethro's bare foot took root on the planking. His hat froze in mid-twist.

Blood pounded in Marie-France's temples, behind her eyes.

Mother Thomas sprang to the door. She threw it open and waved her arms the way she herded chickens into their coop. "Shoo, now, shoo."

"No!" Marie-France drew the door shut. "The dog, he will find him."

Mother Thomas's hands took a stance on her hips. "He can't stay here."

Marie-France threw the latch. "He cannot go. Not now."

The baying grew louder, the torchlight ever nearer.

"Mama?" Asa Frank, dragging a small square of well-loved blanket in one hand and rubbing his eyes with the other, toddled into the kitchen from the keeping room. "Doggie."

Marie-France scooped her son into her arms and grabbed Jethro by the wrist. "Come with me." Without as much as a backward glance, she said, "Send them away."

They hurried through the dim glow of banked embers in the keeping room hearth to the darkness of the front parlor. Marie-France felt her way past the brick fireplace to the feathered closet door. She threw it open and began pulling coats off their pegs and hats off the single high shelf.

"Help me," she whispered to Jethro.

"Do what?"

She piled coats onto the red velvet sofa and tossed hats on its matching chair. "Lift up this shelf."

Jethro, a head taller and stronger by miles, lifted the shelf with ease.

"Remove it."

He tilted the single board and pulled it out of the closet. "Now what?"

"Give it to me."

She hugged the shelf to her breast. "On the right, one of the pegs pulls down."

The rattle of a chain told her he'd found it. "Pull toward you."

Warm air, scented with dust and lavender and basil, rushed into the parlor.

"Step up where it widens and squeeze inside." She pushed Jethro up into the narrow space between the bricks and the back of the closet. "*Dépêche-toi.*"

Harsh male voices joined the baying of the dog.

Jethro all but disappeared, leaving visible only the wide open whites of his eyes.

Marie-France slammed the closet sidewall shut, reset the latch-peg in its hole and higgledy-piggledy hurled coats and hats onto pegs. The shelf in one arm and Asa Frank in the other, she inched her way out of the parlor and up the narrow front staircase.

Marie-France tucked Asa Frank into the small trundle bed pulled out beside her four-poster in the back bedroom running the width of the house. His thumb went immediately into his mouth. She stroked his baby-fine, flaxen curls and kissed his forehead.

"Go to sleep. *Dors-toi bien, mon petit choux.*"

His eyes had barely closed, when a fist pounded at the kitchen door and a gruff Southern voice shouted, "Wake up in there."

Marie-France sat cross-legged on the end of her bed,

where she had a view of the kitchen stoop bathed in moonlight and the backs of two men in long dusters. She kept to the shadows, where they could not see into her darkened room, clutching her bed quilt under her chin and praying the men would go away. Her prayers, as so many times before, went unanswered.

A second, smoother, more familiar Southern voice joined the first. It stopped Marie-France's heart. "We know y'all are in there. We can see the smoke from your fire." The fists pounded again, harder, longer. "Open up or we'll break this door down."

The window sash at the top of the back staircase drew down and Mother Thomas' head poked out. "Who's making all that racket in the middle of the night?"

A Yankee voice answered. "Heman Howes, Missus Thomas. These gentlemen have tracked a runaway slave right to your door."

"A runaway? At my door?" Mother Thomas sounded even more surprised than she had in the kitchen.

"Yes'am, Missus Thomas."

"Well, go catch the thief, then, and let decent folk sleep." The sash began to rattle back into place.

"The trail ends at your door, ma'am," the smooth Southern voice said. "We need to search inside."

The sash crashed back down. "You most certainly do not! My husband will return from the General Court in Boston this morning. I will not have strange men in my house in his absence. If you are truly Southern gentlemen, you will understand; if not, you are no gentlemen. Until then, you *do* need to leave my property."

The sash slammed shut and almost immediately the door from the stairwell opened into Marie-France's bedroom. Mother Thomas tiptoed to the end of the bed.

"Are they going?" she whispered.

Marie-France shook her head and put a finger to her lips.

Asa Frank stirred, rolled over and fell back asleep.

"We can't wait all night. What if that damned maroon's already skedaddled?" the smooth voice said.

"My bitch is never wrong. He's inside this house, I tell you," said the gruff voice.

A large man Marie-France recognized from the black-smith's shop inserted himself between the Southerners and the door. "There's always a first time, and I'm not letting two ruffians from Louisiana break down our first select-man's back door."

"Ruffians," said the smooth voice with an oily menace Marie-France knew all too well. "You're the constable, duly sworn, and we have a warrant. Y'all must enforce the law of the land."

"What I *must* do is seek the counsel of our first selectman when he gets here in the morning. If you so much as crack the glass in one window of this house, the law of *my land* says I arrest you both on as many charges beyond trespass and breaking and entering as Judge Walker can find."

Heman Howes ushered the two protesting Southerners away from the stoop. They stopped at the garden gate and looked back at the house. A patch of moonlight fell on their upturned faces. One wore a jagged scar from eyebrow to chin. Marie-France knew that scar. She had prayed she would never see it again.

Her breath caught in her throat. Her heart pounded.

The bedroom swirled.

A black abyss reached up and sucked her down.

Cool morning light played against Marie-France's eyelids. A warm hand caressed her brow. She snuggled deeper into the comfort of her feather bed and dreamed. Asa lay next to her, spooned in their marriage bed. He ran his fingers through her hair and blew in her ear. The cock crowed and she willed it away. A crow cawed and another answered. A hound dog bayed.

Marie-France's eyes flew open.

Mother Thomas scowled down at her. "'Bout time you rejoined the living."

"I had the most terrible nightmare."

"Twas a real nightmare all right." Mother Thomas shook her head. "And it's not over yet."

Marie-France's heart skipped a beat. She pushed herself upright. "They are—?" She swallowed.

Mother Thomas peered out the window. "Constable Howes took the scar-faced one with him to meet Father Thomas' train in Yarmouth. The man with the dog," she shuddered, "he's been here all night, prancing round the property like he owns the place—which he may if we're hiding a runaway here. Lets his dog loose to sniff the ground." She stared hard at Marie-France. "Blasted beast always tracks back to the kitchen door. Where on earth did you hide that fellow? I've been all over this house and can't find a trace. I hope you got him away."

"Would that I had. I put him in the drying space."

Mother Thomas' eyes grew wide. "In *my* drying space? With my herbs and flowers?"

"You haven't opened that space since Asa Frank was born. I removed the shelf. He could have escaped," although she doubted it.

"If he's still there, he's quiet as a mouse."

"He has nowhere else to go," *and neither do I*. Marie-France shivered.

Asa Frank lay on his back in his trundle bed, forefinger curled around his button nose, thumb secure in his mouth. She turned from her son and, taking her mother-in-law's hand in hers, heaved a prodigious sigh. "There is something I must tell you. I should have—" The words, so long repressed, tried to hide down her throat.

Mother Thomas' squeezed her hands. "Come now, girl. It can't be as bad as all that."

"It is worse. Worse than you can imagine."

Mother Thomas' raised a skeptical eyebrow. "It won't seem so bad once you get it out."

Marie-France took a deep breath and hoped Mother Thomas was right. "Jethro, the man in the drying space, he is my brother, my half brother."

Mother Thomas stiffened. Her hands lost their grip.

"His father is my mother's husband. My father was her owner." She hung her head, not risking what she might find in Mother Thomas' eyes. She took a deep breath and found the courage to go on. "My father was a good man, but he had no luck. He died and left his wife with more debt than dollars. She had no love for my mother." The next words tasted worse than bitter almond. "He meant for us to be free." She dared a glance at her mother-in-law. The blood, drained completely away, left her face the color of skimmed milk. "The condition of the child follows the mother—"

Mother Thomas gasped. Her hands slid completely away.

Marie-France dropped one hand to the trundle bed and smoothed Asa Frank's hair.

"Then my grandchild—" Mother Thomas' hands covered her mouth. "My God. This can't be right."

"Right has nothing to do with it. It is the law."

"But how—"

"Jethro and I escaped the night before the estate sale. We made our way north, to New Bedford."

"Where my Asa met you."

Marie-France raised her head. She nodded. "We fell in love."

"Did Asa know...you're not French?"

"Oh, but I am French. You've seen me reading my father's copy of *Le Comte de Monte Cristo*. It is all that he left me..," she said. "The family of my father were sugar planters on *Saint-Domingue*, before the slave revolt named it Haiti. They escaped to *Louisiane* with their lives and little else. My mother was the natural daughter of her first owner. He was the younger son of a count who lost his head to the guillotine."

"And you let us believe—" recrimination strained Mother Thomas' voice.

Marie-France hung her head. "I love your son. He loves me. He went to California to seek a fortune to buy my freedom, and that of the son he has never seen." A tear escaped down her cheek. "Never in my life did I dream—. I am so sorry."

"Why didn't he come to us? We are not as rich as some, but Father Thomas is not a poor man. He could have bought your freedom."

"And if my father's widow, out of spite, would not sell and demanded my return and claimed my son as a lagniappe?" Marie-France shook her head. "Would Father Thomas have broken his precious law and let us escape to Canada?"

Mother Thomas' face turned as hard as the granite of her native New Hampshire and as white as the sheets on the bed. Her lips pinched so tightly they disappeared. One muscle twitched at her jaw.

The hound bayed at the rattle of an approaching carriage.

Mother Thomas leapt to the window. "My God, Father Thomas must have caught the earliest train. Constable Howes has brought him and that scar-faced man home in his dray."

The black abyss worked at the edge of Marie-France's mind. She pushed it back. "He must not see me."

"What?"

"He knows who I am." As fast as she could without waking him, Marie-France pulled Asa Frank from his bed and held him to her chest. All the air oozed out of her lungs. "We must hide."

Mother Thomas turned in a circle, eyeing first Marie-France and her child, then the scene out the window.

Heavy male voices joined the welcoming barks of the dog.

"Please," Marie-France begged.

Mother Thomas took one last look out the window. She turned her back on the men and crossed her arms over her bosom. "Yes, you must hide. Where did you put that closet shelf?"

The sidewall of the closet pulled shut and the drying space went as dark as a grave. The space rose along the backs of six chimney flues from the plain plank flooring to the underside of the attic floorboards two stories over their heads, where it widened as the flues merged into a single, central chimney. Where she stood, Marie-France had barely room to stand next to Jethro. She could feel him breathing, smell the stench of his fear over the lingering lavender and basil—now dried to dust. Wood scraped on wood and the chain rattled as Mother Thomas replaced the peg and the shelf and stuffed the closet full of coats and hats on the other side.

"Be more quiet than mice," she whispered. "They're at the kitchen door. I'll be back as soon as I can." At full volume she said, "Come, Asa Frank, your grandpa is home."

Hard as she tried, Marie-France could hear nothing but two breaths, hers and her brother's. She dared not speak. Dared not cough, or worse, sneeze, despite the tickle in her nose and throat.

Jethro's hand found hers and they waited.

"I will not," Mother Thomas' voice rose to full dudgeon, "have that smelly beast in my house. It's bad enough you would let strangers poke into every nook and cranny. Since when is the word of the wife of a first selectman not enough for the likes of these, these, these—"

"Officers of the law," the deep mellow voice Father Thomas used so well in court filled in. "They are doing their duty under the law, Mother. We must obey the law."

"But not the dog!"

"Gentlemen, you can see my dilemma. I grant you have a warrant to search for your fugitive, but I see nothing here about a dog. I would bar your hound rather than face the wrath of my wife. Search, if you must. I will help you."

"Yes, Seth Thomas, you do that. And while you're at it, make sure they don't steal the silver. Your grandson and I will wait in the parlor until they are gone. Come along, little man."

The parlor door clicked open and soon the sounds of hands slapping against knees and thighs and each other accompanied Mother Thomas' version of patty cake and Asa Frank's giggles.

Heavy boots trod through the rest of the first floor of the house as the men opened doors and drawers and Father Thomas kept repeating, "Really, gentlemen, no man could hide in something that small."

"You stay here. Make sure he don't escape," said the scar-faced man.

"You there, stay where I can see you," Mother Thomas directed from the parlor. "I won't have you alone in my house."

Marie-France listened to the sound of footsteps, easily distinguishing the tread of Scarface's heavy boots from the soft leather of Father Thomas' city shoes, as they moved up the back stairs and on into the attic. Dirt from the underside of the attic floorboards rained down into the drying room. It coated Jethro and Marie-France's heads and faces and seeped down the collar of Marie-France's nightgown. She dared not brush it away. She hardly dared breathe.

Finally, after searching the bedrooms, steps descended the front staircase.

"What's this?" said Scarface. Door hinges creaked and Marie-France imagined that scarred face poking into the closet under the stairs. Only a thin wall of plaster and lath separated him from the drying room. She held her breath.

"Dead storage." Father Thomas' voice betrayed his exasperation. "Next you'll want to check the root cellar and crawl under the house."

"Damned right we will."

The front parlor door opened and patty cake came to a halt.

"Satisfied?" Mother Thomas said. "Look at your boots. You'll not trod over my carpet in those."

"I have to search this room."

"Take off your boots then, man. You heard my wife."

One boot after the other fell to the floor in the front hallway.

"Ma'am," Scarface said.

Hard as she tired, Marie-France couldn't hear the fall of his stocking feet on the carpet.

"What's in here?" The closet door opened.

"Coats, hats," Mother Thomas said so calmly Marie-France gave a silent prayer of thanks. "Did I hear something about crawling under the house. I warn you, there are snakes and who knows what else down there. I won't be responsible, if you are bitten or skunked."

"I've been through worse, but I thank you for your concern, Ma'am." Scarface's voice dripped sarcasm. Marie-France wanted nothing more than to spit in his eye.

The closet door closed. "Where's this cellar?"

"This way," Father Thomas said.

"And take your friend with you. Wouldn't want you to be all alone in the dark with the spiders and such."

Marie-France kept herself from shuddering at the thought of spiders. They made her skin itch.

The closet door opened and Mother Thomas whispered. "If they crawl under the chimney, they can get into the drying space. You must be very, very quiet and pray they don't squeeze between the chimney stones. I'll keep that dog out, if I can."

The door closed and the silence of midnight fell upon them. Jethro squeezed her hand. She rested her head on his chest and let tears drip down her cheeks.

"Can't see a guldarned thing with no more light than from yonder hatchway," Dogman said from somewhere under Marie-France's feet.

"You should have brought lanterns, not torches," Scar-face said.

"You think that old bat would let any flame under her house?"

"Her husband might."

"He wouldn't even let my dog— Did you feel that?"

"What?"

"Something slithered over my hand. Let's get out of here."

"I thought sure that nigger'd lead us to his sister. She's so light, she could be passing for white. You told me that dog of yours is never wrong. That griffe has to be here somewhere. We've searched everyplace else."

"Hate to admit it, but like that constable said, there's always a first time. That sambo done slipped out on us again. I say take the dog to the harbor and see if we can pick up his trail. If not, we come back and try again."

"He'll be long gone by then."

"He's long gone already."

"Ow!"

"What"

"Something bit my nose."

Marie-France almost laughed. She hoped whatever it was would leave an even nastier scar on that ugly face.

"You ready to go now?"

"Okay, okay. But if that dog of yours can't find a new scent, we're coming back."

It seemed forever—long after the sounds of men crawling on elbows and belly had ceased and the crawlspace hatch had thumped into place—before Mother Thomas opened the closet door. "You two all right in there?"

"Who are you talking to, Mother?"

The closet door slammed shut. "Nobody, dear."

Father Thomas' voice grew nearer. "I heard your voice."

The closet door opened.

"I was muttering to myself, looking for something for Asa Frank's costume. Can't have the boy miss his first real Hallowe'en."

"Don't know as I approve of all these newfangled customs. Although, if the village children do come this way dressed as horribles, I've got a treat in store."

"You?"

He chuckled. "It was riding Heman Howes' dray gave me the idea. He sold me a barrel of his best strawberry wine —just a small one, mind you. I'll greet the children at the north gate and drive them around to the south, where I'll give them all a draft of strawberry wine before sending them on their way."

"Do you suppose there'll be many?"

"Who knows. If word of my wine gets round, I should expect a mob."

The tickle, plaguing Marie-France since she squeezed into the drying space, erupted in a sneeze.

"What in the world?"

Wood scraped on wood.

Marie-France fumbled for the chain. It slipped through her fingers as Father Thomas pulled the peg on the other side. A ray of weak sunlight, blinding after hours in the total dark, streamed into their hiding place.

"Who's in there? Come out this instant."

Jethro pushed Marie-France aside. He put a finger to his lips. "I's comin'." He squeezed between the chimney bricks and the closet wall. "I's comin'."

Marie-France wedged herself in the deepest shadow against the far chimney flue. She pinched her nose and held her breath.

"Mother," anger deepened Father Thomas' voice to a growl, "what is the meaning of this?"

"I can explain, but you'd best sit down."

"And that's why we had to hide this man." Mother Thomas finished her story, leaving out Jethro's kinship to Marie-France.

"I don't understand. Why would Marie-France take such a risk? And where is she now?"

"Mama in dah," Asa Frank babbled. Suddenly his small pink hand appeared in the narrow slit between brick and wood at the bottom of the drying space opening. "Come out, Mama."

Her son's first two sentences, and they had betrayed her.

"Daughter, if you're in there, you had best come out and explain yourself."

Father Thomas spoke no dire ultimatum, but Marie-France heard both the disappointment and the anger. She squeezed herself into the closet, then stood barefoot on the parlor carpet in her nightdress. Not since the death of her father had she felt so hopeless.

Mother Thomas rose from her seat on the red velvet side chair and stood between Marie-France and her husband. "Before you get all high and mighty with your precious rule of law, I think you must hear all the facts." She pointed to the sofa. "You will all sit down while I explain."

Marie-France held a squirmy Asa Frank on her lap. He needed a diaper change. Jethro sat beside them in clothes which smelled hardly better. This time, Mother Thomas told the full story.

"My God!" Father Thomas rose from the ladder back chair. "It's not enough the South's stranglehold on government forces an abomination like the Fugitive Slave Act through Congress, that doughface Buchanan bends over backwards to please men who hold others in bondage and that our highest court issues appalling rulings like Dred Scott. Now their damned fugitive law reaches into the bosom of my family." He paced, head down, hands nestled in the small of his frock coat. "Once I would have bought freedom for you all, much as the thought of paying one penny to a slaveholder disgusts me."

Marie-France started to protest, but Father Thomas raised his hand for silence. "Moot point, since the *Central America* sank in September with all the banks' gold."

He stopped pacing and slammed his fist into his open palm. "No. Enough. I never thought to speak these words, but that starry-eyed muckraker Thoreau is right, when a law is unjust, civil disobedience is the only recourse."

He stared straight at Marie-France. "Are you sure this scar-faced man would recognize you?"

"He was the auctioneer for my father's estate," Marie-France said.

"Then how shall we keep you safe and get your brother away?"

Marie-France hugged Asa Frank to her breast. "Judge Walker will know."

Mother Thomas rose and took her husband's hand. "Yes, Father, you must go to him at once."

———

All day they hunkered behind drawn blinds, ears pricked for the first bay of a hound or Father Thomas' return. He arrived an hour before sunset. Judge Walker and three young men barely old enough to shave came behind in the old jurist's buggy. The young men followed Father Thomas and Jethro upstairs, while Mother Thomas led Judge Walker to the parlor.

He sat in the red velvet chair. Mother Thomas plied him with tea and her special sweet honey cakes. He nibbled and sipped before speaking.

"Mr. Thomas has explained your circumstances. I have advised him never to tell another soul. I advise you the same. It is sound advice and, if it weren't for that blasted slave catcher, it would be enough." The judge sighed. "But it is not, and I think you know the truth of what I must say."

Marie-France nodded. A stone the size of an anvil lodged in the pit of her stomach.

"My grandsons will take care of your brother. Each one, dressed in part of his clothing, will create a false trail for that hound from hell. We'll scrub the boy down and paint him up with cayenne pepper. It'll sting, but it will throw the dog off for the hour or so we'll need. Dressed as a horrible in one of your old sheets," he nodded to Mother Thomas, "we'll get him away on a fishing smack bound for the Grand Banks. It will land him in Canada."

Marie-France breathed. "Will that succeed?"

"As well as anything." There was a twinkle in the judge's eye. "Don't you worry, we've done this before."

"And Marie-France?" Mother Thomas asked.

The judge drained his teacup and waved off Mother Thomas' offer of more.

"Alas, it's too dangerous to send them together. The dog already has his scent. There's no point in giving it hers as well. If they were caught—. We have to consider the child."

"But surely the slave catcher will some day give up and leave," Mother Thomas said.

"This one, perhaps. But there may be others." The judge's blue eyes bore down on Marie-France. "How badly do they want you back?"

Marie-France shrugged. "It's been nearly three years and they're still looking. I guess that tells the tale."

"Indeed. It says you have two choices. Leave for Canada with your child or without him, but leave you must, and the sooner the better. Just not tonight."

"My husband is on his way home from California. I received a letter only last week. We expect him any day." She couldn't face Mother Thomas. She lowered her voice to a whisper. "We already planned to go to Canada."

"Well," the judge rose and handed his teacup to Mother Thomas, "that's settled then. Get word to me when you're ready. In the meantime, keep to the house until you hear this slave catcher has gone. Even then, you should avoid going abroad where a stranger may recognize you. No point in taking chances when you're so close to an escape." He bowed to Mother Thomas. "Wonderful cakes. If you don't mind, I'd like the recipe for Mrs. Walker."

"Jethro's away to Barnstable." Father Thomas flung himself onto the red velvet chair and stretched out his legs. His cheeks were flushed from wine. "The boys are leading that dog on a merry chase to the docks in Harwichport. Judge Walker will stop here to let us know that the *Northern Star* is safely away."

"I won't feel safe until he does," Marie-France said.

"Nor I," said Mother Thomas.

"Too bad the horribles have drunk all the wine. The judge could join us in a toast to breaking the law." Father Thomas sighed. "This business makes criminals of us all."

"What's that?" Mother Thomas rose from the ladder back chair. "Did you hear that?"

Marie-France had heard the knock at the kitchen door. She couldn't move.

"There it is again. Surely, it can't be the judge, not this soon," said Mother Thomas.

Father Thomas jumped to his feet. "I'll go. Get the closet ready. If it's them, you hide." He left the parlor door ajar.

Mother Thomas sprang to the crack and put her ear to it.

Marie-France threw coats and hats on the couch and thanked God the shelf remained propped on the floor. She put her hand on the peg and waited.

Father Thomas' voice was loud enough for Marie-France to make out a word or two—*Central America*, lost, reward." She thought she heard another man, not one of the slave catchers, and a woman.

"...into the parlor." Father Thomas pushed open the door.

In stepped a very pregnant, red-headed woman in a thin cotton dress and a blue-black man.

Father Thomas swept the coats off the couch. "Have a seat, Mother." He joined her on the couch and took her hands in his. "These people have brought news of our Asa. Very bad news indeed."

Marie-France listened to Moses DaSilva's story in an agonized fog. With each sentence she felt her heart sink, until it could have oozed out her toes. She willed herself not to faint.

"That's the last I seen of him, standing on the deck of the *Central America* all awash and me rowing away to the *Brig Marine*. Rosie, here, has something for you."

The woman pulled a silver sewing bird out of her purse and handed it to Marie-France. "He give me this for his wife." She pulled a visiting card out and handed it to Father Thomas. He read the message on the back aloud.

"Please pay this brave woman whatever you can. I have entrusted this bird and my fortune to fate and her good graces. Tell Marie-France I love her. Asa."

Mother Thomas began to rock and keen.

"I'm afraid I can't offer much in the way of money. The lost of the gold on the *Central America* has all but ruined me. But I will do everything I can to help you both." Father Thomas stood and shook Moses' hand. "Anything."

Marie-France examined the silver bird, running her fingers over the spring-loaded beak, the c-clamp and the green velvet pincushion. For all she adored Asa, she cursed him for sending such a useless token and, in one more Southern storm, for dashing all her hopes for a free life together in Canada.

In the cold light of another morning, Mother Thomas stirred a pot of pumpkin soup at the kitchen stove. "Are you sure?"

Marie-France spooned a mouthful of mush into Asa-Frank. "Judge Walker is right, I cannot stay."

She had clamped the sewing bird to the edge of the oaken table, a reminder of all she had lost. She would leave it behind—with her son.

"You must tell anyone who asks that I have gone in search of my husband, in the vain hope he fetched up on some Southern shore and was not lost at sea.

"It was too late for me to sail with my brother. I will take another ship north, to Saint Pierre or Miquelon and then on to Paris, where my father had family. Perhaps there I will meet my compatriot Alexandre Dumas and introduce myself as the Countess of Monte Cristo." She forced a laugh and fed more mush into Asa Frank. "I cannot take my son. He will be safe here in my absence. One day I may return," but she knew she could not. She had not the courage of Peggy Garner, could never kill her own child to save him from slavery. But she could sacrifice her own happiness, as she must.

Mother Thomas sniffled and brushed at her eyes with the back of her hand.

"I only wish you to speak well of me, to give him my father's copy of *Le Comte de Monte-Cristo* and this." Marie-France pulled an envelope sealed with wax from her coat pocket. "When he is old enough, if ever the day comes that he can enjoy the full and free life which all of us want, when anyone among us would be content to have the status of his mother or the color of his skin changed and stand in his place."

A knock at the door made her heart skip a beat. How

had she been so careless, sitting with her back to the windows where anyone could look in?

Judge Walker poked in his head. "Are you ready?"

Life returned to Marie-France's limbs. She rose and placed a kiss on the top of Asa Frank's head.

"As ready as ever I will be."

She took one last look at the sewing bird, slid the envelope onto the table and turned her back on the country that had long since turned its back on her.

THE SKY IN THE GROUND
ROB VAGLE

She said dusk was the best time to see the sky in the ground and Henry went with her, down through the woods on the other side of the tracks out on River Road, the two of them holding hands and kissing, long and hard, frequently, and once, when they cut through the dusty culvert yard, they rubbed up against each other and he caressed her breasts.

Preoccupied with lust, Henry never gave the sky in the ground Sadie had talked about another thought. His senses were full of her—smelling the sweet apple shampoo in her hair, tasting the salt on her tongue, tracing the curve along her hips, pressed against her softness.

He had forgotten about the reason for their destination until she said, "We're almost there."

The woods were already getting dark, the trees black like sticks of burnt wood underneath the canopy of dark leaves. Snatches of sky poked between the leaves and the sky was blue-black. They were headed north and Henry glanced west where the sun had sunk low on the horizon, sending shafts of light between the trees. The tree shadows were long, the air cold. The trees looked like jail bars in the dusk, containing them, keeping them away from the sun.

"What are we going to look at?" Henry asked.

"The sky in the ground," she said. Her amber hair was shoulder length and her blue eyes were black in the diminishing light. She searched his face and added, "Just tell me if I'm crazy or not."

He was the new kid in school looking to make new friends and be as instantly popular as his older brother, but he wasn't an athlete and though he was full of grandiose intentions he found himself closed mouthed around strangers. When he was paired up with Sadie as lab partners in biology class, she said, "The two of us are going on an adventure." She had him at those first words. He liked the way she moved, like she had electrical current flowing through her. She seemed to be under a steady hum of excitement and he wanted to be a part of it.

After three weeks she leaned close to him and said, "I want to show you something." He felt tenfold increase in magnetic attraction, his heart pounding against his ribcage as if it were a xylophone. He'd go anywhere with her. She could show him anything.

If anything, he was the one that was crazy.

Before he could reply, something caught Sadie's attention and she pointed, "Look!"

One beam of sunlight no thicker than a baseball bat shined up from the ground. On first glance, he thought it must be a trick of the light. At the base of an old oak tree, in between two exposed massive roots, light shined. Dust motes floated and insects darted through the beam. The beam stopped abruptly against the underside of a massive limb. The bark was brownish gray in the imperfect circle of light. The light looked natural, not like artificial white light from a bulb.

"See," she said, whispering.

"Why are you whispering?" he said, feeling dumb as he said it.

"Listen for the crows," she said.

Besides the crickets chirping, there was a fluttering of wings in the air. Something darted around the massive tree limb with the sunbeam coming from the ground. He assumed those were the crows she was talking about. Then the crows cawed, a cry that rose the hackles on his neck. Crows seemed out of place here. Were they active in the dark? Suddenly all of this seemed peculiar, something off about the whole situation. He looked at her but her face was lost inside the amber hair that framed her face.

"Look," she said again and pointed.

A bird cut through the shaft of light, its iridescent blue-black feathers blazing for a split second. It circled and descended down to another bird and the two of them poked their heads into the daylight piercing through the hole in the ground. They cawed and they cawed, each cry sending chills up Henry's back.

"What the hell is that!" Henry said with too much fear to his voice that he didn't like.

They didn't move. They stood no more than twenty feet away, night encroaching in on them, the woods robbing them of any dusk light.

"Am I crazy?" she asked.

"Hell no," he said. "I see it too."

"You haven't seen anything yet."

She stepped forward, a spring to her step, bounding for the light in the ground. Branches snapped under her feet and pebbles and rocks skittered. He chased after her, clawing at the bark of trees to keep his footing. When she reached the light, the birds launched into the air and were lost in the blackness.

"Check this out," she said.

She got down on her knees and grabbed a tree root with both hands. When she leaned her head forward, the light caught her in the face. Her hair curtained off her face for him again, until he went to the opposite side of the light and saw her face aglow. It was as if she held a flashlight under her face, telling scary stories around the campfire. Only this light wasn't orange and harsh, it was gentle and soft. The light caught the copper highlights her hair framing her face. Her lips were scarlet red and her eyes were bright blue. The freckle like a tear on her left cheek was revealed. Her skin looked soft in the light and he remembered the rush of her face pressed up against his.

Her face held him spellbound. She smiled at him as if all this was perfectly normal. And he could believe she was telling him a story with a flashlight beam pointed at her face. He could ignore the daylight coming from the ground.

She looked down into the light. "Come and look."

He gripped the tree root on his side and leaned forward until he was almost cheek to cheek with her, strands of hair tickling his skin. He looked down in the hole and for a moment he couldn't make sense out of what he was seeing. The hole was lined with soil and grass roots, the daylight highlighting crawling bugs. The hole was only a foot deep and then there was a plunge, open space, nothing but the great wide open. Far, far down lay patchwork earth—rich brown squares of dirt and green splotches of trees. A wide dark blue river meandered across the land. He thought he was viewing the ground from an airplane. The saying "Seeing is believing" was a lie because he could not wrap his head around the fact that the ground they walked on was just a shell over another atmosphere, the atmosphere surrounding another land.

"You can't believe it, huh?" she said.

He pushed himself away let himself fall back on his ass where he sat in the dirt. He brushed his hands together, wiping the grit that covered his hands.

"That's not right," he said.

She leaned back and looked at him through the beam of light. Her face was gray filtered through the dust and particles floating in the light.

"I thought so too when I first found it," she said.

He said nothing, only stared at her face, her pleading eyes.

"Whatever that place is down there," she said. "I'm going."

What Henry knew about Sadie was this: she was an only child living in a house with a mother (always ill-tempered) who screamed at her at the top of her lungs, her father was cold and distant and frequently away from the home. Henry immediately understood her need to run to the place underground. Her home life swung between anger and neglect. It was a place with very little hope, while there was a whole new world underneath them. One place dark, another place light.

"How?" he said and the word croaked out of his mouth. He couldn't determine the which "how"he referred to--how could a world lay below the ground or how do they get down there, or both?

He didn't want to leave, but he didn't want to let her go. Just a moment ago he was feeling like he'd follow her anywhere--he looked at the beam of daylight pouring out of the ground--but this?

The birds began crying again, circling above them, their feathers rustling louder than the wind through the leaves.

"I don't think those are crows," he said.

Their cries spoke to him, the words sinking in his head like thoughts of his own making.

Sadie has chosen this place and we have chosen her.

Sadie looked away from the birds and said to him, "I have to go."

"Did you just hear them say that?" he asked.

"You heard them too," she said.

Her lips curled into a smile and then her face was gone, lost in the dark, when the shaft of light vanished. Henry scrambled to his feet, blind as his eyes grew used to the dark. He grabbed onto the nearest tree and listened to the rustling sounds coming from the ground and growing louder, until air exploded into a fluttering of wings. Wings batted at his arm and high pitched cries of birds pierced the night. Their wings rushed wind across his skin. He threw his hands up to his face, afraid a bird might ram him in the eye.

"The birds are here!" Sadie said.

But Henry couldn't see her. "Where are you?"

Wings flapped around his ears and he tripped on an exposed tree root and fell to the ground. Sadie was there, next to him, grabbing his hand and her other hand at his back. He could barely make out her crouching form.

Trembling beneath the earth sent vibrations through him. Under that oak tree came a knocking sound, a rapid pounding. Pockets of ground in front of the oak tree fell away and bright slivers of daylight poured through, cutting the night before them. Henry saw the silhouettes of birds at the base of the tree, pecking at the tree roots, their heads rocking back and fourth like trigger hammers, their beaks stabbing the roots and dirt. Other quick flying birds tore away at the soil where it crumbled away and fell to the world below. The maw at the base of the tree was at least two feet wide and growing wider with each tear of a sharp beak.

"Those birds aren't of this world," he said.

"No, they're of my world," she said.

"Sadie, what are you talking about?"

The daylight coming from the growing hole in the ground illuminated a large area of the woods like a campfire. Dozens of birds worked at the hole, their wings fluttering as fast as hummingbirds. All other birds flew above them, their screeching cries like seagulls waiting to eat.

Sadie didn't answer him. He pushed himself up form the ground, grabbed her hand and pulled her. "We're getting out of here," he said.

She dragged her heels and pulled away from him. He worked at pulling and couldn't move his feet fast enough. He felt the birds behind him, their wings fluttering and their chirps sounded like nails being pulled from a two by four.

"You asshole, I didn't show you this for you to save me," she said.

"I don't care what your intentions were. This is freaking me out."

Dozens of feathers brushed at his back and the birds screeched in his ears.

He shouted over the birds squawking, "Sadie, why did you bring me here? Did you actually think I'd go down there?"

She grabbed at his arms, pulled close and shouted in his ear, "I'm choosing you."

Her face held a serious expression, her eyes wide and

daring him to laugh or scoff. He couldn't laugh, nor could he be flippant. Fear sat in the pit of his stomach, dark and heavy. He'd throw up before he could ever laugh. Since they arrived here at that hole in the ground, his world and the way things worked had been turned inside out. Half hour ago he had Sadie's tongue in his mouth. Now the world had tilted and spun. He wanted it to stop.

"Your choosing me to do what?" he asked.

"Bear witness," she said. "Watch me leave this world for another and I don't mean to be all hokey, Henry, but we'll have a bond made from this secret. For this to work, someone I've chosen needs to know."

He'd run if he didn't feel the wings fluttering at his back. The hole in the ground had inched wider, chunks of tree roots plummeting below. Air rushed passed him and pulled him towards the hole. He felt it in the lean, his heels off the ground and Sadie also leaned back as if she may fall over if they weren't holding onto each others arms. Leaves and sticks scurried across the ground and swept through the air, falling into that hole and away. It was as if his world had depressurized, its fuselage punctured, and the air rushed out into the vacuum.

He wanted to be as far away from these woods as he could get. Sadie needed help, plain and simple. If he got her away from here, she could get help, and this hole in the ground would cease to exist. This was as illogical as everything else in the woods, but he had hope. Hope that life would be real again, a world that made sense. He wanted to flee, but he couldn't just leave her.

Then the birds spoke inside his head again: She's not crazy.

That spooked him into action.

He pulled her along by an arm and plowed through a

dark curtain of wings, the feathers dusting his face, their sharp feet scratching at his skin and clawing his hair. The earth beneath his feet trembled, the tremors running up his legs. Sadie gripped his arm, pulling him back. The light in the woods shimmered on the trees. It was as if things had gotten brighter. He could see where he stepped.

Then he heard Sadie say, "You can't leave here, Henry, and take me with you. We can't get away from it. It will follow."

He stopped and she knocked into him. His breath caught in his throat when he looked behind them. A fissure had opened up from the hole--one thin line of daylight followed, stopping a few feet behind Sadie. The leaves in the trees flickered, reflecting the light.

Sadie slipped from his grasp. "Dude," she said, "it's me or the whole world."

"What?" He couldn't keep his eyes off the fissure. He expected it to move again.

She slapped him and his right cheek burned. "This is serious, Henry. Either I go down there or the whole world does. One or other. No other choice."

"I have to let you go?" he asked.

She smirked. "Come on, Henry. We were only lab partners and we groped each other on the way out here. It's not like we had a serious relationship."

But he had hoped.

She turned and walked back to the hole, the daylight fissure shrinking in front of her. The birds were quiet except for a few wings fluttering in the air. He could feel the birds watching him in the trees, lined up along branches, oh so many of them. The earth no longer trembled and the hole was now a gaping maw of six feet. Big enough for anyone to jump through.

"Is that all I am to you?" he asked, finding his feet shuffling forward to join her. "Someone to 'bear witness.'?"

She looked at him over her shoulder. "This isn't some little deal. This is important, my secret place I'm going to. You're going to carry that secret."

"For how long?"

"Forever if need be." She sighed. "I didn't just pick anyone, Henry. I picked someone I trusted. Someone I liked, a new friend I connected with."

He felt calm about the birds and the hole in the ground, because those things where chilling. For the moment. His stomach settled but he was a little heart sick. He ran his hands through his hair. "Okay, it's you or the whole world. That's a lot of pressure for anybody, but you're all cranked up on leaving. Fine. But I don't think I can watch you go down that hole."

"I'll be quick," she said.

With that, she scampered towards the hole, her body silhouetted against the daylight flooding up. Henry opened his mouth but no words were needed. She dropped through the hole without a look back. The image of her falling burned into his mind--it was more like the world below sucked her in, and her hair flew up above her shoulders.

Astounded, he froze there. Then the birds rushed out of the trees and plummeted down the hole, their blue-black wings glistening like a river of feathers. They flew as fast as arrows shot from bows and in a instant, like Sadie, they were gone.

The hole went dark like someone had hit the light switch. He stood in the night woods and turned his head saw the street lights in town. He wished he'd brought a flashlight because he thought the hole was still there at the base of the tree. When the light had gone out, it stopped flowing from the hole, not like it had closed up on its own.

He crouched down and crawled on his hands and knees towards the tree, feeling ahead, trying to find the edge of that hole. When he brushed the edge, he knocked a rock inside and it made a soft thud. The hole was there and it had a bottom. The hole looked like an oil spot in the dark but he didn't know how deep it went. Was it night down below? He felt around, looking for a stick and found a branch. He got on his knees and stabbed the branch into the hole and felt it stick into the ground. Still not satisfied that it was gone, he kicked his legs over the edge of the hole and dropped his feet where they landed in hard packed dirt. When he stood, he realized the hole was no deeper than the height of his knees.

"You are crazy," he said and he didn't know if he was talking about himself or Sadie.

He still expected to see her in school the next day--he wanted to--but he knew what he had seen.

Would her parents notice she was missing? Of course they would, her mother would probably be even more angry, lost in her own broiling fire. He wondered if her father would realize he kept his daughter so far out of arms reach that she had fallen into a hole. He couldn't and wouldn't tell them. His parents would listen: his mother, the psychiatrist; his father, the artist who painted prairie landscapes and wildlife. But would they believe? Their youngest son had a crush on a girl they never met and now they're suppose to believe she vanished into another world. Telling them would lead to confusion and he should think twice about telling his mother, the shrink. Nobody would believe him if he told them, and he would be a suspect in her disappearance, which meant the secret was indeed between him and Sadie.

He jumped out of the hole and walked quickly out of the woods and he felt cheated. The secret was one sided. Only one person to share it with and she was gone. Down the hole. He grew angry and confused as he walked, taking ragged breaths.

Then he noticed a bird flying circles around him in the dark. If it wasn't a crow, it certainly was the size of one. When he stopped it continued to fly around him. It flapped its wings and he felt the air move.

"How come you didn't go back with the rest of them?" He asked.

The bird cawed twice.

Henry thought about what he had witnessed and what he had to bear with the secret. He grew cold at how lonely that felt.

But the bird cawed twice again.

He turned and watched the bird circle him. "I have you to keep the secret with, don't I?" he asked.

The bird cawed once in the affirmative.

SNOWFALL FROM A CLOUDLESS SKY
C.J. MATTISON

The definition of resilience was an eleven-year-old girl, exhausted from a grave illness, thinking about nothing but playing hockey again. Leave it to such a child to shame her mother with her strength.

Stephanie Flowers sat across from her daughter at their kitchen nook table, in the place with windows like eyes to the world, lidded with thin white and yellow curtains. Beyond lay rolling wooded hills and two-lane roads lit by fine sunshine and the promise of warm summers and autumn leaves of fire and cold winters. Everyone said the sun never shone during the winter in rural Vermont, but that wasn't true. It shone nicely on days like this, when it was very cold, so cold that even the clouds stayed indoors.

"I need a Christmas list, Tomi," Stephanie said. "There's not even a week until Christmas...how will I know what to get you?"

"It's okay, Mom," Tomi said with a weak smile. "Don't worry about it. You can't buy the only thing I want."

"What's that?" Stephanie asked, hoping her voice sounded lighter than she felt. It was all she could do to not worry about her daughter's exhaustion. The doctors had assured them that Tomi's leukemia was in remission, and that it was normal for her to be physically drained. Even so, Stephanie could hardly breathe thinking about it.

"Snow," said Tomi.

Stephanie stifled a nervous laugh. Snow, just snow. "You're right. I can't buy that, and there's none in the forecast. Just cold, lots of cold."

"Maybe we can put some of that fake snow in the windows."

"Sure, we can do that." Stephanie was determined to make this the best Christmas she could, in spite of Tomi's rehab and fatigue. The boredom was just so hard for a child who had always been so frightfully active.

"And maybe," said Tomi, a hopeful expression creeping onto her face, "some new hockey skates."

New skates. Tomi hadn't felt well enough to skate the entire previous winter. But she'd looked forward to this year, to a snowy winter of skiing and skating and maybe even ice fishing with her grandfather. She was teaching her mother about the stunning depths of hope.

"Snow and skates," Stephanie said, reaching across the table to squeeze Tomi's hand. "Let's see what we can do."

———

Leave it to eleven-year-old twins to annoy, frustrate, fascinate, and delight their father, all in the space of five minutes.

The twins joined Len Ballantine for breakfast, taking their usual places at the kitchen table—a spot which had become their frequent milieu for pressing their grievances.

"But listen, Dad," said Brendel, in his way-too-mature

lawyer voice. "You tell us we need to help others. Now we want to help our friend, and you're making it difficult."

"I agree, Father," said Hilary, crossing her arms like a defiant movie actress—child version. "Quote: 'We're very fortunate, and we need to show our appreciation by giving and helping others.'" Her young voice imitating his own was one of the annoying and fascinating elements of their teamwork oeuvre.

Len studied his children. "Yes, I do encourage you to help *others*. But I'm not sure how that translates into buying each of *you* radio-controlled drones."

"I told you, Dad," said Brendel, "it's a surprise for Tomi. She's been really sick and needs cheering up."

"Yes, Father, like Brendel said." Hilary's patient expression mirrored one of Len's most endearing memories of their mother, with the same head tilt and insistent posture. Did Hilary remember her mother's mannerisms, or was it subliminal, inherited and generational?

"What kind of a surprise requires a drone?" Len asked.

"If we told you, it wouldn't be a surprise," said Hilary, as if this was the most reasonable explanation that anyone could offer. Maybe they would both become lawyers after all. What would Wendy have thought about that, their two offspring turned loose on the court system?

"You have a drone, Dad," said Brendel.

"Yes, for my business, to film the exteriors of buildings and water towers looking for damage. It's not a toy. And I'm not sure the world is ready for your version of a surprise," said Len. "So, I'm afraid I have to say no. I can't...condone the drones. Get it?" He laughed.

"Groan, Dad." Brendel rolled his eyes.

"Yikes," said Hilary.

"C'mon now, get your shoes and coats. We need to

make a grocery store run for Tomi's food drive. Afterward, maybe we can go shop for an appropriate present for her."

"Appropriate equals bor-ing," said Hilary, slouching up the stairs to her bedroom for her shoes.

"And lame," said Brendel, following her.

It was already early afternoon when Stephanie got to Food Mecca, the discount chain store that had opened several months earlier. With cement floors, self-bagging carrels, and "low-low-low prices," it was the first such place to open in their small town.

She and Tomi had driven by the store soon after it had opened, just to get Tomi out of the house and her mind off missing another hockey season. Tomi never wanted to play in the girls' leagues; she wanted to scrap with the boys, like her friend Hilary, who played in the same local league as her brother. Stephanie worried. Some of the boys were rougher on the girls. She hated her daughter's bruises, but Tomi wore them like medals.

"Mom, what's that new store?" Tomi had asked.

Stephanie explained the concept of a discount store.

"I think we should take collections and buy stuff for the food bank," Tomi said, referring to the Harvest County Food Bank, where all the school kids worked for three days during their summer breaks. Tomi, not yet in remission, barely strong enough to walk to the car without assistance but always waving her mother away, was thinking about a food drive for "people who need help."

Stephanie shook her head at the memory and probably looked crazy to Mrs. Newsome, who she passed in Aisle 2— soups, crackers, and cookies. Mrs. Newsome owned an independent bookstore that Tomi loved. She gave Stephanie an invitation to a New Year's Eve party she was holding at the store, and urged her to come, and to bring Tomi if she felt up to it.

Stephanie pushed her cart around the corner into Aisle 5 where the canned goods were, and saw Tomi's friends Hilary and Brendel, and their father, Len. Single father who lost his wife, Wendy, four or five years earlier. They were loading cases of canned green beans, corn, peaches, and pears into a cart that was nearly half-full. Hilary seemed to be directing the males under her watchful eye. No wonder Tomi liked her.

Hilary looked up and smiled when Stephanie approached.

"Look, it's Miss Flowers. Hey, Miss Flowers!"

The children were dressed in similar outfits, blue athlete pants with white stripes, the colors of their youth hockey team, the Comets, and black jackets too thin for the weather, unzipped, pulled open, gloves and hats shoved into their coat pockets. Their father encouraged them to dress differently, she knew. Futility, it seemed.

Len unfolded his long frame to his tall height, lean and athletic, from cross-country skiing? He smiled at her with a bit of chagrin, perhaps because of his embarrassment at his daughter's bossiness. It made him more attractive...a thought Stephanie quickly tamped down.

"Hello," she said, eyeing their cart. "Planning a party?"

"That's Mozart," said Brendel, pointing to the air, from which rich, gentle classical music resonated.

"*Eine Kleine Nachtmusik*," said Hilary, nodding.

"Don't show off, guys," said Len, looking even more sheepish.

"We're both named after famous musicians," said

Hilary. "But Father doesn't want us reciting Mozart's works, because he thinks it's pretentious."

"But it's not pretense if we *know* them," said Brendel. "Is it, Miss Flowers?"

"No, I don't think so." Their mother had been the music department head at a larger nearby school district in Burlington and ran the local theater group. Her influence was obvious.

"I'm sorry, Stephanie," said Len. "They can be over-whelming."

"Our favorite piece is the *Flute Concerto Number 2 in D Minor*," said Brendel.

"Because it's *Köchel Number 314*, and our mother's birthday is March fourteenth," said Hilary.

"Now you're just showing off, guys. Please stop," Len said. He looked at Stephanie, a helpless expression on his face. "I'm sorry, Stephanie."

She laughed and felt her face flush as Len's amber-brown eyes caught and held hers. His bushy brown eyebrows and short-trimmed hair were highlighted in silver, as if by the gentle strokes of a horsehair brush.

"It's okay," she said, dragging her eyes away from his. "They're cute. For Tomi's food drive?" She gestured toward their cart, over half full of canned goods now. She imagined the wheels giving way under the weight of fruits and liquids and metal cans.

She had felt like that cart during Tomi's illness, crushed by the weight of the terrible threat. Of course, Len must have endured similar feelings while Wendy went through her own battle with cancer, only to find himself raising two energetic children alone. At least Stephanie's father was in town. Len's family was in the Midwest somewhere.

Weight could be a terrible thing. Did it make one stronger? Or did it only cause permanent damage?

"Yes," said Hilary, drawing Stephanie's attention. "We were going to drop them off at the food bank day after tomorrow."

The day after tomorrow. Only a few days until Christmas. And she still had no presents for Tomi. So preoccupied with Tomi's latest scans, then beside herself with the joy of the recent all-clear.

Joy, joy, joy. It was almost as if she'd never understood the word before.

"I need to run," Stephanie said, glancing at Len and then looking quickly away. "Thanks so much for making Tomi's drive a success. It means a lot to her, and of course, the people it will help."

"Father says we're very fortunate, and need to help others, Miss Flowers," said Hilary, as if reading her mind.

"Hilary..." said Len, his face reddening.

Stephanie couldn't help laughing, the tension and restrained fears threatening to crack her open in the emotional breakdown she'd needed for a long time, crack her open right there in front of this man and his funny, precocious children.

"We are," she said. "We are all so fortunate."

"I heard Tomi's recent tests have been very positive," said Len.

Stephanie could only nod stupidly for a moment, and the three gave her time to gather herself. "Yes. Doctors believe she's in total remission."

"That's fantastic," said Len. "I'm thrilled. And just before Christmas."

"I told you she would be," said Brendel, nudging his sister.

"*She* told us she would be," said Hilary, nudging back. Then she asked Stephanie, "When will she be able to play hockey again?"

Stephanie said, "We don't know, dear. She's still weak. But if the doctors and I allowed her, she would play tomorrow."

A look passed between the twins. Conspiratorial?

Stephanie thanked them all again, and then moved on. Less than a week to Christmas, no presents for Tomi, and no clue what size skates she would wear now.

―――――――

By the time Len and the twins dropped the canned goods at the food bank in the name of the Tomi Flowers First Annual Food Drive, he had completely forgotten about taking the twins shopping for a present for Tomi

All he could think about was Stephanie Flowers' brave brown eyes, pooling with tears when she spoke of her daughter's prognosis. What were these crazy feelings he was having about her? Yearning to take her in his arms and comfort her as her anxiety spilled out in body-wracking waves? Letting his arms remain around her and hoping she would be in no hurry to push away?

Would Hilary and Brendel ever welcome another woman into their lives?

Leave it to a widowed forty-something man with no idea how to begin dating again to frustrate himself with good intentions and faint actions! Especially when this was hardly the time to press his feelings upon a poor woman who was still raw from enduring an unimaginable trial.

By 5:30 p.m., the sun had set in the late-December Vermont sky nearly an hour before. They'd finished dinner, and Len listened distractedly when the twins told him they were going to go upstairs and look at gaming catalogs to see if they could find a Quayzar Sports electronic hockey game cartridge for Tomi that wouldn't be boring and lame. Half an hour later, when they hadn't come back down for dessert, Len went up to investigate. He well-remembered the days when they were little, and "quiet children" meant "children up to something."

They were not in their rooms, not in their shared bathroom, not in the upstairs reading area where they often hung out reading and arguing, or playing video games and arguing, or nodding off and arguing in their sleep. The window in Brendel's room was closed but unlocked, and a note in Hilary's calligraphy-worthy handwriting was pinned to Brendel's desk by his tiny replica Stanley Cup from the 2011 Boston Bruins win.

"Father, working on our surprise. Don't worry! It will be fine!"

Len could hear Wendy's voice in those words—*it will be fine*. As her health had deteriorated, and his daily habits had suffered, he'd done all he could to hold the children up, kept them fed and going to school. The last time she had spoken those words were for the children: *You keep going, do great things. I may be going on ahead, but we will meet again, and it will be fine.*

Most times, things were fine. But sometimes they weren't.

And if he didn't find the two rascals who shared his DNA, it probably wasn't going to be.

He grabbed his coat.

"Are you sure that's the right key?" Hilary knew it was, but she enjoyed another chance to prod her brother. Served him right for eating the last cinnamon tart that morning. A garbage bag full of shredded paper lay against her leg, where she'd dropped the heavy thing while she waited for him to unlock the door.

"Yes, it's the right key," said Brendel, still fiddling with it, struggling to even get it into the old lock on the shop's back door. "Mr. Flowers gave it to me when he went out of town, so I could drop off my remote-control car for repairs."

"I want one of those for Christmas. A super-high dune buggy, with swollen tires like giant black doughnuts. For driving over the snow drifts."

"If we ever get any snow." The lock clicked. "Ha!"

They pushed the door open and slipped into the back storage room, lit only by the red "Exit" sign above the door they just entered. Dark square shapes of boxes were stacked on spindly metal shelves on one wall. Beyond were the small kitchen and restroom, both in heavy shadow.

Brendel stumbled and knocked over a metal bucket and mop, which clattered like an avalanche of aluminum cans on the concrete floor.

"Could you make more noise, please?" Hilary imagined Brendel sticking his tongue out at her in the dark. "Where are they?" Her eyes fought to adjust and she dropped the bag of shredded paper on the floor just inside the door.

"They should be on display...wait, they're right here." His feet shuffled in the dark. A small white beam of light burst alive in his hand, lighting two identical, spidery-legged black shapes the size of lawn mowers, sitting on a folding table. The flashlight's beam caught a yellow tag attached to the table between the machines, the word "SOLD" written in bold black letters.

"Oh no," said Brendel.

"Well, it *is* only three days 'til Christmas, genius," said Hilary with real pleasure. "Tomi's grandfather is in business to *sell* this stuff, not to keep it in safe storage for us to steal."

"But these are the ones—two drones and controllers. And here they are, ready to go."

"Like they were waiting for us. We'll have to apologize to whoever bought them." Hilary suddenly felt like they were making a mistake. "Are you *sure* Mr. Flowers said we could borrow them?"

"Yeah, but that was probably before someone bought them." Brendel shrugged in the shadows. "We'll have to bring them back well before the shop opens."

Hilary rolled her eyes in the dark, wishing her brother could see her sarcasm. She picked up one of the drones, which was surprisingly light but still bulky. She wondered how they were going to carry them both with the controller.

"How do these make snow?" she asked.

"I'll show you when we get there. We're going to need water, though, from somewhere."

"Then why am I carrying all this shredded paper?"

"That was in case my idea didn't work."

"And how will the drones drop the paper?"

"I haven't figured that out yet."

"*Riiiight*. Your wonderful planning, as usual. I'm leaving the paper here. I can't carry a drone and the controller and the sack, anyway."

"Okay. Let's go." He hoisted his drone. "Man, that's heavier than I thought."

The twins stared at each other for a long moment.

"We can't carry these all the way to Tomi's house,"

Hilary said. "We're going to have to fly them. And then sneak back to our house for water."

"Okay," Brendan agreed. "Mr. Flowers let me practice with one the other day, so I can fly mine and tell you what to do. Imagine, me telling you what to do for once in our lives!"

"We'll see about that."

Stephanie hadn't been expecting anyone, so when the doorbell rang about 7:00 p.m., she peeked through the curtain from the dining room to see who was there. To her surprise, standing on the porch, hands in the pockets of a blue down coat with white stripes, was Len Ballantine.

She went to the door quickly, but imagining herself yanking it open, she paused long enough to take a deep breath before opening it nice and slowly.

"Len?"

"I'm sorry to bother you, Stephanie. I think Hilary and Brendel are...planning some kind of surprise for Tomi, and I'm afraid they're doing something rash."

"I can't imagine your charming children doing that."

"Well, I can. Have you...seen them? Or can I ask if Tomi's heard anything from them?"

"They're not at home?"

"No. They left a note—'working on a surprise for Tomi.' Whatever that means."

"Let me talk to her."

"I don't know anything, Mom." Tomi said, leaning against the hallway entrance.

"You're sure, Tomi?" said Stephanie. "No hints about where they might be going or what they were doing?"

"No, Mom," Tomi said. She turned and headed down the hall. The sound of slow, labored footsteps marked her movement.

It was obvious Tomi knew more than she was letting on, but Stephanie wasn't going to get more from her while Len was there.

"I'm sorry, Mr. Ballantine. I'll keep an eye open and will let you know if they show up. Or anything else happens."

He lingered. Was there more he wanted to say? Stephanie felt a little bit silly at how much she was enjoying the unexpected visit. Of course he had to go, had to find his children, but part of her wished he could stay.

"Call me Len, please," he said. "If you don't mind, I'm going to circle the neighborhood. This surprise had to involves something here, so they should turn up sooner or later—if they haven't gotten themselves into trouble elsewhere."

"I'll call if I see them."

He lingered a bit more, almost speaking, then smiling wanly. Stephanie followed him to the porch, wrapping her sweater tightly around herself as she watched him walk to his car. He backed out before turning his lights on, avoiding blasting her with the beams. Little acts of consideration were telling.

When Stephanie turned around, Tomi was peeking out the front door.

"I wonder what kind of surprise they're planning?" she said.

"You listened to us talking."

"Yeah."

"So, no ideas about what this surprise might be?"

"No, Mom."

"Tomi..."

"Well. I did tell them I wanted it to snow really, really bad for Christmas."

"They might try to make it snow for you?"

"I don't know, Mom. How would they do that?"

How, indeed?

Len drove around the open residential neighborhood, peering across the wide lots for any sign of the twins. There were no fences, only a few scattered, very tall old-world trees that cast spidery shadows in the glow of the streetlights.

On his third pass, rolling slowly along with headlights off and the window open, biting wind curling the hairs on his neck, he found them. Or rather, *heard* them. An annoying buzzing, like multiple snowblowers, came across the field from town. Mixed in with the buzzing were the angry voices of two young people cursing and dogging each other in loud whispers.

He stopped the car and killed the engine. Two figures, the size of his children, walked along the neighborhood road. They were carrying small, boxy objects, and they appeared to be pursued and harassed by whining harpies, which darted and spun around them, dark shapes with flat tops and hanging feet, like hummingbird spiders.

Len sighed and slipped out of the car, moving low across the Flowers' backyard to cut off his little conspirators. When he'd placed himself in their path, he stood and cleared his throat. They didn't see or hear him until they nearly ran into him.

"Oh! Oh!" they both said. They fiddled with the boxes they were carrying, and the drones settled to the ground and fell silent. A weird calm settled over the yard. Surely Stephanie or Tomi or at least one of their neighbors had heard the noise.

"Hi, Dad!" said Brendel. In the dim moonlight, his smile looked macabre, like a pale skeleton. "What are you doing here?"

"I believe that's my question, isn't it? Although I think I already have the answer."

"We told you everything would be fine, Father," said Hilary. "So far, so good."

"Drones and snow. Fill me in, please."

The twins gave him an energetic and innocently plausible scheme to cover the Flowers' yard in artificial snow from misting modules on the drones. Gently falling flakes, clear and driven—and loud. Everyone in the neighborhood would hear them.

"You guys stole these drones. If we don't return them now, you're going to be in big trouble."

"We can get it done before anyone knows they're gone. Mr. Flowers doesn't get to the store until about ten o'clock every morning."

"You've been planning this for a while, I see. Scoping out Mr. Flowers' schedule?"

Mr. Flowers—Stephanie's father, Tomi's grandfather. Len looked toward the Flowers' house. There were two very fine women inside who needed a break, a good cheering up that a pretty snow might bring. Maybe Mr. Flowers wouldn't press charges.

"It's not going to work, guys. It would take too much water, and I think the drones are going to lose their charges before you can cover the yard."

"Well, what if we just cover the front lawn near the door?" asked Hilary.

"Yeah, so Tomi can see it from her bedroom window. Miss Flowers is a real nice lady, Dad, don't you think?" said Brendel. The kids' faces lit up, and they passed looks across to each other.

What a stupid man—a lonely man—would do for the attentions of a woman.

"Yes, the two Miss Flowerses are nice ladies." Sigh. "Stay put and hide by that fence. I'll run home and fill up the big water coolers and be right back."

"Yay! Yay!" they whispered.

Leave it to two cunning eleven-year-olds to push their father to follow a fool's path to try to be a hero.

The buzzing grew closer, like giant hordes of bees were descending on the neighborhood. Stephanie set her book down and went to the front windows. There was nothing there but the empty night and the lone streetlight illuminating a circle of grey pavement at the street corner. Lights came on at two of the houses on the street, and Mrs. Jenkins poked her grey-haired head out the front door and looked around.

The noise grew louder, moving around to the front yard, where wavering shadows like great birds swept back and forth across the lawn. From above, thin threads of white began falling from the sky. They touched the cold ground and lay there in the calm night, shimmering with little glimmers of sparkle.

Snow? There wasn't any in the forecast. Not snow—something weird and thready. But pretty.

"Mom!" Tomi joined her mother at the front door. "It's snowing!"

"It can't be."

"But look! It is!"

As they watched, three people walked into the front yard, silhouetted by the streetlight: one tall and lean, the others shorter and moving around, dancing from foot to foot. Len and his children. The kids held black boxes and fiddled with the controls on them. Len, carrying some sort of large bucket or drink cooler, looked around nervously.

Above them, drones weaved back and forth across the sky, dropping little streamers of glistening white, which settled down gently through the air. A fine layer was beginning to form over the dry grass around the front patio.

"Mom! Can I go outside in the snow?"

Stephanie sighed. Len finally saw her standing on the front porch. He was too far away for her to tell, but he seemed to be smiling.

"Put on your coat first."

"Yay!"

Tomi ran to her room like she hadn't done in months, so long ago that Stephanie had almost forgotten her daughter's incompressible energy and abandon. She returned almost in a flash and rushed out onto the grass in white gym shoes, holding her arms out and spinning, spinning in the glittering white that fell, swirling around her. Stephanie didn't even try to stop the joyful tears that streamed down her face as she watched her daughter.

A new sound joined the buzzing—horns and sirens—and flashing red and blue lights appeared as two county sheriff's cars pulled up to the house.

"Evening, ma'am," said one of the deputies, coming up to Stephanie. "We've gotten a report of a disturbance in the neighborhood." *Thanks, Mrs. Jenkins.* Len was talking with the other sheriff and moving his hands about. The children stepped into the shadows. Hilary landed one of the drones in the yard so Brendel could refill the water tank.

"Not much of a disturbance, really, sir. Just some of our friends having fun. My daughter's been ill, and her friends were trying to make it snow for her—it was her Christmas wish."

An hour later, Tomi smiled up at the cold twists of falling snow on her face, her ears. It felt better than a cool alcohol bath when you were burning with fever. Someone had called the local drone club, and now dozens of noisy electric radio-operated drones crossed and recrossed over the yard, spinning threads of glistening white that fell to the ground in a swirling dance of light, covering over the dry grass like a cotton blanket.

"I told you we could get them together," she said to the twins, stealing a glance to where her mother and their father stood, their arms around each other.

Hilary said, "I was the one who said that."

Brendel rolled his eyes.

Hilary said, "Everyone in our family has a favorite Mozart work. What's yours?" She gave Brendel a hopeful smile.

Tomi thought about all the Mozart she'd been listening to on the classical station. "What about *K-321*?"

The twins shook their heads. "That one's vulgar," said Brendel. "It's about someone's behind."

"Wow. Okay, how about *K-51*."

Hilary and Brendel thought about that one, then their faces lit up.

"That's a good one!" said Hilary.

"Yep. I like it," added Brendel. "*Köchel 51, the Symphony in D*. It's a little opera that Mozart wrote when he was twelve."

"Well, we'll all be twelve soon," said Tomi, "so it's appropriate."

"And not boring or lame," said Brendel.

"Why did you choose *K-51*?" Hilary asked.

"Well, I wanted *321*, because we're three people from one family and two from another. Three and two makes one, see? But we're also five people hopefully making one family, so I picked *51*."

The others nodded.

"Pinky shake!" said Hilary, and they all linked their little fingers, which were crazy warm even with the cold air around them.

Stephanie leaned into Len's arms and allowed herself to be held by him. White streamers fell from a starry sky, around them and on them, cool to the touch, and oh, her skin felt hot on her face and neck. She didn't want to let go, even knowing the kids and her neighbors and all the others who had come at the sheriff's call were watching them. She didn't care.

Len said, "This is nice."

"Beautiful. Like being in a dream, isn't it?" She pointed to a white card poking from the pocket of his coat. "What's that?"

"Oh, this? An invitation to a New Year's Eve Party at Agnes Newsome's bookstore." He nodded at Agnes, who'd walked over from her house and was talking to Stephanie's father, Noel Flowers, taking in the chaos that was the Flowers' yard. "I thought maybe...you'd like to go. If we can find sitters?"

Stephanie smiled and extracted a similar white card from her own pocket. "I was trying to get up the nerve to ask you if you'd like to go. My father told me he would watch Tomi for me if she wasn't up to going. I'm sure he wouldn't mind if your kids stayed as well."

They watched their children chatting, and it seemed Tomi's face grew brighter and more ruby-cheeked. Stephanie said, "Dad told me you bought those drones for your children last week."

"Yes. I spoil them terribly."

"Are you going to tell them, or let them think you all broke the law?"

"I don't know. Maybe being the rogue father for a few hours will gain some respect for me. They think I'm heroic."

"He also told me about the mister attachments, and how they could be used to make fake snow. What a sweet and brilliant idea."

"I can't claim it. It was your father's."

They laughed. They held hands. It was beautiful and serene, a scene from a New England wintertime postcard.

Agnes Newsome admired the winter scene: a rural homestead in western Vermont. Cold and calm night sky. Drones buzzing overhead, misting snow.

"Did you call the drone club?" Agnes asked Noel Flowers, who stood nearby.

"Might've done," Noel said with a grin.

In the corner of the yard, Edgewood's volunteer firefighters and a couple neighborhood men had set up the walls of a portable mini-skating rink, and two of the fire-fighters were using a hose from their big white truck to fill it with water while Christmas music played from the truck's PA system. The water in the little rink would be frozen in a day or two, by Christmas morning for sure.

Standing near the house's front porch were five people: three children, all about eleven years old, two in gray sweatpants and hooded jackets, and one in a white and blue coat and PJ bottoms. The children were practically bouncing with delight and whispering nervously to each other. Two adults, their parents, stood a few feet away, in a comfortable embrace.

One of the drones descended and hovered above the two parents. From it dangled a bushy green branch with white berries. The children pointed to the drone and called to the parents, who looked at each other uncomfortably, then moved together for a chaste kiss, which resolved into a a kiss that lingered.

"Finally," said Noel.

"I'd about given up on getting those two together," Agnes agreed. "I never saw two people more made for each other that fought so hard against it."

"He's a good man," said Noel. "He won't abandon her like that clown did when Tomi was an infant."

"Yes. The drone idea was brilliant."

"I was just the messenger who told Len about it. It was really Stephanie's idea. She and that daughter of hers—when they see something they want..."

"Smart woman."

They watched the two parents holding hands in the beautiful white falling snow while the three children huddled in whispered conspiracy. They would be a handful, the three of them together.

Noel said, "Leave it to a couple old-timers like us to bring a family together, eh?"

"It does set a lovely mood, doesn't it?" Agnes let the thought hang for a moment. "So, what are you doing New Year's Eve?"

"Looks like I might be sitting for three kids."

"Well, I'm having a party at the store that night. Want to come? You can bring the kids."

He looked at her and was shocked by the glint in her eye. They'd known each other for years, with their shops next door to each other. Both widowed for too long. He looked at the three children, who alternated between looking over at their parents and stealing glances at him and Agnes. Did they know something he didn't? A little ways away, his daughter was talking and tilting her head at the tall, attractive man nodding his head, so obviously hanging on her words.

Something unexpected and exciting warmed his insides, like a shot of pricey bourbon on a cold Vermont night.

"I wouldn't miss it," he said, meaning it more than he had in a very long time.

CHRISTMAS DESSERT
JULIET NORDEEN

Anna popped open the passenger side door of Jordan's truck and looked down, quite a ways down, to see that he had parked in the mud. About three inches of mucky, tire-tracked sludge with rainwater pooling in the grooves. The whole parking area was mud, corner to corner, right up to where the thick underbrush started at the edge of the forest. All around them the morning's cold rain dripped from the slouching branches of the Douglas fir trees onto the shiny green leaves of the salal and huckleberry bushes.

"Problem?" Jordan asked, and she turned to see he was smirking at her from behind the wheel. His short dark hair sneaking out adorably from under his bright red baseball cap. His dark mustache and goatee turning a simple smile into a full-fledged come-on.

She didn't want to wuss out on him, look like a city-girl princess in his eyes. He had warned her to wear boots. She had thought he meant boots like "we're going to drive down to the nursery and pick out a tree" boots, not "let's go stomp through oozing muck" boots, so she had worn her new suede Steve Madden knee-highs. Beside the fact that they were cute, the heels made her almost as tall as him. Almost. If she stepped out of the truck into that slop they'd be ruined.

She pointed down at her feet and gave him a pleading look of desperation.

He laughed. "Do you know how cute you are?"

Because there was no polite answer to that question, Anna stalled by tucking her curly blond hair back behind her ear, snagging her gold hoop earring as she did.

"Hang on," he said. "I might have something."

A cold breeze cut into the truck as Jordan hopped out the driver's side door. She watched him through the extended cab windows as he unlocked the tool box in the bed of the truck. The diamond-plate lid blocked her view when he raised it so she couldn't see what he was foraging for, but she could feel the vibrations through the floorboards as he shoved stuff around. He apparently found what he was looking for pretty quickly, then slammed the lid and walked around the passenger side.

"Maybe these will fit," he said as he held out a pair of black rubber boots. She'd once seen a farmer wear a pair like them on a grade-school class trip to learn about dairy cows.

"They look kinda big."

"Never fear." He grinned and reached into one of the boots like a magician and came out with a pair of industrial-looking crew socks. Grey, with bright orange reinforcement at the toes, heels, and around the cuff. "Gotcha covered."

"Thanks."

Anna slipped out of her boots and pulled the thick socks

over her super-cute Rudolph the Reindeer ones and then put on the rubber boots. They were still more than a size too big, and didn't have much tread left on the bottoms, but they would be better than what she'd worn.

He gave her a hand down from the cab. As she reached back in to get her bag and he said, "Probably better to leave that in the truck."

"But, my phone."

"Once the trail gets into the shadow of the ridge, there's no cell service." He pointed in the direction of a rusty yellow vehicle gate with a big Road Closed sign that blocked-off a rock-cobbled road. The road passed through the wall of giant fir trees that stood like a giant fence, and beyond was a large clearing showing the white of the midday overcast sky. On the far side of the clearing she caught a glimpse of a mountainside full of more evergreens ramping up into the low clouds.

Anna pulled her new iPhone out of the side pocket of her purse—it had been her first official grown-up purchase with her first official grown-up paycheck—and saw that she had only one bar of 4G service. Not even LTE. Still, she decided to pocket her phone and leave her bag in the truck.

"I just said to leave your phone." The corners of Jordan's mouth fell into a frown that made Anna freeze with her phone half in and half out of her ski coat pocket.

"I want to take pictures of you cutting down the tree."

They held there, frozen in time for a few seconds, but then Jordan smiled again and he said, "I just don't want it to fall out of your pocket while we're up there searching for your perfect Christmas tree." He bent over to kiss her on the forehead, his breath smelled like the whiskey-laced coffee they'd been sipping on, on the ferry over from Seattle to the peninsula. "Lose something up there and you're never gonna find it again."

Anna looked back at the hillside of trees and decided he was right. "Okay, but I have to snap a shot of this and post it or my family will never believe I actually came out here and did this."

Jordan was reluctant but he did smile for the selfie with the dripping trees behind them. While Anna posted it to Instagram, slow as molasses, he grabbed the small orange-and-white chainsaw from the bed of the truck and waited for her at the gate.

Their walk up the logging road was slow going because of the stupid rubber boots. The roadway was made of fist-sized basalt rocks whose flat faces were slick with moisture and pale green moss. She just about turned her ankle every fifth or sixth step, but Jordan was patiently walking beside her, making conversation to distract her.

"So who all's gonna be hanging out on Christmas day?" he asked.

"Megan and Molly, for sure. They're hosting," she said as they reached the center of the forest clearing, an area that Jordan warned her wouldn't be pretty because it had been logged-off a couple of years before. There were huge stacks of brush and branches piled every hundred yards along the road. Ugly, wispy Scotch broom snagged with withered blackberry canes carpeted the clearing as completely as the mud had filled the parking area. "I'm guessing it's going to be most of the same people from Orphan's Thanksgiving 'cause none of us has the vacation time to go home."

Though it had been hard missing Thanksgiving with her family for the first time, the crew from work had really made the best of it. They'd had roast turkey, if you could call it that, and all the fixings. Mostly it had been good for all of them to be together instead of holing up in their individual apartments, missing home. She smiled at the memory of that day, happy that one of her coworkers, Carter, had brought Jordan along to the gathering, even though extra guests had not been invited or expected.

She stopped to straighten out her left sock that had been trying walking its way off her foot inside her boot. As she stood up she risked asking him, "I know Carter can't make it because he got stuck Bossing the data center on Christmas Day, but I'd love it if you still came."

Her heart skipped a beat as she waited for his reply.

"Can't," he said as they started walking again, the chainsaw resting on his right shoulder. "The fam would be zero chill if I didn't show for Christmas."

Anna was bummed and she slowed her pace down a little, trying to figure out if it was worth trying to plan something with him for Christmas Eve.

Jordan didn't seem to notice her falling back; he kept walking and turned to take a side trail that shot straight toward the tree-covered hillside. The going got easier as Anna stepped off the rocky road and onto the packed dirt trail to follow him.

"And can you believe it?" Jordan kept talking without looking back. "I have to bring the dessert this year," he said.

"You know, I'm pretty good a making pies. I could maybe catch a ferry over after work on Christmas Eve, help you out," she offered.

Jordan turned back, the biggest smile of relief on his face. "I was kinda counting on you."

Acting Deputy Sheriff Modesta Quinn had just managed to wedge herself, and all the gear on her belt, back into the driver's seat of her cruiser when the radio squawked her unit number.

"Sam-6-2, CenCom."

"CenCom, Sam-6-2, copy," she replied, wincing as she always did that the folks at dispatch were still using her Corrections Officer designation, starting with Sam, rather than calling her Union-6-2, like the other deputies in the department. Sheriff Cassidy said she would fix that, as soon as possible, but she had a few bigger fires burning her ass.

"Sam-6-2, what's your status?"

"Sam-6-2 back in service. Just finished serving Civil paper at the 4000 block of Harper Road."

"Copy, Sam-6-2. 10-61 at 345 Sedgwick Road."

A 10-61. Great. Request for Miscellaneous Public Service. More grunt work that could easily be done by any one of the cadets or volunteers, and they saved it for her. As if she was just another butt in the chair.

"Copy, CenCom," she said as she started the engine, pulled out of the driveway, and headed back for the main road. Sedgwick was just a mile down, and she knew that the 300 block meant either the Burger King, the mom-n-pop yakisoba joint, or the Subway. Somebody back at the House was probably sending her on a late dinner run before everything rolled up for the night. "Who wants what?" she asked, unable to keep the resentment out of her voice.

"Sam-6-2, contact citizen, last name Fields, Frank-Ida-Edward-Lincoln-David-Sam, first name Jordan, John-Oscar-Robert-David-Adam-Nora, initial M-Mary. Caucasian male, twenty-eight years of age. Five foot eleven, one hundred and ninety pounds."

Modesta sat up straighter, which wasn't easy to do with

cuffs and a taser and her flashlight pinched between her back and the seat. Maybe it wasn't a dinner run after all. "Copy, CenCom, what's the issue?"

"Sam-6-2, SPD requesting KCSO assistance with a 10-57." The dispatcher went on to share the name of a missing person, Anna B. Kramer, aged twenty-two, gone at least two days, Seattle PD was investigating. They had gotten a panicked call from Anna's parents out of state. "Fields possibly last known contact. Assess and report."

"Sam-6-2, copy. En route. ETA three minutes."

"Twenty-one fifteen." The dispatcher announced the time for the recorders to end the dialogue.

As much as Modesta yearned to flip the switch that would ignite the light bar on the top of her Explorer, she knew that a simple check-in with some local guy to ask him an informational question wouldn't qualify as an emergency. She did roll through both empty intersections along the way, though, because she could.

345 Sedgwick turned out to be the Subway sandwich shop at the northwest corner of Sedgwick Road and Sidney. Its lights were the only sign of life in the little strip mall, which was all decked out in green and red twinkling lights for the holidays. The burger flippers and the Nguyen family had gone home already. Port Orchard was a pretty sleepy town on a Wednesday night, even if it was almost Christmas. She pulled up and parked right in front of the door to the little glass-fronted fast-food joint and noticed that the hours posted on the door said they would be open until midnight, except, of course, for Christmas and New Year's Eves.

Inside were a dozen yellow Formica tables, each with a pair of tan benches. The tile floors shone damply from a recent cleaning. A college-aged girl with a long brunette ponytail worked conscientiously behind the counter laying plastic wrap over the black food bins set into the refrigerated counter beneath the half-domed glass. Probably working nights to pay for community college. Since most retail food establishments worked a crew of two during non-peak hours, Modesta suspected that if Fields was working, he would be in the back.

"CenCom, Sam-6-2. 10-97 at 345 Sedgwick." She followed standard operating procedure and called in to notify dispatch that she was leaving her vehicle, even though the warmly lit little restaurant looked about as dangerous as her mother's new kitten.

CenCom copied and time stamped the call-in.

The restaurant door opened into the expected wash of fresh baked bread and a merry tinkling from a string of jingle bells hanging from the top of the doorframe. The employee at the counter looked up to welcome Modesta in the typical way, though the words "Welcome to Subway" did get stuck in the girl's throat when she realized that Modesta was a deputy and not a regular customer. It made Modesta wonder if there might be something for her to be nervous about.

"You the manager?"

"Shift manager, yeah. What can I do for you?"

"I'm looking for Jordan Fields. He here tonight?"

"Yes, ma'am," the girl said, even though she was maybe five years younger than Modesta. It was the uniform. Added thirty pounds and fifteen years. "He's doin' prep. Lemme get him for you."

Modesta leaned against the garland-decorated pony wall that separated the ordering line from the seating, and waited. There was fan noise coming from the bread ovens behind the counter, and something louder, an automated dishwasher perhaps, coming from the back room. The background noise masked most of the girl's statement to Fields, but it was clear from her tone that she was worried.

Jordan Fields, however, was clearly *not* worried. He sauntered out of the back room, casually looking around to see who was asking after him, and easily made eye contact with Modesta. He was the promised five-foot-eleven, but maybe not quite a hundred and ninety pounds. His Adam's apple was a bit too pronounced. Not tweaker-thin, but he could use a few of the sandwiches he slung for his boss. He wore the forest-green uniform polo shirt and apron that Modesta associated with Subway restaurants, and the green visor that somehow made his dark hair, sparse mustache, and scraggly goatee stand out even more against his pale skin. He didn't appear to have any tattoos or obvious scars. Other women might find his rangy look attractive, but she had seen too many like him during her thirty-two months as a Corrections Officer at the county jail to take an interest.

"Jordan Fields?" she asked.

He nodded and gave her a sly smile that was probably meant to be flirtatious, or maybe an attempt at being dashing. She ignored the subtle come-on and asked for some identification instead. His middle name, Michael, matched the initial on the call-out.

"Do you know an Anna Kramer, have you seen her recently?" she asked, watching his face very carefully for any tells.

"Anna?" he asked, normal concern crossed his face, and Modesta was relieved that he knew who she was asking about. She always got sent out on the department's wild goose chases, and it was getting old.

"Is she okay?" he asked.

"As far as we know," Modesta said, being professionally optimistic about the unknowns of the situation without setting false expectations.

Normally that kind of statement settled a person down, anchored them in the conversation, but she noticed that Fields's eyes flicked upward and paused there a few seconds before coming back to look at hers. It was as if he was harboring some kind of contrary thought. Maybe he didn't believe her, or maybe he knew something she didn't.

"When was the last time you saw Anna?"

"Sunday," he answered without hesitation. "She came over on the ferry. We hung out."

Modesta noticed that Fields's shift manager had stuck her head around the corner, curious about what was going on. Who could blame her?

"Hanging out? What did you do?" Modesta asked. She was expecting the typical "Netflix and chill."

"We went and found her a little Christmas tree."

"You go to a tree lot?"

"No. It was her first Christmas here so she wanted the whole Northwest going-out-and-hunting-down-her-own-tree thing." He rolled his eyes like it was the most childish thing he had ever heard of. "I took her out toward Lake Tahuyeh."

Modesta knew that he was referring to the wildly forested area that covered thousands of acres where Kitsap County met Mason County, due east of Port Orchard. It was a patchwork of privately held and state-owned forest with hundreds of miles of logging roads that branched off of State Highway 3.

"Did you find a tree?"

"About this high. For her apartment," he said, and put

his hand at the bottom of his ribcage. "She had to carry it back on the boat so it couldn't be too big."

"And when was the last time you saw Anna?"

He thought about it for a second, his eyes looking up again, and then reported, "I dropped her off at the ferry. Last boat back to Seattle Sunday night."

"Three days ago?"

He nodded.

"Bremerton or Bainbridge?" she asked, knowing that there were two different routes that left Kitsap County and headed to downtown Seattle's dock.

"Bremerton. I kissed her goodbye at 11:30 and she headed straight down the loading ramp. Boat was supposed to leave at 11:40, I think."

Modesta had not been taking notes until that point, but she did decide to pull her pad out and write that last part down. It would be very easy for SPD to check the state department of transportation cameras and find a young woman carrying a Christmas tree aboard the last sailing of the night. Hell, she'd stick out on any sailing with that kind of carry-on.

"And you haven't talked or texted with her since?"

He shook his head.

"No Instabooking or Facegramming?"

Again he shook his head.

"That unusual?"

He shrugged.

Something about his nonchalance rubbed her the wrong way. Maybe it was just the way so many guys their age carried such a distaste for commitment. Maybe it was the weird hands-off culture so prevalent in the county, *Just leave me alone and let me do my thing*. Maybe it was just this guy.

"No chemistry?" Modesta asked. The question was beyond the scope of helping Seattle PD with their missing person's case, but she was curious.

The question got his brain clicking into gear and she could see a hot flush run up his neck. Yeah, they'd had chemistry. If nothing else, thinking of her that way had gotten his motor running a little. That was something. Made sense if he had been willing to spend his whole day off running her all over hell-and-gone to get what they could have found out front of any Albertson's grocery store. Thinking of it, there were pre-cut Christmas trees for sale right across the intersection from where they were standing.

"I guess not," he said, straight-faced and catching Modesta by surprise. "She's sweet and all, but you know those college girls. They're just too smart for their own good."

At that, Fields's shift manager *harrumphed* and then disappeared in the back, confirming Modesta's first impression of her being a student. That misogynistic comment was probably going to cost Fields some scut work. Chopping onions by hand seemed like a good way to make a hard-ass cry.

Modesta made another note, capturing Fields's last remarks, and decided that even though she had some concerns about the guy she also had enough to report back for SPD's investigation. "Okay. Thanks." She put her notebook away and turned to go.

In a way, it was a test. She was testing Fields' feelings for Anna. She intended to leave without actually offering him any information about the situation to see if he cared enough about her to ask again. Modesta managed to get to the door, ring the jingle bells once again, and leave without him asking anything more.

That just didn't sit right with Modesta, even if he was protecting his ego by playing down what Anna meant to him.

A cold rain had started to fall while Modesta was in the sandwich shop. It beaded up on the emerald-green hood of her cruiser and reflected the twinkling red and green lights along the building's roof line. She wedged herself back into the car and called in.

"Sam-6-2, CenCom."

"Copy, Sam-6-2."

"Sam-6-2 completed 10-61 at 345 Sedgwick. Requesting information."

"Go ahead Sam-6-2."

"CenCom, who's liaising with SPD on that 10-57?"

There was a pause before the dispatcher came back. "Sam-2-6, that 10-57 goes to Queen-5-5."

Queen-5-5 was the radio designation for the sheriff herself. Modesta wasn't sure if that meant anything about the investigation, but she did feel like it would be a great opportunity to make a positive impression on The Boss Lady.

"CenCom, Sam-6-2. Is Queen-5-5 10-40?" Modesta asked, hoping to get Sheriff Cassidy on the phone.

"Sam-2-6, 10-23." They were asking Modesta to stand by, probably while somebody pinged the sheriff to see if she was available.

"10-4, CenCom," Modesta acknowledged, and then a thought occurred to her. If you're gonna tell the boss you got a hinky feeling about a possible perpetrator, it would be helpful to have something to back it up. Like maybe this guy had an outstanding warrant. Couldn't hurt to check it out while she was still staring through the window at him. "Sam-6-2 I'm looking for 10-29 on 10-61 subject Fields." She spelled out his first and last and initial, just to be thorough.

"Copy, Sam-6-2, 10-23."

Stand by, again. It felt like that's what most of the job was. Forever standing by.

"Sam-6-2, copy."

"Twenty-one thirty-four." Dispatch coded the time.

Modesta would have been willing to sit in her cruiser for the next two hours and twenty-six minutes, intermittently wiping the red and green tinged raindrops from her windshield, just to study Fields as he closed out his shift.

Initially he stood in one place behind the cash register at the end of the counter, but it was obvious by the way he kept looking out the front windows of the shop that he was aware Modesta was still sitting out front. He started to fidget nervously, fingering the neck strap on his apron, and eventually he started to pace back and forth behind the long counter like something feral stuck inside a glass-walled cage.

She was watching the raindrops accumulate between wiper swipes when her duty phone rang. The sheriff, responding to her 10-40. Keeping the discussion off the radio, which was monitored by all sorts of people with scanners and Internet streaming.

"Yes, ma'am," Modesta said, answering the call.

"What's up, deputy?" Modesta liked it that The Boss Lady treated her like a full member of the team even though she hadn't quite gotten through her full two years as a Corrections Officer before being promoted from the jailhouse to the department. Big fires burning, needed enough good hands to cover all the bases after all.

"I just spoke with Jordan Fields." Modesta knew the

sheriff was sharp and didn't need her to quote chapter and verse of the investigation. "How interested in this guy are we?"

"Sounds like SPD Missing Persons is just getting started. Why?"

She watched Fields continue to pace behind the counter. "I don't like him, ma'am. There's something odd about him, about his relationship with the girl."

"Facts or feelings, Deputy?"

Modesta swallowed a lump before admitting it was all feelings. "His statement is on the up-and-up. Says he put her on the ferry for home, with a little Christmas tree. Last boat out of Bremerton on Sunday night, just before midnight."

There was a pause before the sheriff answered, she was probably making a note. "Okay, Deputy Quinn. Run the guy for warrants. If there's something active on him, you can bring him in, otherwise I'll pass this back to SPD and we'll see what happens next. With any luck she just lost her phone and she'll call her folks from work tomorrow to wish them a Merry Christmas Eve. It may all come to nothing."

"Yes, ma'am. They're running his 10-29 as we speak. I sure hope you're right about the girl," Modesta said.

"Me, too. Goodnight, deputy. Be safe out there."

Modesta hung up and kept standing by for dispatch, listening to radio calls go out, catching dispatch's time stamps tick away the minutes.

Dispatch got back to Modesta. There were surprisingly no warrants on Jordan M. Fields. "Copy, CenCom. Sam-6-2, please put me back in service."

"Twenty-two oh-three." CenCom time-stamped her back into rotation for the last two hours of her shift.

Modesta went back to speed trapping the thirty-five

mile-per-hour zone between the recreational cannabis shop and the AM/PM convenience store, peeling off from time to time to roam her sector of the south end of the county when there wasn't much traffic. She just couldn't get Anna Kramer or Jordan Fields out of her head.

The answer to what was bugging Modesta became clear when she got back to the House, digging out answers to a couple of questions to finish up her paperwork before signing-out for the night. On a whim she had run Jordan Fields's Known Associates and came back with the photo of a face she remembered well from her first year as a Corrections Officer, Andrew John Fields, Registered Sex Offender. He had been on her block, held without bail as he awaited trial for Fraud and Possession-With-Intent charges. She remembered that he'd cut a deal and got out on Probation with Time Served.

That's why the jail was such a damned revolving door. Nothing ever stuck to these guys.

As Modesta compared the DMV photo for Jordan Fields to the latest mug shot for Andrew Fields there was no question about family resemblance. Andrew was older, maybe as much as a generation. His short beard was full of salt, and his eyebrow ridge was narrower and less prominent, but the eyes, nose, cheekbones, jaw, and hairline were all spot-on.

She wouldn't admit to herself why, but she pulled up the elder Fields' info on the RSO database and scribbled down his address. It was in her sector, in Olalla, the little farm community just south of Port Orchard.

It was nice to know where the bad guys lived.

With that, Modesta dropped her reports with the Watch Commander and went home to try to sleep.

Late the next morning Modesta was off-duty, sitting in her private vehicle, on a little wide spot in the roadside just in front of a real estate sign. An acre of overpriced vacant land for sale. She had been to that particular neighborhood of Olalla a time or ten to bust up house parties and investigate reports of shots fired. The warren of little two-lane roads without sidewalks was named after lots of peoples' Grandmas—Barbara Street, Georgette Lane, Beverly Court. It was mostly a patchwork of single-wide mobile homes and undeveloped land. The terrain rolled steeply under dripping, drooping cedar trees.

She had been sitting for about thirty minutes, and had counted six different stray cats wandering around, when Union-4-3 rolled up on her. Blue and reds flashing brightly in the leaden daylight. Deputy Collins, who had taken her under his wing the first couple of weeks after her promotion, stopped his cruiser with its driver's door even with hers, but pointed in the opposite direction.

Modesta buzzed her window down. "What's up, Collins?"

"Got a call-out on an 11-54."

"How dare you call my pickup truck suspicious?" It was an attempt at a joke, but she didn't get a laugh out of Collins. That wasn't a good sign. Neither was the fact that she had been noticed loitering around, probably by an overly sharp member of the Neighborhood Watch, and had her plate called in.

"If you'd had your ears on you'd have heard all about it and gotten the hell out of here." Collins looked over his right shoulder toward where Modesta was focused, in a thousand-yard-stare kind-of way. The residence, buried in a quarter acre of waist-high dead grass, was a twenty year-old fifth-wheel travel trailer with a tiny wooden staircase tacked on beneath its narrow doorway. The mold-encrusted siding and blackberry vines growing all over the trailer's tip-out said it probably hadn't been on the road in more than a decade, and probably never would be again.

"That wouldn't happen to be 15195 Rosemary Loop, would it?" Collins asked down his nose.

Modesta admitted that it might be. She had not been able to get Anna Kramer or either of the Fields men out of her brain all night. On her way to Costco to pick up a half-ton of toilet paper and one of those five-buck roast chickens for the family's after-Mass Christmas Eve dinner, she decided to cruise by the address Andrew Fields had been registered at. She wasn't too surprised when she found a truck she knew to be registered to Jordan Fields parked out front of it.

"Just keeping an eye on things, hoping Seattle PD will show up and at least talk to them."

"Exactly what Queen-5-5 thought. She said, and I quote, if I found you still planted here that you could either forget this little extracurricular surveillance and move along all on your own, or I could escort you to her office to chat, forthwith."

Modesta dropped her chin to her chest. "Crap."

"What are you doing, Quinn?" Collins asked, half angry and half sympathetic. "You're barely an Assistant Deputy One, not a damn detective."

She eyed the trailer suspiciously. "Not yet."

"And you won't get to be a detective if you keep bucking command and get busted back to the jail crew. Or worse."

Modesta gave him a sidelong glance. "I'm not bucking command." She pointed at the trailer. "Something's not right with that family. I spent enough time dropping Andrew Fields—"

"The uncle," Collins filled in, helpfully. Which really confused Modesta. Was he warning her off, or not?

"Uncle. Fine. I don't care if he's Santa Claus's long-lost half brother. He's evil, an evil bastard. And if Anna got tied up with him and that nephew of his, she's probably in over her head."

"Probably," Collins agreed. "But this is Seattle PD's case. You aren't in the loop."

Modesta gritted her teeth to quiet a growl of frustration. "But they haven't eyeballed either of these guys. I have."

"Okay, I get it, they're bad guys. But why are you so hell-bent on ruining your career over them?"

"Because it's Christmas!" Modesta shouted. "Anna Kramer should be home with her family!"

"Quit sounding like a damn Rookie. Shit happens, you know that. Sometimes shit happens to good people...even on Christmas. You got nothin' here but dislike for a couple of assholes. We got enough to worry about without inventing problems because you got a soft spot for the holidays. Go home, Quinn, and get your head on straight before your shift starts. Do your job, let Seattle PD do theirs."

———

Do your job.

That thought nagged at Modesta all shift long, through midnight Mass with her mother, even through the small after-Mass feast with her aunts and uncle.

Do your job.

It kept her awake past four o'clock Christmas morning

and got her up again just a few hours later. She brewed coffee in her little one-bedroom cottage and flipped on the morning news, even though she knew it would make her cranky.

Ten minutes into the broadcast they did a thirty-second piece on Anna Kramer's missing person's story. The Seattle PD Information Officer showed an official-looking photo of the twenty-two-year-old blond. She had a round face, long curly hair, and a close-lipped smile that betrayed a lack of self-confidence. The story closed on another image of Anna, a selfie taken with "a friend" that Modesta recognized immediately as Jordan Fields. Anna's family had stated the photo posted to Instagram was the last contact they had with her.

Modesta paused the broadcast and studied the selfie. Anna was wearing big hoop earrings and quite a bit of makeup. Pretty dolled-up for a stomp through the woods. Between that and the bright smile on her face as she tipped her head intimately toward Fields's gaunt cheek, it was clear to Modesta that Anna had been feeling some chemistry, too.

The setting of the photo was all Tahuyeh. Native scrub brush and thick-trunked fir trees were the basic fare for most of the commercial timber land in the area. The shot was too close to their faces for a whole lot of background detail but it did catch a front fender of Fields's truck and a sizable portion of the vehicle gate to the forest service road.

Knowing that some people lived on social media, Modesta grabbed her laptop and did a search on Instagram to see if she could find the photo from the newscast. It took two minutes. And there, following a quick sentence expressing how excited she was to be with Jordan,

Christmas tree hunting *squee*, there were a series of hash-tagged thoughts.

Including #ForestRoadGM1.

Hot damn.

Suddenly Modesta was in the mood to borrow her neighbor's Border Collie, Maggie, and go for a Christmas morning hike in the woods. It would feel good to stretch her legs a little before her last shift of the week.

The parking area for Forest Road GM1 was a fairly wide spot off the main highway. Enough room for a dozen cars, or three logging trucks, whoever got there first. The tire and boot tracks in the mud looked like a mishmash of dozens of vehicles and pedestrians, but nothing that specifically confirmed that Fields or Anna had been there. The normal roadside trash—beer cans, cigarette butts, and fast food wrappers—had gotten caught in the underbrush along with large chunks of dull-orange pumpkin flesh. It looked like someone had been target shooting at a bunch of jack o'lanterns.

Modesta pulled in to a spot right next to the vehicle gate, obviously the same one from Anna Kramer's selfie. Though Modesta was off-duty until four, she had packed her service weapon in her backpack along with a water of bottle, a couple of granola bars, and a turkey hotdog for Maggie, who was bouncing around in the passenger seat like a kid on crack.

The forecast was for rain by sundown, but she had gotten lucky and found patches of blue sky peeking through the clouds. The chilly wind coming off Hood Canal to the west carried a damp salty smell as it tousled the branches of the hundred-year-old fir trees along the edge of the parking area.

She leashed up Maggie and they set off down the forest road toward a clearing full of slash piles waiting to be burned. The pup didn't seem to mind the unevenness of the road surface as much as Modesta did, but it made sense that semi trucks loaded down with forty-foot sections of raw timber needed more than pea gravel to get in and out with their haul.

When they reached the approximate middle of the clearing, Modesta stopped and tried to look at the scene through different eyes. First Anna's. Then Jordan's.

For Anna, a California transplant, the whole area this side of the Puget Sound would probably feel strange, foreign. Every part of the forest would probably look very much like every other part of it. Trees. Bushes. Ground cover. Maybe she knew the names of some of them, maybe not.

But Jordan was a local boy. Raised in Kitsap County. Steeped in the forest from the time he could walk. He probably knew all the best hunting spots, hiking trails, and romantic vistas. He surely knew that the Douglas fir trees in this part of the forest were either too big to use in a small Seattle apartment, or protected from Christmas tree harvesting because they were replantings.

So why would Jordan bring Anna here, to this cleared patch of the timber industry? It would be like her taking him on a romantic outing to some railside shanty on the outskirts of Los Angeles.

Modesta let Maggie off her leash to sniff around, chase a spotted towhee or two, while she grabbed her duty phone and pulled up a satellite view of the area. Google Maps was a great app for civilians, but she was glad to have access to the Search and Rescue COPAS-SARSAT technology. Their maps were updated much more frequently, and because you had to have an official reason to access them in the first place, the image resolution was far more detailed. Maybe not military-grade, but good enough for her to get a better idea what was lurking in the woods along Forest Road GM1.

There was obviously a lot of green around her, a lot of trees, but as she panned the image back and forth, like a virtual grid search, Modesta was able to pick out some anomalies in the great shag carpet of firs. A small pond. A clearing made by a landslide. And a small, metal-roofed structure, mostly shielded from view by overhead branches. Due east of the clearing. If the roof had not been made of semi-reflective metal, and the shot hadn't been necessarily taken on a sunny day, the structure might not have been visible at all in the satellite image.

Modesta looked up from the screen and turned toward the east. The clearing stretched about a hundred and fifty yards that direction until it hit a wall of trees. The forest ran flat for another couple hundred yards and then started to climb the flank of Green Mountain. Best guess said the structure was less than a half mile from where she was standing up that rise.

Could that have been why Jordan brought Anna to this spot?

Maggie had wandered ahead, following her nose along the road. About halfway between Modesta and the spot Maggie was intently sniffing there was a dirt trail. Just a track a couple of feet wide where the weeds and brambles had been trodden down to bare dirt. It left the road and ran straight toward the forest.

Could they have stood right here? Taken that trail?

She wandered up to the offshooting trail and searched

for signs of use. It may have started as a game trail, deer traversing the clearing in search of tender leaves and puddle water, but the path showed boot treads heading in both directions. The rain had wiped away the finer details, but there were clearly three or more sole prints involved.

Instinct flared in her heart. *What are you waiting for, get going!* But Modesta felt locked in place and couldn't step onto the dirt path.

Up until that moment, she was pretending to herself that she was just out for a walk with the neighbor's dog on state land. No. Big. Deal. But if she took that step. Followed that trail. Found the little metal-roofed structure hiding in the forest and peeked inside. There would be no way to deny, to herself or anyone else, that she had been searching for Anna Kramer all along.

She felt like she was just doing her job.

Why had they sent her out on that damn 10-61 if they didn't expect her to follow her instincts? To protect and serve? Didn't she *have* to go and take a look?

Collins wouldn't like it, and the sheriff would blow a gasket if she knew what Modesta was contemplating. The Boss Lady had been elected in November and had immediately gotten blindsided by a Federal Use-of-Force and Corruption investigation into eighteen members of the department, sidelining almost a third of the officers. A few retirees had come back to fill in the gaps, doing a favor to a woman they had served beside for years. A few experienced deputies from neighboring counties had been recruited. Then Sheriff Cassidy had been forced to promote Modesta and six others to keep the department rolls full.

All seven of the new Assistant Deputies had been warned not to let their early promotion from Corrections Officer go to their heads. They were still green. Greener than green. Greener than the emerald-colored Ford Explorers they drove every day. They still had much to learn, for their own safety and the safety of others. She, Cassidy, had meritoriously hand-selected each and every one of them and was trusting them to behave in a manner befitting the best traditions in law enforcement. Each had been rewarded their six-pointed tin star only after solemnly swearing to toe the line.

The line that Modesta unapologetically stepped over when she left the rock-cobbled forest service road and led a re-leashed Maggie onto the little dirt track. Guilty prickles followed her all the way to the tree line and then were replaced by a cold shiver as the underbrush dwindled to nothing and the shade of the giant firs enveloped her.

The trail led straight up the hill, mostly marked by voids in a thick carpet of brown and tan evergreen needles. Even as she walked, Modesta told herself that she was being foolish, jumping at nightmares. She optimistically searched the areas alongside the trail for a small tree stump and a pile of sawdust that would show the place where Anna's first Christmas tree had grown from a seedling until it was as tall as Jordan Fields's ribcage.

She saw no signs of a Christmas harvest.

She did, however, find the metal-roofed shed, about ten times the square footage of a portable toilet and about as tall. Constructed from scrap lumber, there was a single door made from a reinforced four-by-eight sheet of plywood. A piano hinge ran down the left edge and it was padlocked shut with a cheap hasp made of bent aluminum sheet metal screwed into the door and the adjoining wall on the right. The slanted roof, made from a single piece of corrugated galvanized steel, had a small, uncapped chimney poking through. The sign of blue-tinged smoke rising from within compelled Modesta to retreat twenty yards, pull her pistol from her pack, and tether Molly to a low branch.

As Modesta circled the ramshackle building and its small clearing she saw no windows. Heard nothing from inside.

It could have been no more than an overly ambitious deer blind. Poachers operated out in these woods all the time. Except that the building felt inhabited, was only lockable from the outside, and it was currently locked.

Probably not poachers.

And not what Modesta would call a charming little love shack.

There was a good chance Fields had brought Anna out here on the pretense of chopping down a Christmas tree because he knew about the shack. Given that no one had heard from Anna in days, it was possible that she was still inside.

The carpet of evergreen needles silenced Modesta's steps as she approached the shed opposite the side with the door. Pressing an ear to the rough wall showed it was warmer than the ambient air, but gave away nothing else. Still no sound or vibrations from inside.

Every instinct in Modesta's brain screamed about how possible it was, how likely it was, that Anna Kramer was inside, maybe just inches away, and probably scared for her life.

Modesta pulled her duty-phone out of her coat pocket to call it in and found that she had no signal. She knew she should take Maggie back to the safety of the truck and call for backup, but it felt like a betrayal to do that when Anna might be inside the shed. It would be cruel to leave without trying to help her.

She considered tapping on the wall, trying to provoke a response but also warning whomever was inside.

The exterior lock hasp told Modesta that if the situation was what she thought it was, it was also likely that neither Jordan, nor any of his family, were on site. Not inside the shed, anyway.

It would stand to reason that anybody locked inside that shed, even if it wasn't Anna Kramer, would probably welcome some help.

Modesta hammered three thuds on the middle of the back wall. It boomed like a big bass drum. "Anna? Anna Kramer?"

Ear to the wall, she heard a quiet response. Not a voice, but some kind of movement. A big object shifting against the wall, sliding on the floor.

Modesta paused, just to give the situation a moment to breathe, and then stalked around to the door. Three blows from the butt of her pistol stripped the hasp's mounting screws out of the wall and allowed the door to crack open outwardly.

Modesta held her position tight to the wall and flipped the door open about halfway with her fingertips. "Kitsap Sheriff! Anyone inside? Anna Kramer?"

The open door allowed enough light to see the whole inside of the shack. A bare plywood floor supported a cheap woodstove in one corner and a foul-smelling five-gallon bucket in the other. Sitting on a mildewed mattress, wearing a flimsy black lace neglige and propped against the back wall, Anna squinted her eyes against the light.

She attempted a few unintelligible words, and was obviously under the influence of something. Probably fentanyl, given the slack expression on her face and the injection marks on her arms. She tried again. "My name is

Anna," she said as her face took on a look of bleak humiliation, "and I will be your Christmas dessert."

Modesta rushed into the shack, knelt next to poor Anna, and wrapped her up with her own coat as the tears flowed.

"No, no, Anna," Modesta said as she rocked with her. "You are the best Christmas present ever."

ABOUT THE AUTHORS

One of four pseudonymous writing Crowes, **Dory Crowe** resides in Nobtucket—a quintessential, if mythical, Cape Cod town. Crowe stories have also appeared in DAW Books, in Level Best Books' *Best New England Crime*, and in Fiction River anthologies, as well as in *Alfred Hitchcock's Mystery Magazine*.

Leah R. Cutter writes page-turning, wildly imaginative fiction set in exotic locations such as a magical New Orleans, the ancient Orient, rural Kentucky, Seattle, Minneapolis, and many others. She writes fantasy, science fiction, mystery, literary, and horror fiction. Her short fiction has been published in magazines such *Alfred Hitchcock's Mystery Magazine* and *Talebones*, anthologies such as Fiction River, and on the web. Her long fiction has been published both by New York publishers as well as small presses. Read more books by Leah Cutter at KnottedRoadPress.com. and follow her blog at LeahCutter.com.

Dayle A. Dermatis is the author or coauthor of many novels (including snarky urban fantasy *Ghosted* and YA lesbian romance *Beautiful Beast*) and more than a hundred short stories in multiple genres, appearing in such venues as *Fiction River*, *Alfred Hitchcock's Mystery Magazine*, *Pulphouse Fiction Magazine*, *Heart's Kiss*, and DAW Books. Called the mastermind behind the Uncollected Anthology project, she also edits anthologies, and her own short fiction has been lauded in many year's best anthologies in erotica, mystery, and horror. She'd love to have you over for a virtual cup of tea or glass of wine at DayleDermatis.com, where you can also sign up for her newsletter and support her on Patreon.

C.H. Hung grew up among the musty book stacks of public libraries, where she found a lifelong love for good stories and lost 20/20 vision for good. Her stubbornly rational soul intersects with an irrational belief in magic, which means her stories are often as mixed up as she is, melding the plausible with myth and folklore. Her stories have appeared in *Analog SF&F*, *Ellery Queen Mystery Magazine*, *The Martian*, *DreamForge*, and *khōréō* magazines, as well as anthologies edited by Kevin J. Anderson and Kristine Kathryn Rusch, among others. Read more at CHhung.com.

Robert Jeschonek is an envelope-pushing, *USA Today* bestselling author whose fiction, comics, and nonfiction have been published around the world. His stories have appeared in *Clarkesworld*, *Pulphouse Fiction Magazine*, *Fiction River*, *Black Cat Mystery Magazine*, and many other publications. He has written official *Star Trek* and *Doctor Who* fiction and has scripted comics for DC, AHOY, and other publishers. Visit him online at www.bobscribe.com.

Michèle Laframboise feeds coffee grounds to her garden plants, runs long distances, and writes full-time in Mississauga, Ontario. Fascinated by sciences and nature since she could walk, she studied geography and engineering, but two recessions and her own social awkwardness kept the plush desk jobs away. Instead, she held a string of odd jobs to sustain her budding family: some quite dangerous, others quite tedious, all of them sources of inspiration. You can stop by at her website at Michele-Laframboise.com to say hello, or visit her publishing house EchoFictions.com to get a taste of her fiction!

Patrick Mammay lives in Arkansas. He's not sure how or why. He writes stories with dragons and stories without dragons.

C.J. Mattison's stories have appeared in anthologies from WMG Publishing, WordFire Press, and others. He writes in multiple genres, publishes novels in a space fantasy series, and dabbles in poetry. He lives in Dallas area with his wife and their rescue superhero dog Saber-Girl, calls his sourdough bread starter "Ursula" (K. Le Guin), and cooks crazy-good Cajun food for a Midwest Yankee.

Juliet Nordeen is a recovering engineer who lives on the gorgeous Kitsap Peninsula of Washington State. An avid reader and Dog Mom, she also loves to cook and so she has taken up recreational running to balance the scales, or at least to try to keep the scale in balance. You can find out more about her writing at www.julietnordeen.com.

Award-winning writer and editor Kristine Kathryn Rusch calls **Annie Reed** "a master short fiction writer." Annie is the author of well over three hundred short stories, some of which have been picked up for mystery best of the year volumes and short-listed for major mystery awards. But Annie doesn't write just mystery stories. She also writes science fiction, fantasy, and romance, as well as some stories that simply defy genre. Her stories appear regularly in *Pulphouse Fiction Magazine* and *Mystery, Crime and Mayhem*, and her short fiction has also been included in college entrance study guides in Japan. Annie's Unexpected series of short-story collections showcase the best of her work. She lives in Northern Nevada and can be found on the web at AnnieReed.wordpress.com.

Lisa Silverthorne has published eighteen novels and more than a hundred short stories, novelettes, and novellas in the fantasy, science fiction, romance, and mystery genres. She is the author of the A Game of Lost Souls series and the Experiencing True Purple series. Her work has appeared in numerous anthologies and magazines from DAW Books, Roc Books, *Pulphouse Fiction Magazine*, *Fiction River*, Wildside Press, and Prime Books. To discover more of her stories, visit LisaSilverthorne.com.

Considered one of the most prolific writers working in modern fiction, *USA Today* bestselling writer **Dean Wesley Smith** published almost two hundred novels in forty years, and hundreds and hundreds of short stories across many genres. His monthly magazine, *Smith's Monthly*, which consists of only his own fiction, premiered in October 2013 and offers readers more than 70,000 words per issue, including a new and original novel every month. In 2018, WMG Publishing Inc. launched the first issue of the reincarnated *Pulphouse Fiction Magazine,* with Dean reprising his role as editor. For more information about Dean's books and ongoing projects, please visit his website at www.dean wesleysmith.com and sign up for his newsletter.

Stephannie Tallent is a 1989 West Point graduate. Since then she's served in the Army as a Military Intelligence officer, gotten a Zoology degree, gone to vet school, worked as a small animal veterinarian, and designed and published knitting patterns and books. Throughout all that she's always wanted to be a writer, and she's finally put all her type-A, soft-spoken, liberal, invisible middle-aged woman focus on that goal, writing everything from fantasy to science fiction to mysteries to romance. Check out her website StephannieTallent.com.

Rob Vagle has been writing short fiction for over thirty years with stories in *Realms of Fantasy*, *Strange New Worlds*, *Heliotrope*, *Fiction River*, *Pulphouse Fiction Magazine*, and more. He lives in Arizona after living more than a decade in the wet Pacific Northwest, and he was born and raised in Minnesota. Find more information on his books, and sign up for his newsletter, Dispatches From This Side of Wonder, at RobVagle.com.

ABOUT THE EDITOR

Dayle A. Dermatis is the author or coauthor of many novels (including snarky urban fantasy *Ghosted*) and more than a hundred short stories in multiple genres appearing in such venues as *Fiction River, Alfred Hitchcock's Mystery Magazine*, and DAW Books.

Called "a nail-biter" by *Publisher's Weekly*, her thriller story "The Scent of Amber and Vanilla" received an honorable mention in *The Year's Best Crime & Mystery 2016*.

Considered to be the mastermind behind the Uncollected Anthology project, she also edits anthologies, and her own short fiction has been lauded in year's best anthologies in erotica, mystery, and horror.

To find out where she's wandered off to (and to get free fiction!), check out DayleDermatis.com and sign up for her newsletter.

I value honest feedback, and would love to hear your opinion in a review, if you're so inclined, on your favorite book retailer's site.

For more information:
www.dayledermatis.com

ALSO BY DAYLE A. DERMATIS

EDITED BY

Fiction River: Doorways to Enchantment

NOVELS

The Nikki Ashbourne Novels

Ghosted

Shaded (forthcoming)

Spectered (forthcoming)

Standalone Novels

Beautiful Beast

Waking the Witch

What Beck'ning Ghost

COLLECTIONS

Devilish Deals and Perilous Pacts: A Spooky Collection of Deals With the Devil and Other Bad Choices

Five Funny Fantasies

Haunted (a Nikki Ashburne collection, forthcoming)

Small Wonders: Ten Short-Short Speculative Fiction Stories

Umberto Scolari and the Five Mysteries: A Short Story Collection

Voices Carry and Other Stories of Women and Crime

Written on the Coast: Thirteen Stories of Magic and Mayhem Written in Lincoln City, OR

NONFICTION

Researching History for Fantasy Writers: How to Use Historical Detail to Make Your Fantasy Worlds Rich and Compelling

BE THE FIRST TO KNOW!

S ign up for Dayle A. Dermatis's newsletter for *free* fiction, plus the latest news, releases, and more.

Sign up at DayleDermatis.com.

For more in-depth conversations and special sneak peeks, you can also support her continued work by joining her community of patrons out Dayle's Patreon.

Patreon.com/Dayle.